HER NAME WAS
CHARLIE

Published in the UK in 2021 by Old Swan Press

Copyright © Frank Jones 2021

Frank Jones has asserted his right under
the Copyright, Designs and Patents Act, 1988,
to be identified as the author of this work.

This book is a work of fiction, and except in the case of historical
or geographical fact, any resemblance to names, place and
characters, living or dead, is purely coincidental.

Paperback   ISBN 978-1-8384337-0-3
.epub eBook   ISBN 978-1-8384337-1-0
.mobi eBook   ISBN 978-1-8384337-2-7

Cover design and typeset by SpiffingCovers

HER NAME WAS
CHARLIE

FRANK JONES

To my mother
Elizabeth Jones
1912 – 1959

Contents

SIX MONTHS EARLIER 1

1..3

2..17

3..34

4..51

5..64

6..75

7..84

8..95

9...105

10..115

11..117

12..123

13..130

14..141

15..151

16..157

17..168

18..177

19..185

20..200

21..213

22..223

23..237

24..249

25..258

26..270

27..291

28..303

29..315

30..319

31..323

SIX MONTHS EARLIER

She lay staring blankly at the ceiling as she felt the dread slowly descending, covering her like a shroud; he was coming again. She started to tremble as the memory of his voice began to infiltrate her mind, and there was nothing she could do to stop it. Her breathing became heavier, faster. She plunged her head backwards into the pillow and grabbed fistfuls of the bedclothes as the creeping anxiety continued to spread throughout her body, smothering her mind, twisting her stomach. Her brow glistened with sweat, as blades of pain stabbed her chest. She started to pant breathlessly. As the panic tightened its grip, she closed her eyes. Once again, his evil whisper was reaching out from the grave, to exact its revenge.

Whore... Bitch... Burn in Hell...

'Dear God, help me – Please, make it stop...'

You killed me... you killed me... you evil bastard...

'It wasn't my fault.'

You're going insane... I'll drive you mad... completely mad... you lunatic...

'It wasn't my fault... It wasn't my fault...'

You killed me, you, nasty, deranged bitch. Burn in

Hell... burn in Hell... you dirty slag...

For five torturous minutes his voice raped her trampled mind until, gradually, eventually, the horrific vision of the past began to evaporate from her thoughts. Her breathing started to regulate. Her grip relaxed, as the psychological stampede slowly disappeared. But, if there was any crumb of comfort to be had, it was that now, the attacks were coming fewer, and further, between.

1

Like a cat stalking an unsuspecting sparrow, a Mini Cooper moved slowly along the skewed lines of moth-eaten Sierras, Cavaliers, Fiestas, Novas, et al, until it spotted a space. It drove past, then carefully reversed in, engine still running, wipers still wiping. Across the Universe emanated plaintively from the speakers, as she sat completely still, half-listening to the song, gazing out, robotically, through the windscreen. *What am I doing here...? What, exactly, am I doing in this God-forsaken place?* What started off as an ill-thought-out blatant act of maternal defiance had now, in the cold light of day, transmuted into the most ridiculous idea she'd ever come up with, and she was scared shitless at the thought of the consequences. As the anguish began to build, she pushed the doubt to the back of her mind and switched off the ignition. As the engine died, the wipers lazily relaxed into their sleeping position. Twenty seconds later, the song came to an end. She turned off the radio, wondering if anything was going to change *her* world. The only sound that remained was that of a thousand spears of rain, hammering defiantly onto the roof of the car. Continuing to gaze out, as if in a trance, a flash of grey caught her attention; two squirrels, over near the factory wall, were frantically giving chase to each other, in their courtship display. Quick as lightning – onto the oil drum, down to the cinders, up onto the fork-lift, back to the oil drum, down onto the cinders. A gentle smile almost found its way to her lips.

She placed her head back onto the headrest and closed her eyes. Once again, doubt began to cast its shadow. As thoughts of *him* crept into her mind, her breath began to nervously tremble through her lips, her stomach started to tense. She opened her eyes, leaned forward, and stared through the windscreen, focusing intently onto the bonnet. *It's metallic blue, the rain is bouncing off... It's metallic blue, the rain is bouncing off... It's metallic blue, the rain is bouncing off...* continuously tumbled through her mind as, taking long slow breaths, she banished every other thought, silently repeating her mantra as she concentrated on the bouncing rain. She continued breathing deeply until, gradually, her feeling of calm returned. Gently stroking her fingers across the top of the steering wheel, she gave a sigh of defeat. No, it wasn't going to work. She'd have to give up on the idea. Go home and grovel to her mother, for forgiveness. She turned the engine on, pushed the lever into first, then the Mini, threading its way back through the skewed lines, slowly emerged and headed toward the car park gates. As it stopped, to give way to the never-ending stream of Monday morning traffic, she thought of *him*; he'd won again, beaten her into submission, from his grave. She squeezed the steering wheel as a seed of defiance began to grow within her mind, turning into a thread of determination,

You're not going to win, again - I've had enough of

you... I've had enough.

The Mini reversed, then did a U-turn.

***

Ten minutes later the downpour had eased, to intermittent spots. The time had arrived, no turning back. She slipped her fingers behind the handle and pushed against the door. A gush of cold, damp air invaded the warm cocoon of the car. She stepped out: twenty-five, tall, statuesque, beautiful. Reaching back in, she lifted out her trench coat, pulled it on, then took her bag off the passenger seat. She looked at Cooper and didn't want to leave him. Behind her, through the massive, opened jaws of the factory, came a distant cacophony of an alien world, presses stamping, hydraulics hissing, drills screeching, voices shouting. She pressed the remote. He clunked. She turned.

It stood before her, huge, dark, imposing. From the foundry chimney a pall of acrid black smoke lazily searched its way to the clouds. As her eyes took in the scene, the words *ARBEIT MACHT FREI* stumbled clumsily through her mind. It wasn't too late. She could still turn around and go home. Admit defeat... to her mother... to herself.

As she made her way toward the gaping jaws, she could never have imagined the life-changing journey upon which, she was about to embark.

***

After three polite knocks, 'Come in,' squawked a young voice. She entered, to be greeted by Zeta, a slim, blond-haired woman of twenty-two.

'Hello,' said Zeta, chirpily, her blue eyes smiling over the rim of her tortoiseshell glasses. 'Is it Charlotte?'

'Yes,' she said, with a smile.

'Have a seat,' replied Zeta, rising from her desk. 'I'll just see if Mister Hardcastle's ready to see you.'

She sat, and watched Zeta totter to her boss' door, knock, then enter. Her eyes were drawn to a large, framed print of The Chinese Girl, looking sadly down on her, as if saying, *'This is your last chance, get out now while the going's good.'* Her breathing trembled. The ogre was right, *'I've never heard such a ridiculous idea in all my life. Have you gone completely mad?'* She stood quickly, and took two paces toward the exit, when, 'Mister Hardcastle will see you now,' said Zeta, holding the door open. 'Here she is, Mister Hardcastle.' She paused for a few seconds. 'He's waiting...' mouthed Zeta, in a whisper. She hesitated, then moved toward his office, and entered. Fifty-seven, of stocky build, with a face that vaguely resembled an unsuccessful boxer, he rose to greet her. As Zeta was about to close the door,

'Zeta...' he said, 'be a love, and bring us two coffees.'

'Black no sugar, please,' Charlie added.

They sat opposite each other, separated by his green-leather topped desk.

'Who are you, again?' he said sternly, with an icy gaze.

'Charlotte...' she replied, with the hint of a smile. 'Charlotte Stuart... *Sir.*'

'Are you, indeed...,' he said, busying himself with some papers on his desk.

'Well, *Miss Stuart,*' he said, 'then his eyes narrowed, and his lips cracked into a warm smile, as he extended his hand, 'welcome to Nelson's'.

Chapter 1

Dot's domain within the factory was the balls-up area, or, to give it it's correct title: The Rectification and Small Assembly Area. It was where production cock ups were sent in a vain hope that any engineering misdemeanours might be given the kiss-of-life, or at least be salvaged, from becoming scrap. Small assemblies were also carried out when needed, various nuts and bolts, from different parts of the factory, congregating to be married together, before being completed, then sent to the stores. It was a cushy number, the supply of work being intermittent. Dot, being a shop steward, had been allocated this job as it could be picked up and put down at the drop of a hat, allowing her to be called away, periodically, to deal with union matters. Dot's long-forgotten outpost of a once-proud, now crumbling, entity limped by, from week to week, like the rest of the lame-duck factory, under the reluctant ownership of octogenarian twins Archibald and Reginald Nelson.

'How are the injections goin?' Dot said, with a mumble, through a mouthful of Yorkshire tea and a sloppy, chocolate chip cookie.

'Me bum's like a pin cushion. I can't sit down.'

'You don't need that palaver. Let nature take its course.'

'Change the bleedin record, will yeh?'

Dot, admonished, gazed at the dregs of the milky tea, in the chipped Simpsons mug. Her eyes moved to her overall, and the four biscuit crumbs resting on her thigh. As she was about to brush them off, Joan's hand reached down, and scattered them away. Dot heaved a stretch and managed to precariously balance the mug, onto the corner of her workbench.

'There isn't a day goes by, that I don't think of that lovely, little...'

'How many more times?' said Joan, abruptly.

She snatched Dot's mug, in frustration, swirled the dregs of tea around, then lashed them through the metal grating of the drainage grid. Dot raised her head, and their eyes met. Joan looked, into the plump, round face that gazed submissively back. Dot was Hardy, to her Laurel. Joan's lips widened into a half smile, as she silently asked Dot's forgiveness. It was one of *their* moments, when words were superfluous.

'The new girl starts today,' said Dot, with an exaggerated huff. 'Just my friggin luck, having to wet-nurse a new starter... Still, I better look after her, the poor bugger's been out of work nine months.' Her eyes glazed over, as a vision appeared in her mind. She imagined the poor unfortunate: twenty-five, not got two ha'pennies to knock together, buying her clothes from charity shops and jumble sales, maybe a single mum, fighting against the odds to make a better life for herself, and her kids, driving around in some death trap, living on a crap council estate, surrounded by rusty cars, and barking dogs.

'*Dot*'

'Wha?' she said, with a start.

'Will y'wake up? Y'were at it again.'

'Was I...?'

Grumbles aside, Dot was inwardly please at the prospect of having an *assistant*. The thing she couldn't figure out, though, was, she had very little to do, anyway. How could she share that with someone else? Hardcastle had told her the new starter was being employed on a temporary contract, but this was like a red rag to a bull, where Dot was concerned. She was determined to fight for the girl to be upgraded to a permanent position. The ghost of dear Uncle Harry pointed the way, to Dot's conscience. She could see the future; she'd take the girl under her wing, unto her bosom, like mother and daughter, give her a break. Her glance moved over Joan's shoulder. In the distance coming down the alleyway, towards the area, was Zeta, accompanied by an official-looking woman. Dot slid her ample, arse cheeks sideways off the chair, and stood. 'Here's Zeta, with someone – looks like a visitor.' She picked up her oil-stained sheet of A4, as they approached, and began to jabber, to Joan.

Joan was thirty-eight, manageress of the Nelson Engineering Ltd., canteen. For her and Dot, think chalk and cheese. Five foot-five, slim, dusky blond, straight hair, as opposed to Dot's brunette curls, and chubby features. She was bubbly, cheerful, a natural comic, to Dot's eternal doom and gloom outlook on life. Joan had played out this scenario many times. 'Right,' she whispered, then continued with an in-depth monologue, regarding the complexities involved in the preparation of a three-gallon batch of lump-free custard.

'Morning, ladies,' said Zeta, with a chirp.

Dot grunted an acknowledgement, as Joan looked in awe at Charlie. Dot also looked her up and down, awaiting the grand pronouncement from Zeta, with regards to her purpose for being there. She was obviously an intrusive snob: that arrogant swagger as she approached, the trench coat, the angora sweater, the sprayed-on jeans. Her appearance: nurtured, elegant. From her freshly cropped, jet-black bob, to her unblemished, porcelain complexion. From her size-six waist to her towering, six-foot height. Charlie hadn't opened her mouth, yet Dot, had already heard her speak a thousand words, make a hundred statements. Dot decided to stamp her authority on the situation. No toffee-nosed, stuck-up visitor, no matter who she was, was going to take priority over the shop steward. Especially on a Monday morning, when Dot had a fully loaded shotgun itching to have its triggers squeezed.

'What the Hell's goin on?' she said with a bark.

Before young Zeta had chance to come back with one of her oratorical gems such as, 'How do you mean, like?'

'D'you think I've got nothink better t'do than stand here all day, waitin for the new girl?'

Job done.

Impression made.

Authority stamped.

'The new girl?' said Zeta, having now fully recovered her power of oratory.

'I've got union business to see to,' said Dot, as a smile crept across Zeta's lips. As Zeta's smile grew in width, Dot was taken aback.

'Worra *you* smirkin at?' she said, with a snarl.

She couldn't look at Dot any longer. She turned, and glared at Charlie, with an expression that cried, *'throw me a freaking bone'*. Charlie felt a tickle of amusement dance across the surface of her lips.

'Have you not twigged on, you?' said Zeta, with a chuckle, turning back to Dot.

As she was about to growl, *'What the bleedin hell are you talking about?'* Zeta lost her battle to stifle the chortle, that bounded from her mouth.

Whahahahaha…

Charlie allowed herself a tad of a titter, which didn't

escape Dot's evil glare.

That Was It. Best friend's daughter or not, how dare this trumped up, back-stabbing, social climber, attempt to belittle Dot, in the presence of The Visitor. The anger and rage began to rumble. Joan took a step back, and decided to make a swift exit, disappearing in the direction of the canteen. Zeta coughed nervously. Dot looked her straight in the eyes and inhaled.

'Dot - Charlotte. Pleased to meet you,' said Charlie, extending her right hand. The gesture completely threw Dot out of kilter. Charlie had suddenly ridden to Zeta's defence, and thrown her the *freaking bone,* she desperately needed. Dot's glance was distracted from Zeta, to The Visitor. She reigned in her anger, to take stock of the situation, lowered her gaze, and looked at Charlie's rigid hand.

'That's what I've been trying to tell you,' said Zeta. 'This *is* the new girl - it's Charlotte.'

Dot looked from Charlie's proffered hand to her face, then back to her hand. Impasse. She withdrew her hand. Bearing in mind she was standing with her back to him, as he burst into a banshee-like wail of: It's Now or Never, it's entirely understandable that Rick's sudden, vocal explosion almost caused Charlie to dirty her knickers, with fright. She swung around and glared at him. All her composure, understatement, elegance destroyed in one fell wail. Dot was inwardly delighted to witness The Humiliation of Charlotte. Her cheeks inflated, as she pursed her lips with barely concealed laughter. Rick, ear-phoned to the max, was oblivious to Charlie's presence, as he pulled the pallet truck backwards. He came to a halt, with a soaring rendition of *kiss me, my darling, be mine tonight,* and began dragging two stock bins-full of small assemblies off the forks of his truck, and shoving them into position with his foot. Zeta looked at Charlie, and just before a full-blown guffaw exploded from her mouth, managed to spit out,

'You don't have to be a mad to work here – but why be the odd one out...?' *Whahahahaha...* (snort) *Whahahaha...* (snort)

Dot didn't laugh on a Monday. Monday was Martyr Day. When she read her missives to The Faithful: the rubbish weekend she'd had, the crap passengers she'd ferried around in the taxi, the fact that Dave wanted to get back with her, but the cow he was living with wouldn't let him (this one was entirely a figment of her imagination), and of course, the burden of being a single, hard-up mum of five kids. But the good news was, she'd been asked out on a date.

'One of me passengers, Saturday night. About fifty-five. Gorgeous. Spoke beautiful. I couldn't do it though. I still love Dave.'

That was the official version. The missive to be read to The Faithful. She'd already spoken to Joan on Sunday morning, and told her what really happened:

'He fell into the cab, pissed as a fart, breathed ale fumes all over me, and says, Alright, gorgeous, any chance of a date? then burped, in me face.'

'So, Dot,' said Zeta, 'what do you think of your new assistant...?'

As Rick walked away, without even noticing Charlie, half-hidden by Dot's ample frame, Dot paused. How, on earth, could she answer Zeta with the truth? She wanted her new assistant to be dragged kicking and screaming to Madame Guillotine. Any chance of salvation had disappeared, the second she heard Charlie speak; a husky, middle-class accent, where they pronounce *all* the letters, like: working not workin, going not goin, shirking not shirkin. They probably said, shaite not shite. Dot was always suspicious of anyone, who wasn't an obvious card-carrying member of The Proletariat, but when they turn up looking like Charlie, well, if there was one thing Dot despised it was snobbery.

'Mr Hardcastle has told me all about you,' said Charlie, attempting to break the ice.

'I bet he has,' said Dot, her voice as cold as a pathologist's scalpel.

Two seconds passed. The wall of silence was deafening. Charlie began to realise what she was up against. What can you say to elicit a conversation from someone, who's obviously determined to blank you?

'Well, I best get back, Mr Hardcastle will be looking for me,' said Zeta, then she turned, and headed back to the scintillating world of personnel records. Another impasse. All her GCSEs, A Levels, 1st in English Literature, and time at law college hadn't prepared Charlie for this. She was stumped. Welcome to the real world.

Dot huffed under her breath. She had so much union business, to get through, and here she was, wet nursing a new starter. Not *just* a new starter, but some toffee-nosed snob, who was taking the bread out of a deserving case's mouth. Dot remained stony-faced: the Sphinx in a green overall, and Hush Puppies.

'I've never worked in a factory,' said Charlie, clutching at straws.

She could have bitten her tongue, at the crass obviousness of the statement. Dot sarcastically muttered, 'Y'don't say,' as her eyes bored into Charlie's face. Assistant or not, she had to be gotten rid of. Apart from it undermining her credibility with The Faithful, how could Dot, who looked like a charity shop on legs, have an assistant that looked like a frigging model? She decided to lay her cards on the table. 'Look girl,' she said, there was then the statutory, three seconds pause. 'I'm not tryin to get rid of yeh, but you don't give me the impression that you're cut out for this place.' Charlie was about to reply, as Dot continued. 'The like of you shouldn't be slummin it in a dump like this.' Charlie had had enough. 'Well, thank you very much for your obvious concern, but I've had enough bloody lectures to last me a lifetime,' she said, abruptly. Dot was taken by surprise. She feigned her best glare, to make Charlie realise who she was talking to.

'I'm sorry, Dot... I shouldn't have sworn at you.'

Strangely enough, the short, sharp exchange had managed to impress Dot. A microscopic hint of admiration stirred, within her portly frame. During the uncomfortable pause that followed, Charlie heard a voice within her,

Just turn around and go home... It was a stupid idea anyway. She ignored it.

'Is it worth my while, removing my coat?'

The only reply was a cold silence, as Dot averted her gaze.

Just turn around and go home...

There was a pause, then,

'Very well, Dot...' she said, resigned to the situation 'It was nice meeting you. Goodbye.' She turned and began walking back toward the alleyway. Dot, watching her go, heaved a sigh.

Just my luck. Why did she have to be a bleedin snob? tumbled through her mind.

Charlie was five yards away when she became disorientated, then realised she was walking in the wrong direction. She hesitated, turned, looked down to the opposite end of the alleyway, regained her bearings, then began walking back. Dot had developed a liking for the taste of Humble Pie. It wasn't Humble Pie she was eating of course. No, she was being magnanimous in victory. Plus, the fact that it had suddenly dawned on her, that the shit would hit the fan, when Hardcastle found out what had happened. She racked her brain, to quickly come up with something middle-class, that Charlie would relate to, then, out blurted, 'I've gorra Rolex.' Charlie stopped walking.

'Oh, wow,' she said, sensing a chink in Dot's armour, 'They're really good…'

She had to make this work. How could she go home and face the ogre? She had to stand on her own feet, prove her wrong.

'You'll be joinin the union…?'

'Of course.'

Three seconds passed. Charlie rekindled the momentum by saying, 'How long have you had it – your Rolex (she was about to say *watch* but thought the best means of attack would be to butter Dot up, by emphasising the fact that it was a *Rolex*).

Dot ruminated, eventually speaking in a robotic monotone.

'The kids got it me… for me fortieth, last year…' she gazed down at her workbench, as thoughts of her children appeared in her mind; the only semblance of any hope, any love that remained in her life. Absent-mindedly, in an almost inaudible whisper, she said, 'I'll have to get it fixed…'

Had she been the type, the word's, '*You don't say?*'

could have quite easily smirked off Charlie's lips. She wasn't. She could have tittered, at the very idea that Dot owned a genuine, Rolex watch. She didn't. She'd already clocked Dot's Hush Puppies; one brown lace, one black, the genuine article, but they'd seen better days. The sort of bereavement clutter that relatives donate to charity shops, where they languish for weeks on the shelf, until the front doorbell rings, and someone like Dot walks in, with one pound fifty, burning a hole in their pocket.

Her eyes glazed over in a mist of tears as her bottom lip began to quiver.

'Dot... are you alright...? Dot...?

2

Nelson Engineering Ltd. was founded in 1901 by Ernest Nelson, and now, one hundred years later, such a state of apathy prevailed from his two sons down, that nobody had even remembered it was the firm's centenary year. Thriving during both world wars, due to government contracts to produce armaments, the company entered a gradual decline in the 1970s', the main reason being the disinterest of its two owners, who never wanted to inherit the business, anyway, and the number of petty, unofficial strikes and industrial disputes, led by Harry Smith, Dot's firebrand, union convener uncle. The unions might have been brought to heel by Thatcher, but as the eighties gave way to the nineties', Nelson Engineering ploughed its own furrow, allowing pig-headedness, on both sides, to survive, with the two Nelson brothers hoping to eventually off-load the place onto an unsuspecting imbecile, and the remnants of the union hankering for a return to the glory days of wielding power. So, as the two sides bickered and squabbled amongst themselves, the weeds grew higher, the railings got rustier and the roof developed more leaks. It was almost by a miracle, that the factory had managed to stumble its way over the line, into the new millennium. It was a relic from a bygone age. This was the scenario that Charlie had, unwittingly, let herself in for, on the day she walked into the place.

* * *

Apart from the shock he'd given her three hours earlier, with his caterwauling, she hadn't seen Rick, since. That was about to change.

'Who's he?' she asked, as he, singing an unbelievably out of tune song, backed into the area, pulling his pallet truck. Dot ignored her question. Rick turned, and, for the first time, his gaze enveloped the understated, elegant form that was Charlie - standing next to the Sphinx in the green overall, and Hush Puppies. *'Jee-zus'* hissed imperceptibly through his teeth, and he immediately averted his glance, and carried on working in a feigned, nonchalant manner, pretending he hadn't seen her. Simultaneously, his gut was wrenched in, his chest pushed out, and his shoulders reigned back. He could feel her eyes upon him, undressing him. He tore off one of his leather gloves, and wiped the non-existent sweat from his brow, with the back of his hand. He ran his fingers through his black hair, and rubbed the back of his neck, as he put on a show for her. He slowly laced his fingers back into his glove and pulled it tightly down over his outstretched hand. *Drive her wild with anticipation,* he thought, *make her wait... Right, I'll turn round now and let her cop a load of me packet.* He heaved a manly, world-weary sigh and turned. Unfortunately, his macho posturing had been as much use, as a pot of stale piss. Charlie and Dot hadn't been taking a blind bit of notice, they had their backs turned. He had to make a quick decision, *how to approach the new girl?* Should he become the Strong Silent Type, or maybe, she'd prefer the laugh a minute, Mister Nice Guy. In the end, he thought *play it cool:* Cool Hand Rick. Removing his earphones, he sauntered up to them, 'That's the lot for now, Dot.' True to form, she completely blanked him. Charlie looked at him in a shy, girl meets boy, kind of way. Their eyes met. A polite smile of acknowledgement graced her lips. Rick's *play it, cool* composure crumpled under the weight of his involuntary wink. *Bollocks,* he thought, *I've fucked it up, already.*

As Rick waited for a reply from Dot, Charlie waited for a reply from Dot. In the ensuing seconds, her eyes drifted back to Rick. He was wearing a black tee-shirt, with: Triumph Motorcycles emblazoned across the chest, with a pair of blue jeans, and black work boots. Six foot-two, broad, muscular, and handsome, yet with an anachronistic, slicked-back quiff of black hair, which made him look like a fifties' rock & roll star. She guessed, he was about twenty-eight, thirty, and as far as you could get from the usual, limp-wristed, arrogant, chinless wonders, that normally made a play for her. He spoke in a soft, yet manly, voice.

'Aren't you gonna introduce me, then…?'

'Rick, Charlotte, Charlotte, Rick – also known as *little-dick.*'

She could sense Rick's embarrassment, at this uncalled-for insult. As his hazel eyes turned toward her, she smiled reassuringly, and held out her hand.

'Charlie will be fine, Rick.'

He returned her smile, removed a glove, and took her hand into his palm. Without a word he shook her hand in a firm, but gentle, manner, as if holding a captive bird. Dot was doing her best to ignore this, as a whirlpool of anger began to swirl within her. She turned her back on him. He heaved a sigh, and realised it was going to be a long time before she finally let the bone drop from her jaws. Resigned, he turned, without a word, took hold of the handle of his pallet truck, and traipsed off, pulling it behind him.

'Trainers'll do,' said Dot, looking down at her boots. 'Have a look at the *Sportyman* gear, out the market. It's shite, but, at least, it's cheap.'

'Right,' said Charlie, 'Sportyman,' buttering Dot up, then, she seized the moment to steal a glance at disappearing Rick. She'd thought, his cheeky wink was sweet, evoking a childhood memory of her beloved, Sir Reginald. Rick, on the other hand, was looking for a gas oven, to put his head into.

As Joan approached from the canteen, clutching another half-pint mug of tea,

'I don't believe it,' she said, in exasperation to anyone within range, 'he's just rung up, '*Where's me maggots?*' She took a deep breath, as she reloaded the Gatling gun, then once more opened fire, into No-Man's Land. 'I got home last night, after eight hours in here, workin me fingers to the bone, and there he is, spread out like a lettuce, in front of the telly, gas fire blazin away. I thought he'd died of carbon peroxide poisoning. '*I fell asleep, watching Blue Peter,*' he says. He's as much use as a wet fart. I flung them down the bog. Dirty, horrible things.' Dot and Charlie stood transfixed, like two pot dogs, watching Joan. 'How can anyone in their right mind be expected to live with someone, who keeps maggots in the fridge?' Joan began smashing the lock off another case of ammo, with the butt of her rifle. Charlie turned, and looked quizzically at Dot.

'He goes fishin on the canal,' Dot said, with a murmur.

'What does he catch?'

'Supermarket trolleys.'

Joan lined them up in the crosshairs of her sights. 'He's been goin three times a week, for the past six months. I wouldn't mind, if he come home with anythink worth eating, but does he? The only thing he's ever caught, was a cold. Are you married…?'

Charlie's eardrums felt like they'd just gone ten rounds, with Muhammad Ali. Such was the relief when Joan's staccato-like barking came to a halt, that the interminable drone of the factory resembled the delicate strains of Beethoven's Moonlight Sonata.

'*Shit!*' she thought. Her automatic pilot switched off, and there was Joan standing in front of her, waiting for an answer. *What did she say?* exploded in her head. Then, lo, the heavens opened, and the sky turned a golden yellow, as Saint Dot descended on a cloud of incandescent mist, took pity on the poor child, and delivered her from evil.

'She said, are y'married?' repeated Dot, eagerly awaiting the reply.

'Only you can't tell nowadays,' Joan started to rattle again, 'with people being married, and not wearin a weddin ring. I ask yeh? Bein married, and not wearin a weddin ring. That's as hard-faced as pissin through someone's letter box, then knockin on the door and askin how far it went.

Three seconds of stony silence passed.

'No… I was once engaged…' said Charlie. 'Sort of.'

'What d'you mean, sort of?' said Joan. 'You're either engaged or you're not.'

'I'd rather not discuss it any further.'

Dot's hackles began to rise. *Snotty-nosed cow. How*

dare she talk to us like that, slithered through her mind.

'Here's your tea,' said Joan, thrusting the mug into Dot's hand,

'You coulda took the bleedin teabag out,' said Dot, with a growl, as she scooped the offending article out of her mug, on the point of her Biro. She flicked the teabag with the skill, and grace, of a knife thrower. Unfortunately, Dot's skill and grace in launching the teabag wasn't matched by her skill in judging its trajectory. On its way to the litter bin, a damp and smelly Walker's crisp box, roast chicken flavour, *splat!* The flying teabag came to an abrupt halt, as it hit the wall, four feet above the crisp box. For the first time in months Charlie laughed. Not just a polite titter, but an enormous belly laugh, and when the teabag, seconds later, gave up its grip and dropped with a *plop!* into the crisp box, she almost became hysterical. Dot looked, sternly, at her. By now, the tears of laughter were flooding down Charlie's cheeks. It was one of those occasions when something mildly amusing touches a nerve and erupts into uninhibited guffaws. Maybe it was a relief, a safety valve, for the pent-up anger, grief, and despair that she'd been subconsciously holding in, since that horrific day at her granny's house. Her laughter started to subside, and her breathing began to regulate. As she searched through her bag for a hankie, Dot had misgivings. She didn't trust her. That laughing couldn't have possibly been genuine, she was trying to ingratiate herself into the clique. No chance. Middle-class cow.

***

Dot leaned on Joan's serving counter, which doubled as

a garden fence, and extolled the virtues of camaraderie amongst the work force. The rubber, double swing-doors swished apart, and now, stripped of her baggy overall, Charlie strode in, her slim, nubile figure being lustily caressed by the eager gaze from the male-dominated queue. She bought, a large apple and a bottle of spring water. Dot chose, a meat and potato pasty, double chips, and a big dollop of mushy peas. Rick was already sitting at a table, swigging from a carton of milk, when Dot, carrying her amply laden tray, and Charlie, nibbling her apple, passed him.

'Oops,' said Dot as she nudged the side of his head with her right elbow, sending the milk surging down Rick's windpipe, causing him to cough, splutter and wheeze. Charlie couldn't help noticing, that Dot had done her evil deed on purpose, and felt mildly sympathetic towards Rick's embarrassing plight, not to mention mildly apprehensive, about Dot's obvious, bullying nature.

'He denied it point blank,' said Dot, as the two sat at the next table to Rick. 'Uncle Harry would've sorted him out, as will I. If they think they're gonna sell us down the river, I'll have us all out, pickets the lot.' As the words emerged from her lips, Dot felt what she hadn't felt for a long time; a feeling of pride, determination, swelling within her breast. Charlie felt that she'd been transported, back to the eighties.

'What do you mean, sell us down the river...?' she said to Dot.

Dot paused. Rick was straining to hear the conversation. Dot noticed this, and decided to fan the flames of his fear, and curiosity, with a totally bogus story.

'There's a group of Japanese comin,' she continued, in

a sinister tone. 'My guess is, it's to size up the place, prior to a buyout, and what's the first thing you do before you sell a factory?'

'Well… if it was me… I'd… erm…' said Charlie.

She was trying frantically to come up with something that sounded plausibly acceptable if a tad naïve.

'Cut down the workforce,' Rick butted in.

Her penny dropped.

'Reduce the overheads, to make it a more attractive proposition?'

'Reduce the wages bill,' confirmed Dot.

'Redundancies?' asked Rick, as he picked up his plate, moved from his table, and joined them. 'What have you heard, Dot?' Dot gave an enigmatic pause for effect, then replied an unconvincing, 'Nothink,' as she dangled the bait in front of him. She decided that, although her theory of impending redundancies had yet to be confirmed by management, she'd enjoy making Rick squirm with fear.

'We'll all be on the dole, by Christmas,' she said, twisting the knife. 'But we'll go down fightin.'

'I've just spent eight hundred and forty quid on a new aviary,' said Rick. 'It's cleaned me out… Japanese,' he added, 'I don't forget what they did to the British bike industry.' Then he sat, waiting for the fish to swallow his bait. He was *The Man*. The Man Who Knew About *Man* Things, like motorbikes, footy, The War. He was expecting,

'Why? What did those nasty Japanese people do to the British motorbike industry?'

Dot hadn't even heard him such was her sense of loathing for Everything Rick. Charlie looked at him. He looked at her.

Great, he thought, *she's gonna ask me, what they did*

to the British bike industry.

He's waiting for me to ask him what they did to the British bike industry, she thought, as she stifled an impish smile between clenched teeth.

As the few seconds ticked away, she was quite taken with Rick. She admired his air of commitment. Even the hint of bitterness in his voice, she sensed, was nothing more than a smokescreen, to instigate a conversation. He was the millpond, to Dot's raging torrent.

'Yeah,' he repeated, in a last ditched effort to take command, 'I don't forget what they did to Triumph and BSA.' She swallowed a fledgling smile, and could no longer resist, as she decided to mischievously play Rick at his own game.

'And AJS, Matchless, Royal Enfield, Ariel, Vincent,' she replied.

After her words had rolled around inside his head, they set of an inexorable train of thought that was to lead to his inevitable subjugation when, impressed by her knowledge of classic British motorbike Marques, he slowly opened his mouth and, 'Yeah, I know,' grudgingly spilled out. Dot rose to her feet, sniffed huffily, turned, and made her way toward the shop floor. They both remained, still, quiet, like on a blind date, when trying to think up exploratory questions, which are not too probing, or pretentiously profound. Safe, easily digested questions, the answers to which are neither important nor revealing. No questions were forthcoming in either case, then she picked up her bag and was about to stand.

'You don't have to go. Stay for a natter...'

She smiled at him, then stood. As she did, forty-eight, nearby, male heads turned. The great wall of Dot had gone, and now the castle was laid bare. A ripple of dirty whispers began to spread, in increasing nastiness and filth, as lust-filled eyes caressed Charlie. 'Nice arse... look at the tits on that...' As another couple of sexist comments and sniggers, increasing in nastiness, followed, she sat back down onto the chair, and gazed at a plate, as her breathing began to tremble, nervously. Rick looked at her. She glanced at him.

'Take no notice,' he whispered. 'They're just dickheads.'

She rested her elbows on the table and placed her forehead onto her fingertips. She closed her eyes.

It's metallic blue, the rain is bouncing off, echoed through her mind.

He noticed her distress, and showed concern by saying gently, 'Hey, Charlie... are you OK? C'mon, take no notice. They're just a gang of idiots. C'mon...' He innocently touched her forearm, with the back of his fingers. She felt reassured. A moment passed.

'D'you fancy a slice of roly-poly, an a dollop of custard...? It's a bit lumpy, like, the custard – but y'get used to it, after a while... about forty years.'

As chat up lines go, it wasn't the most flattering, but certainly the most original, she'd ever had thrust upon her. But the softness of his voice, the innocence of the question, and his child-like eagerness to please, imbued her with a sense of security. Unlike the usual undertones which accompanied the like of, '*Would you like a ride in my 911?*' His semi-comical question struck the right nerve, and an appreciative smile found its way to her lips. She politely passed on Rick's kind offer, then said she needed some fresh air. He pointed to the fire doors, leading out to the field. She hesitated before she stood, expecting another tirade of sexist filth. She rose to her feet: nothing. The initial novelty had now worn off, and they had more important things to waste their dinner time on.

'Are you coming with me?'

'I haven't had any roly-poly, yet.'

'That's what I like,' she said, with a gentle smile, 'a man who knows his priorities.'

She headed toward the fire doors as Rick stood and headed in the opposite direction.

* * *

As she stepped onto the field, a pied wagtail took off, flew twenty yards, and landed on a hawthorn bush. The May air was exhilarating as she breathed it in, deeply. She gazed into the sky. The clouds had cleared, and she could feel the tentative warmth of the Spring sun filtering down through the fingers of the breeze. As an Easyjet A320 passed overhead on its way to Majorca she gazed up at the big, orange bird. Thoughts of happier times found their way through the darkness, that intermittently clouded her mind, and drifted up toward the jet. She could see them – clear as day. Ordinary people leading ordinary lives: grandads, grandmas, husbands, wives, kids, lovers. Brand new dresses, chinos, tee-shirts, sunglasses. Cases stuffed with everything, but the kitchen sink. All those euros to spend, cheap booze to down, warm sea to frolic in. And in two weeks they'd be on their way back: sunburnt, skint, deflated. Ordinary people, leading ordinary lives. Lucky buggers.

She could hear Elvis singing Love Me Tender, drifting across from the council houses on the far side of the field. She lay down on the grass, closed her eyes and listened to the distant voices of the humans in the canteen: talking, laughing, shouting, being normal. The boring normality of the known, the familiar, the needed. They'd slowly trudged past her in the factory, booted, plodding, round-shouldered, as if they'd stepped out from one of his paintings. She wondered if it would return. *When* it would return? The sanity of boredom. The boredom of sanity. She *had* to start again. From this day forward, for better or for worse. Year Zero. Today's experiences - tomorrow's memories. She *needed* the uncomplicated, anonymous bliss of being one of them. She *craved* to become one of them; one of The Lowry People. Her breathing grew heavier as she began to relax into a doze, then, just as she reached the precipice of sleepy oblivion.

'Didn't they teach you anythin in that posh school?' he said, at the sight of her lying on the damp grass. She opened one eye and looked at him.

'Nothing worth knowing,' she replied, dozily, squinting from the sun, then closed her eye, and carried on listening to the squabbling magpies, searching for scraps in the canteen skip.

'Get up, before you catch your death…'

He looked at her, lying with her eyes closed. God, she was beautiful. Too beautiful. Five seconds passed, then she opened her eyes, and raised herself onto her elbows.

'You've gone quiet. Is something the matter?' she said.

Who was he kidding? He wouldn't have a snowball in Hell's chance, of pulling her. She was completely out of his league. As she looked at him, he looked back, smiled and gave her a cheeky wink.

'Tara, silk knickers, see you 'round - like a doughnut.'

As he turned, and walked back toward the factory, she didn't want him to go.

'What kind of birds do you keep...?'

He turned and faced her.

'Who told you about me birds...?'

'Your new aviary...?'

He paused. What should he do? Ignore her, turn around and walk away, or answer the question? Yeah, he'd ignore her. But just as he was about to turn, his gaze betrayed him as her sensuous crimson lips parted into a magnetic, innocent smile.

'Goldfinches - bullfinches - a pair of siskins,' tumbled feverishly out of his mouth, 'I thought about breeding greenfinches, but they can get enteritis - I wouldn't bother with softbills - Mate of mine used to have a pet Barn owl, fed it day old chicks - Dunno where he got them from - Right, then, I'm getting off.'

'I don't know anything about birds,' she said, in her calming, sultry voice. 'Gran had a budgie... when I was a little girl. A blue one.'

'Australian grass parakeet,' he replied.

'His name was Giacomo.'

'Giacomo...?'

'Puccini...'

'That's posh coffee isn't it?' he said, covering a guilty smile, with his hand.

'La Boheme...? Tosca...? Turandot...?'

There was a pause, as Rick deliberately looked ignorant.

'Let's say he was the Victorian equivalent of The Beatles.'

'The Beatles, now you're talkin my language, babe. Boss band, The Beatles.'

The conversation hit a wall. Five seconds passed as two black-headed gulls landed on the far side of the field, and Elvis stopped singing.

'We better get back in... The bell's gonna go,' he said, hesitantly.

There was no reply. She sat in silence as Roy Orbison began to sing In Dreams.

'Charlie... Charlie...'

'Thanks...' she said, in a quiet, subdued tone.

Before he had time to ask her, *what for?* she continued, 'For what you did... in the canteen.' He had no idea what she was on about.

'You better get up. Your arse is gonna to be soaked.'

'It's my arse, I'll do what I want with it.'

'Sod you, then.'

'Joke?'

'Oh...'

A simultaneous smile of forgiveness almost found its way to their lips, then he proffered his hand. She took it and he yanked her to her feet.

'Have you got a motorbike...?' she asked. 'Your tee-shirt...?'

'How come you know so much about them...?'

She hesitated.

'Someone I used to know... collected classics...'

'What were they?'

'And sports cars...'

There was a pause.

'Why do you stand for it, Rick...? The way she treats to you?'

He knew she was talking about Dot, but as he struggled to justify why, he *did* stand for it, she continued, 'She could be reprimanded, disciplined,' she continued.

She'd caught him off guard, thrown him off course. She

looked into his eyes.

'You shouldn't let anyone bully you, Rick, treat you like dirt. Stand up for yourself.'

The canteen bell echoed metallically across the field. She realised she'd gone too far. But it was a measure of how comfortable she felt in his presence. He was unchallenging, kind, and she'd ridden roughshod over his feelings on her first day. She felt no better than Dot.

'I'm goin,' he said, quietly, as he took one last look into her dark green eyes.

She reached behind and began pulling at her jeans. She smiled submissively as she said, 'Me arse is soaked.' She thought there was a slim chance it might make him smile. She was wrong. Three seconds of uncomfortable silence passed. Then, without a hint of expression, his lips parted,

'I particularly like Madame Butterfly...'

'That's my favourite,' she replied.

'Especially, Un Bel Di.'

'It's beautiful...'

He began walking back toward the canteen. After taking a few steps, he stopped and looked back at her,

'By the way...' he said, hesitantly, 'don't tell anyone I like opera...'

'Okay...'

As she watched him go, a gentle smile tip-toed across her mind then, gradually, found its way down to her lips.

***

Three hours later Dot was sat at her bench, filing burrs off three-inch copper tubes. She became dispirited. Charlie's sylph-like elegance, and distinctive beauty, had brought her own plainness into sharp focus. She'd looked in the mirror that morning, as she was putting on her lipstick, and didn't like the face staring back at her. *Why has he gone? Left me?* She could understand him not wanting to be married to a fat bag anymore, but to leave his kids…?

'Have you finished with this mug?' asked Joan, picking it up, as she obviously had.

'Maybe, he'll come back… He's only been gone a year.'

'Who?' said Joan.

'Wha?' replied Dot.

'You were talkin to yourself again mutterin shite.'

Four seconds passed.

'I'll have to get back,' said Joan. As she turned,

'Dave…'

'You *are* jokin…?'

'Maybe, it's not too late… to pick up the pieces,' she said, submissively.

'I've heard everythink now,' said Joan, in disbelief.

'Maybe I deserved it.'

'Sufferin Jesus…'

'He's a good man. I wouldn't have married him if he wasn't.'

'A good man…? What part of *he's a fucking psychopath*, don't you understand…?'

She had a way of blanking out the things she didn't want to remember, like the pain of childbirth; it was worth it in the long run. It was the only way she could cope. She just wanted him back, at any cost. She could no longer bear the crushing loneliness of her life, making her feel unloved, rejected, worthless. Like the fare, she'd picked up on Saturday night. She felt sorry for him. He was trying to cope, as well. He'd laughed and joked, and breathed ale fumes into her face, but as the Mondeo drove along the ring road and the amber reflections of the streetlights slid methodically up the surface of the windscreen, she'd glanced into the rearview mirror, and could see him, as he sat in the intermittent shadows of the back seat. *'Hello, gorgeous - any chance of a date?'* he'd laughed, as he stumbled into the car. But it was all bravado. Dutch Courage. His way of coping. As she looked at the silhouette of his face, she could pick out the glint of his tears as they trickled slowly down his cheeks. As his sobbing grew louder, she subtly turned up the volume of the radio, but all the tears in the world would be to no avail. Charlie on the other hand, was full of the joys of Spring. She picked up the air gun and switched it into reverse mode, then took an assembly from the stock bin, on the bench. In the oppressive claustrophobia of the factory, she'd already begun to experience a new-found freedom. All she had to do was put this thing onto that thing, squeeze the third thing, then the first thing reversed out of the second thing, and she was being paid to do it. There were no more lectures to digest, exams to sit, timetables to keep, facts and figures to memorise, no more counselling to attend, no more nurses to sob to, no more Prozac to take. She felt as free as a bird.

3

It was the last day of Charlie's first week. Apart from Dot taking an instant, psychopathic dislike to her, things hadn't gone too badly. Dot still managed to retain her hatred of all things affluent within the factory: Charlie. But it had now been relegated to an on/off situation whereby, when Dot wanted something doing, for example a journey to the stores, she'd preface the request with the words, *'Do us a favour, will yeh?'* Now, being as Charlie was (un) officially Dot's *Personal* Assistant, she was hardly likely to come back with a reply along the lines of *'Do it yourself.'* So, she made it her mission to always bounce back with an enthusiastic response such as *'sure.'*

This continual, positive response eventually began to irritate Dot. The plan was, to gradually grind Charlie down, in an effort to punish her, make her pay, for being one of the elite and teach her that, even with all her breeding, class, and affluence, none of it amounted to *Jack Shit* in that place, because she was the underdog. So, there was absolutely no point in her being a snob. As the week progressed, and it had become patently clear to Dot that her plan was beginning to come unstuck, her irritation would transmute into carefully crafted remarks. and ambiguous comments; a specialty of Dot's armoury. They were never spoken directly to the Charlie's face, though. They were always aimed obliquely or muttered. It was the tone they were muttered in however, that belied the true nature of the words. Dot was meticulous in her choice of phrase, to ensure that something that sounded quite sinister, when first spoken could, when repeated back in a different tone, be reinterpreted, laughed off as taken out of context. As the days had ticked by, Charlie had accepted the fact that she and Dot were never going to become bosom buddies. She decided to conduct herself with charm, in adversity. To maintain a dignified silence, whenever necessary. Joan, however, was the crucifix to Dot's antichrist. It was hard to understand, how Dot and Joan had come out of the same womb. Joan had quite taken to Charlie. She'd began to treat her as a younger sister and when you got Joan on your side, it was like manna from Heaven: double chips, extra mushy peas, all the hash browns you could manage, not forgetting double helpings of her famous puddings and custard. The only fly in this ointment was the fact that Charlie was on a starvation diet, of a thousand calories a day. It was this Friday morning when she looked down at her bathroom scales and discovered that, in the space of a mere three days, she'd put on five pounds. It was then, as she stood naked in front of the cheval mirror in her bedroom, scrutinising her skeletal frame, that she decided she had to make a stand. Much as she liked Joan, she really must find some way of declining her intrusive, if well-meant, bourgeoning mounds of sustenance. She'd spent most of the previous evening, trying to devise a feasible excuse, whereby she could speak directly, without being hurtful, be assertive, without being tactless. It was a waste of time. What to do?

She'd hardly seen Rick since Tuesday. Even then it was just for a minute when he dropped off a bin full of assemblies, glanced at her momentarily, and as she smiled back at him, he turned and walked off, impassively. Since then, the stock had appeared as if by magic, when she'd momentarily left the area to go for a pee or gone to have her lunch. When she went to the medical to get a splinter of swarf removed from her finger, she came back, and another bin had appeared next to the bench. Wednesday and Thursday, there was no sign of him in the canteen. She wanted to speak to him. Not to embarrass him by apologising for her inquisitiveness regarding Dot's bullying, but... well... she just *wanted* to speak to him. She missed his voice. The plan of attack was thus - bring in her own bottle of mineral water and apple, together with two slices of crisp bread etc. This would, at a stroke, alleviate the need to visit the canteen, rendering Joan's bourgeoning mounds redundant. Then, making an excuse to Dot, to join her later in the canteen, slip out quietly, with the said emergency rations, find a hidey hole, somewhere where nobody would think of looking, then, eat the aforementioned delicious rations, in secret.

Bingo.

Job done.

That covered Friday. What she was going to do for the rest of her term of employment there, she hadn't figured out yet, but she'd think of something.

'I'm goin f'me dinner,' said Dot, picking up her bag.

It was 11.50 a.m. The time had arrived to pull off her cunning stunt.

'Right oh,' replied Charlie, trying her utmost to sound

common. 'I'll just finish these last few off, then I'll follow yeh.'

Dot sauntered out of the area and carried on walking down the alleyway. Charlie kept her head pointing down at the component as she crooked her eyes sideways, to follow Dot's every move. As the distance increased between the two, she prepared to grab her sustenance and run. *'Balls.'* Dot stopped walking. *'Shit.'* Was she going to turn around and come back? She held her breath. As a second passed, Dot's glance moved to the floor, in front of her. She slowly bent down, reached out her right arm and carefully picked something up, between her fingernails. She straightened up and looked at it. It could have been a pound coin. It might have been a fifty-pence. Whatever it was, she blew on it, then wiped it on the lapel of her overall. She put it in her pocket and carried on walking. Eight seconds later, still under the scrutineering eyes of Charlie, Dot turned left, into the canteen.

'Where's Charlie?' asked Joan.

'She's just finishin off. She'll be down in a minute.'

After a few seconds, as Joan stood poised, ready for the latest assault on Dot's appetite, Dot grudgingly confessed to her that she'd have a piece of haddock for her dinner. When Joan got over the initial shock that Dot wasn't having anything that was encased in a pastry crust, she reiterated that haddock was, in fact, fish not meat. *'I know that, you daft bugger. D'you think I'm bleedin stupid?'* she found the biggest portion of haddock she could and slid it onto Dot's plate. As Joan started to scoop a never-ending portion of chips on, to keep the haddock company, Dot gave the increasingly large portion a reticent stare, and suddenly found her lips beginning to part with the words, 'I don't want no chips today,' slowly sliding out. Joan stopped scooping the portion and gave her sister a look of mistrust.

'You don't want no chips…?'

'No…' answered Dot, guiltily.

'What d'you mean, you don't want no chips…? You've had chips every day, for the last eighteen years.'

Just when Dot was doing so well, her stomach rumbled, and, as she made the lethal mistake of gazing at the thick golden-brown succulent wedges of potato, her salivary glands started pumping spit into her mouth, as her stomach gave a louder rumble.

'Just a few, then,' she said, with a gulp.

Joan scooped half of the chips back into the steel dish then moved sideways, to the mushy peas, and picked up the ladle, about to scoop a couple of dollops onto Dot's plate.

'Erm…' said Dot. Joan hesitated, dollop poised, 'I thought I might have some carrots… instead.'

'Carrots…?' replied Joan, incredulously, knowing full well the last time Dot had a carrot in her mouth was when Maggie was on the throne, if not before. She replaced the mushy pea ladle onto the surface of the thick pea-green slop, and as it slowly submerged into mushy oblivion, she picked up the carrot scoop. Not wishing to ridicule her sister for her obvious, commendable attempt at trying to elevate her dieting intentions to the next level, Joan tumbled a scoop of the orange medallions onto Dot's plate. 'Ta,' she said, dejectedly staring at the sliced carrots, her will to live finally crushed. Then she took the plate from Joan, placed it onto her tray and turned, about to pick up her cutlery.

'Are y'not havin no puddin, then…?' Joan said, with a hiss, which, to Dot, sounded like the voice of Satan. They were the exact words that she was hoping she wouldn't hear. She half turned and cast her glance down at the trays of steaming hot, plump, cherry pie, or glistening inch-thick, flaked almond-topped, lemon sponge. In a last, valiant attempt at self-control, Dot's eyes moved to the bowls of fresh fruit salad: cold, unloved, unwanted, under their coatings of crinkled cling film. Their fate was sealed when Dot's nostrils caught a whiff of Joan's freshly made, creamy custard.

***

Having no idea where she was heading, Charlie made her way as far as she could down the main alleyway. When she got to the end, in the distance, she could see daylight flooding in through two, opened, concertina doors. She reached the doors of the loading bay and burst out, into the sunshine. She made her way to the end of the platform, down the five steps, and between two forty-foot artics. As she reached the front end of the lorries, she hesitated, and saw an area, opposite, that looked just like the sort of neglected place that people rarely went to (she hadn't noticed the large, brown rat). She walked across the turning area, then continued up, onto the rough grass, and gently picked her way between the numerous eight-foot, precariously balanced towers of long-forgotten, wooden pallets. As she reached the far side, the rat slinked away, carrying the pot-bellied remains of a dead sparrow chick, between his teeth.

An ancient, Kwik-Save trolley, minus a wheel, she recycled as a seat, sat down, and opened her bag. She looked into her lunchbox, at the cornucopia of splendiferous things to eat: two slices of multigrain crispbread, a stick of celery, three Piccolo tomatoes, a Braeburn apple, and a nuts & raisin fruit bar. She placed a slice of crispbread into her mouth and closed her jaws. As her teeth compressed it, it snapped like a piece of sun-dried cardboard. There was no taste to it whatsoever, and as she chewed it, she imagined there was probably more taste *in* a piece of sun-dried cardboard. She put the piece of celery between her front teeth and bit it. As she began to chew the cold, crunchy stick of nothing, she gradually began to realise that she didn't want to be there, sitting alone, on that antique, shopping trolley, eating totally boring uninteresting non-food. She kept thinking of Joan's canteen: the hustle and bustle, the smell, the banter, and laughter. But most of all, the food. Her mouth began to salivate as she visualised the pasties, the chips, the chicken curry. She thought back to yesterday - the magnificent mound of bread-and-butter pudding and lumpy custard, that Joan had kindly kept to one side for her. Her stomach grumbled, as if in protest, as she picked up one of the tiny tomatoes and placed it in her mouth. She pressed her tongue hard against the soft body of the fruit, compressing it against the roof of her mouth, and it burst like a little bomb, sending a spatter of pips toward her throat.

* * *

She looked down, at the generous slice of steaming cherry pie; a triangular island surrounded by a hot sea of yellow. She raised her spoon, lowered it vertically, then, with the clinical precision of a surgeon, dissected the pie into four pieces. She singled out one of the pieces then sliced it in half. She scooped it into the bowl of the spoon and smothered it with a portion of the custard. She raised her hand and was just about to introduce the lot to her gaping orifice, when Joan appeared, and interrupted her gastronomic ritual.

'Where's Charlie...?'

Two seconds passed, as Dot decided to either carry on stuffing her cakehole, and mumble incoherently through the mound of semi-masticated, cherry pie and custard, or answer the question first, then shovel the lot in and savour the moment, in peace. She decided on the latter.

'I don't know,' she said, brusquely.

As Dot spooned in the highlight of her day, her taste buds were bombarded with the sharp tang of Morello cherries and the sweet creaminess of custard. Before she had chance to take one chew, Joan shot back with,

'Is she definitely comin in today? Did she say?'

Dot, through a gush of saliva, and a mouthful of slop, blurted out angrily,

'Ill u 'uck off? - Im trin t'ea' me uckin' 'inner...'

Joan stood and waited for Dot to swallow down the mouthful of stodge. Dot, feeling like a condemned man eating his last meal, huffed in exasperation down her nostrils, as she began chewing at double speed. Eventually, after the abomination had been consigned to her gullet, she turned to the still-waiting Joan, and said, with a bark,

'I don't know what she's doin. Alright?'

'I was waitin to ask about y'car?' said Joan indignantly.

Dot had been on a short fuse all week. Not that that was anything unusual, but this week was different. It was down to the fact, that she'd temporarily lost her supplementary source of income. Each weekend, she drove a taxi part-time. The Saturday before, she'd taken a fare home, dropped him off, and was making her way back to The Peacock, when she started having problems with the gearbox. She managed to get the car to crawl back to the pub car park and parked it up.

'Well…?' asked Joan, 'have they fixed it yet, or wha?'

***

She snapped the lid back onto her lunchbox then pushed it into her bag. As she rested her head back against one of the pallets, she looked out through the railings. She closed her eyes and began listening to the extraneous sounds surrounding her: a distant jet, children shrieking, the chirruping of sparrows, someone snoring… *someone snoring?* She opened her eyes and listened. It sounded like someone snoring, coming from within the pallets. She stood, then moved tentatively toward where the sound was coming from. As she came to the end of the pallets, the sound was coming from around the corner. She slowly put her head around and could see a pair of jeans-clad legs. As she got closer, there was Rick. Hardly daring to breathe, she stood and watched him, surrounded by an empty orange juice bottle, a sandwich box, an apple core, and a Mars bar wrapper. She looked at him and felt a warm surge within her. Not wishing to be discovered, she slowly turned. As she took a step, his eyes opened.

'What are you doin here?' stumbled clumsily out of his sleepy mouth.

'I was…'

'I wasn't asleep, just – restin me eyes.'

A smile travelled incognito across her lips.

'You can't afford t'go asleep ere. The rats'd be down your throat, quicker than y'could say…'

'*Rats?* There are no rats are there…?'

'I was pullin your leg…'

An uncomfortable pause bounced between them for five seconds.

'So… this is where you've been keeping yourself…?'

Rick stood and picked up his bottle and sandwich box. He'd just woken and wasn't in the mood for convoluted replies.

'Yeah…' he said with a mumble.

'Right…'

'I asked you what you were doin here?' he said.

She couldn't think of an answer. He'd not seen her for four days but hadn't stopped thinking of her. He'd been trying to get her out of his system. He knew there was no way, the like of her would have a relationship with the like of him, that's why, he'd been deliberately avoiding her. Once bitten, twice shy.

'Have you been deliberately avoiding me?'

'No,' he said, as a rat squeaked in the distance.

'I just wanted to say…' she started. She didn't know what she wanted to say. But she knew what she *didn't* want to say; she didn't want to say she was sorry. She didn't want to rake it back up, embarrass him with an apology.

'Wha…? You just wanted to say wha…?'

A moment passed, as they looked at each other. His desire for her remained.

'I'm sorry…' she whispered, deferentially.

She wanted him to tell her that it was alright. She needed to be reassured that not all men were the same, control freaks, emotional bullies. Not all men force you to look like a skeleton. To submit. Condemn you to a psychiatric ward.

'You've got nothin to be sorry for,' he said, in a tone that was gentle, but manly. As he moved towards her, her heart rose, but he continued past and made his way toward the corner of the pallets.

'Rick...'

Without a word, he turned.

'Please... don't avoid me.'

He was taken aback. His mouth went into a state of paralysis. He didn't know what to say. His brain fired the message, *Don't just stand there, you daft prick, kiss her.* The best he could manage was a clumsy wink. Then, as he turned to leave, he paused and looked back.

'See you round,' he said, almost apologetically.

'Like a doughnut...?'

In the moment that followed, they exchanged innocent smiles, that were betrayed by a look of desire in their eyes.

* * *

'I won't know til this afternoon,' said Dot. 'It's somethink t'do with the bits that hold the gear lever. I've got t'ring them at two o'clock, t'see if the parts have come in.'

Joan looked on as Dot shovelled another spoonful of cherry pie and custard into her gaping manhole. Dot put her hand into her overall pocket and took out a penny. She put it on the table, placed her middle finger onto it and slid it across, to Joan.

'What's this?'

'I just found it.'

Joan picked the penny up and looked at it.

'It'll be lucky,' said Dot. 'Take it with yeh, when y'go to the clinic.'

Dot rescued a last vestige of cherry skin from her bowl, lifted it to freedom, then licked it off her spoon with the tip of her tongue. As Joan turned to walk off, she surreptitiously dropped the penny back into Dot's opened bag. Dot's mobile rang.

'Yeah...?'

'Hello, Dot, It's Laurence...'

'Hello, Lol...'

'Your car's ready.'

'You're jokin.'

'No, we had one of the parts in stock. You can pick it up anytime you want.'

'Thank God for that.'

'I'll see you later, then.'

'Ta, mate. I owe you one.'

'Tara.'

'Tara, Lol.'

***

Charlie was at the workbench, undoing more things from the things. She thought to herself that it might be a good idea, in the fullness of time, if she found out the correct names for all these *things*. Dot was preparing herself for an early dart, so she could go and pick the Mondeo up, and Charlie was being trusted, for the last hour at least, to run the area single-handedly. As Dot slipped off her overall, then hung it up in her locker, Rick appeared coming down the alleyway, pulling his pallet truck. There was a bin of assemblies on it, and Charlie *knew* he was heading her way. She put her head down and pretended she hadn't seen him.

'Right, I'm off,' said Dot. 'Tara.'

'Tara, Dot,' she replied, as Rick approached.

Dot picked up her bag, then made her way down the

alley. Rick looked at Charlie, as she worked. As he turned his back to move the stock bin, she glanced at him.

'How long have you worked here…?'

'Too long,' he said, then became silent.

Maybe I should just give up, wandered through her mind, then she wondered about abandoning the idea of a conversation, just before,

'How come they took you on anyway?' he said, 'when there's rumours of redundancies?'

'I phoned up,' she replied, hesitantly, 'Zeta asked me to come for an interview, and Hardcastle offered me the job. It's a temporary contract, until the export order's been met.'

'Why did they give it to you, when there's thousands of poor buggers strugglin to exist on the dole?'

'Maybe, because I was the one who bothered to phone up?'

Fair comment, he thought.

Before he had a chance to leave, she said, 'So, how long *have* you worked here…?'

He started to speak in a quiet voice, that bore traces of disappointment, betrayal, bitterness. He told of his father, Jim, who had started off in the factory as a machine operator, and been promoted to foreman, then General Foreman, to finish up at the age of fifty-six, as Plant Superintendent. He told her how, at the age of fifty-seven, while driving home from work in his Passat, he'd felt crushing pains in his chest. How he pulled up at the side of the road, and a passing cyclist called an ambulance. How he, and his mother, sat for six hours in the Coronary Care Unit hoping against hope, only to see the last gasp of life drain slowly out of him, as James Kenneth Edwards departed this life. He told how he'd joined the company, at the age of nineteen, to follow in the footsteps of his father, and how he had so much to give, but his ambition, his enthusiasm, was misplaced, as nobody was interested. How three years later he'd made some scrap gears, because the machine was faulty, and was hauled before William Gregory Hardcastle who decided to make an example of him, giving him a written warning, and how Dot called a strike meeting, three weeks before Christmas, and how the workforce voted three to one to carry on working. And how he and Dot walked out in disgust, and spent the afternoon getting plastered in the bar of The Red House. And now, how he just turns up for work, clocks on, gets through the day by singing out of tune songs at the top of his voice, to relieve the boredom, and frustration, then clocks off, goes home, sees to his birds, sometimes writes songs, but mostly sinks pints of Magners cider, mainly with his bandmates, Eddie, Matty and Pete.

***

The number 63 pulled into a halt at the stop. The doors hissed, opened, and Dot stepped off onto the pavement. She walked around to the back of it, waited for a break in the traffic, then crossed the road. In less than two hundred yards she'd be in the company of Laurence. As she approached the garage, she was heartened to see the Mondeo sitting outside the customer entrance. She glanced into it, then continued through the door, into the reception area.

'Dot,' Laurence said with a smile. 'Come on, let's get you done.'

There he goes again, she thought, saucily smiling inside, *comin out with the innuendo.* He'd charged Cresta

Cabs account with the bill, so the car was ready to roll. As he placed the keys into her hand, she felt his fingers brush against her palm. If only she was free and single, she thought... instead of being (sort of) married.

Firstly, being a gentleman, he enquired about her kids, always a good sign. Then, he asked had she lost weight. Dot simpered. Thirdly, he asked if there was any chance of her getting back with her husband. *Why,* would he ask that if he wasn't on the sniff? Having responded with an ambiguous reply, to ensure that she kept him cooking on a low light, he then confirmed everything she suspected when he called to her, just as she was about to walk out the door, and said, 'Let me know, the next time you need a service'. As the words drifted through the air of the reception area then landed like a thousand butterflies onto Dot's awaiting lugholes, she took hold of the knob, slowly, and looked back at him. Anyone else, and she'd have responded with her usual '*Orright*'. But, as Laurence smiled at her, she found her lips sensually parting, and heard herself utter the words of her submission to him, 'Sure... why not?' His phone rang. He answered. She twisted his knob.

As Dot, walking on air, got into the car, started the engine then pushed the gear lever into first - *bliss*. She pulled the car out, onto the main road, and accelerated. She picked up the radio microphone and called Cresta Cabs, letting them know the news. Donna took the call, and while she was on, told Dot there was a fare waiting to be picked up nearby, if she fancied it. Dot didn't normally start her shift until seven but thought she might as well cop for an extra couple of bob, seeing as how she was in the district. She took the fare's name and address and went to pick the woman up.

Mrs Rose was on her way to St Catherine's maternity unit, to see her sister Maureen and new baby niece. As Dot guided the car through three sets of lights, around two roundabouts, past the canal, the retail park, then down the dip and under the flyover, her intermittent chit-chattings to Mrs Rose were interspersed with dreamy thoughts of Laurence and what he'd said to her. At approximately the same time that the car was drawing to a halt under the canopy of the maternity entrance, Laurence was putting down the phone. His lover Damian had just rung to confirm the arrangements for their evening out, at their favourite gay bar.

Dot told Mrs Rose the fare was £8.60. She passed a tenner over, telling Dot to keep the change. As she opened the rear door of the car and turned to get out, Mrs Rose uttered,

'There's summat down ere... under the seat.'

'You wha?' replied Dot, as she imagined her tongue inside Laurence's mouth.

'Down ere...'

Mrs Rose reached down and picked up a wallet. She handed it to Dot, then, as Dot said, *'ta,'* Mrs Rose said, *'t'ra,'* got out of the car and headed into the maternity unit.

Dot's stomach welled with excitement. *A wallet.* She squeezed it between her thumb and forefinger - it felt thick. That nice, fat thick that they feel, when they're bulging with banknotes. She put it onto the front passenger seat, then drove for a mile. Turning the car into a side street, she stopped randomly, outside a painters' and decorators' merchants. The bloke, struggling to manoeuvre the window grille into position, gave her a dirty look as much as to say, *'Can't you see, I'm about to shut?'* Point taken, she moved the car a few more yards down the street then stopped. After craning her neck, to see if any furtive characters, disguised as humans, were lurking in the litter-strewn doorways, she picked up the wallet and looked at it. It wasn't one of Italy's finest, just an old piece of cow, as rough as a bear's arse. Even Dot could see it was cheap and nasty. Something on the front surface caught her eye, and she looked closer at it. Under the faded imprint, of what appeared to be the outline of an island, was the word *Malta*. She could hardly bring herself to open it, imagining it to be stuffed with useless papers, photos and, if she was lucky a fiver. She undid the clip and peeled apart the two halves as if she was opening a book. Her eyes went straight to the back section, and as she pulled the front down, she could see banknotes. *Lots* of them. She greedily plunged her right hand into the wallet and her fingers and thumb locked onto the chunk of paper dreams. Her eyes began to sparkle, as she wrenched the notes from their hiding place. Never, in all her life, had Dot been so happy to see the regal face of Her Majesty.

'Twenty… forty… sixty… eighty… a hundred… a hundred and twenty… a hundred and forty… a hundred and sixty… A Hundred and Sixty-Five…'

A hundred and sixty-five… She clenched the notes to her chest, with both hands, and leant back onto the headrest. She closed her eyes and exhaled a huge sigh.

'Maybe there is a God, after all.'

Then, a smile began to spread across her lips, and as the excitement became too much to bear, she let out a massive shriek of delight.

4

'I'm finished with men, I'm joining the army,' said Charlie, as she arrived back from the toilets, having caught a snippet of Dot and Joan's conversation.

'You're finished with men, so you're joinin the army?' queried Joan, struggling to come to terms with the logic of the statement.

'I used to do aerobics and keep fit before I had my...' she paused. 'I'd like eventually to be in the Physical Training Corps.'

The resentment toward her began to rekindle within Dot. As Charlie put away her bag and took her place at the workbench, Dot studied her every move. She was lean, agile, and moved with the grace of a gazelle. Even her oversize overall, with the cuffs turned up at the wrists and its bagginess, did nothing to divert the eye from the fact that she was inherently sexy. In fact, it made her look vulnerable, childlike; she looked sixteen.

'Bitch,' Dot said, with a huff, under her breath.

'What?' asked Joan, taken aback, as Charlie peeled out a pair of latex gloves from the cardboard box, that sat on the workbench.

'*Ouch,*' she squealed, as she let go of the wristband, and it snapped onto her wrist.

'Look at her,' said Dot. 'Can't even put a pair of gloves on, without it turnin into a performance. Bleedin drama queen.'

She was standing only fifteen feet away, but was oblivious to their conversation, it being drowned out by the extraneous droning, screeching, and whining of the all-pervading machine tools noise from the factory floor. She picked up the air gun and switched it into reverse mode then took an assembly from the stock bin, on the bench. She'd arrived early at work that morning and had decided to repay Dot for the shaky start to their relationship. She'd gone through the rectification area like a dose of salts, brushing vigorously places that hadn't been touched in years. She'd polished their lockers and the workbench and disposed of the stinking Walker's crisp box replacing it with a new McCoy's crinkle cut one (flame-grilled steak flavor) instead. The thought had crossed her mind to tear down the shabby Mel Gibson and Rick Astley posters, but she decided against it; one liberty too far.

'Have y'seen what she's done?' said Dot, casting her head to one side to indicate the disgusting state of cleanliness.

'A new broom sweeps clean,' replied Joan, admiring Charlie's new-found talent for brushing up.

'Not here they don't,' said Dot, venomously, 'they just become old brooms.'

'Well, old broom, you were like her, once,' said Joan.

'I was never like her,' came the tart reply. 'Stuck up bitch.'

Joan didn't like the words being spouted, but what followed next disturbed her even more.

'Pervert...'

'What did you say...?'

'She's gay... a rug muncher... It's obvious,' said Dot. 'She hates men, broke off her engagement, and wants to join the army – fuckin G.I. Charlie. She'll be gettin her head shaved, next. She's a dike.' Dot was sowing the seeds of her next rumour, but on this occasion Joan was in no mood for collaboration. What normal woman wants to be called Charlie? As she carried on canvassing for votes, the electorate slammed the door firmly in her face, when Joan fired back, 'What, exactly, do you call normal?'

'Normal,' said Dot. 'Not a pervert.'

Joan's heart began to thump heavily. Her breathing quickened, as the adrenalin coursed through her veins. Her mind drifted back to those dark, secret times that had stolen the innocence of her childhood. The black spider-like memories that she'd kept buried for so long, once again began to creep back out, from under their stones. She tried her hardest to keep the words in, but they escaped from her lips, 'You don't know what a pervert is,' she said angrily, almost gasping. Dot stared at her. 'Why have you suddenly got on your soapbox?'

'It doesn't matter if you're gay, or straight,' said Joan, her voice heavy with emotion. She'd caught Charlie's attention, who, had glanced across at them. Joan, taken by surprise, shot her a half-smile back. Charlie shouted something to Joan, but she couldn't catch what it was. Joan, with eyes glaring, turned back to Dot.

'There's only two types of people in this world – good ones and evil bastards, who should've been drowned at birth.'

'What are you talkin about?' said Dot, shocked at the

outburst.

'Never you mind,' said Joan.

'*What are you talkin about, I said.*'

'Nothink.'

'How are you gettin on with y'treatment?' said Charlie, trying to sound working-class. She was there – standing next to them.

'Wha?'

'Y'treatment…?'

Joan's emotions were in tatters. She wanted to tear someone's head off but had to restrain herself. Dot, as a subtle insult to Joan, decided to throw Charlie a lifeline.

'I'd be careful if I were you, *Charlie,* she's just threw her rattle out the pram.'

Joan was livid. Dot was smirking. Charlie could feel the quicksand reaching her neck. Here she was, in the middle of a conversation minefield. What should she do? She was trying her utmost to be one of the girls, be normal, ordinary. In the seconds that followed, she thought she had the answer to the pickle that she found herself well and truly in - crack a joke! It was the wrong decision of monumental proportion. She put on her most appealing smile, and announced to the disparate attitudes of her audience, 'Sex could become a thing of the past, couldn't it? Just drop into the sperm bank and ask to see the duty wanker!' Dot, her anti-gay vitriol vindicated, had never laughed so loud since she saw Hardcastle slip on the ice last winter, and go sprawling on his arse. Joan glared at Charlie, in disbelief.

'I'll have you know that me and my Eric, are very happy together. We haven't had kids, yet, but we will. We're funny like that, y'see. We have this old-fashioned idea, that men and women should reproduce – so, you can take your turkey baster, and shove it, as far as it'll go.'

Joan turned and did an impression of a bullet train on its way to Tokyo.

'I think I've upset her,' Charlie said with a murmur, inadvertently coming out with the understatement of the century.

'She'll get over it,' said Dot, then, as Charlie was about to speak, she continued, in a distant tone, 'It's just that... she needs this baby, so much.'

'How old is she...?'

'Thirty-eight.'

The flurry of words dried up. Then, as Charlie made a move to turn,

'What's all this in aid of...?' said Dot.

'Which...?'

'Gettin in early – sortin the place out...'

'It was a mess (she wanted to say *'shithole'*).

'It was lived-in...' said Dot, with a hint of aggrievement.

The words, *it was a lived-in, shithole* cartwheeled mischievously through Charlie's mind, and it was only with the greatest of restraint that she prevented them from transforming into a huge belly laugh.

'Dot... I found an old penny under the bench... you know – one with Britannia on the reverse.'

'I wondered where that got to...' said Dot, as the two women played facial poker, Dot, feeling her stomach quivering with retrained laughter, Charlie rubbing her nose with her fingers, to hide her bottom lip being bitten.

'So, you're not after no promotion then?'

'I'm not after anything... I did it for you – right, OK? I wanted the place to look nice, for you...'

A three-second pause hung in the air, then Charlie

turned and walked back to her bench.

***

Such was Joan's nature, that two hours later in the canteen, she was joking and laughing with Charlie, as if nothing had happened between them.

'And how do they stimulate your ovaries?'

'I've been injectin myself with hormones, every day. I've got it off to a fine art. That's why my bum's like a pin cushion.'

As Joan spoke, Charlie had a look of enchantment in her eyes, as she absorbed and digested every word. Rick sat, tightly gripping his spoon, and with a grimace of disbelief on his face, as his brain assimilated each gruesome detail.

'They inject yeh with estrogen, to get your ovaries to produce a load of eggs. Then, they whip a few out an mix them in a test tube, with a dollop of sperm.'

At this information overload Rick threw his spoon back into his bowl of lumpy custard, and pushed towards the centre of the table.

'Then put the whole lot back into your fallopian tubes.'

Dot had been sitting, silently, half listening to the conversation. She had nothing to contribute. She had things on her mind. It was almost three days since she had been handed the wallet, by Mrs Rose. Three days since she had tugged out the wad of cash and counted it. Initially, she'd been elated. More spare cash than she'd seen in years - just dropped into her lap, to do with as she pleased. She had a phone bill to pay, school clothes to buy. She thought of treating her kids to a *proper* meal, instead of their nightly ritual of chips. So, why hadn't she done any of these things?

What was stopping her? Why after what would be three days in a matter of a few hours, was the hundred and sixty-five pound still intact? Undisturbed? Wrapped in an Aldi carrier bag and secreted under the driver's seat of her Astra? She was *definitely* going to spend it. It wasn't her fault, that the soft bugger had lost it. He should have been more careful. Finders Keepers. Yeah - she was *definitely* keeping it. Serves him right... Why then, hadn't she told anyone about her good fortune? She could have dressed up the truth with a cock and bull story, about winning it on a scratch card or something. But, she hadn't. Why was it still untouched, after three days? She hadn't even broken into the fiver. She owed the window cleaner two months money. The MOT on her sixteen-year-old Astra was looming. No doubt that would be the usual horror story. But when the initial elation wore off, she began to have an attack of conscience. She rung Laurence on the Monday, to see if any of his staff had lost anything, they hadn't, (he also sounded cold and distant on the phone). She was just going through the motions of course. She knew quite well that it didn't belong to anyone, in the garage. It had obviously been left behind by one of her passengers, from last weekend. Then, she thought about handing it in to the police. Yeah, she thought seriously about that one. Even enough to pull up outside the station and sit for three minutes with her engine running. She turned the engine off, took the wallet from her pocket, and was just about to pull on the door handle, when she thought she'd have one last look at the money. One last count. But she gave up on handing it in to the police when she realised that to do so would be to kiss it goodbye. Because apart from the money, there was a credit card, a bank card, an NHS prescription card, and his driver's licence, complete with his name and address. They'd contact him,

'Hello, Mister Silly Bastard, we've found your bulging wallet that you so stupidly lost. And guess what? It's been handed in, by an even sillier bastard than you.'

Then, he'd go down to the police station, pick it up, and probably the ungrateful sod wouldn't even send her a 'thank you' card. But that's how people are nowadays. She *deserved* to keep it. Why shouldn't she?

'Will you two change the subject?' said Rick, more out of embarrassment than anything else. 'I'm bringin sarnies from now on - I come here to eat me dinner, not listen about babies being conceived.'

'So, today's the big day, then?' asked Charlie, delightedly.

'My appointment's four o'clock this afternoon. He won't know what's hit him, whenI get home,' said Joan.

'If I can't get half a pint of sample, out of him, I'll eat my hat!' and the two women giggled, as Rick almost retched. Charlie, overcome by the moment, stood, put her arms around Joan and kissed her on the cheek. Joan stifled her recoil: no smoke without fire.

* * *

Then, there was the redundancy rumour, which refused to go away. And this also, was beginning to look like there was no smoke without fire. Dot's intuition was bomb-proof, in these kinds of situations and if Hardcastle tried so hard to convince her that it was only a rumour, she knew what to expect. The management had called a meeting with the convener and shop stewards for tomorrow.

'There's a meetin tomorrow mornin,' said Dot, followed by her customary pause for effect.

'Really?/What about?' said Charlie and Rick in unison, taking the bait.

'The strike,' replied Dot licentiously, with the sole intention of striking fear into Rick's heart.

'I'm not going on strike,' he said, defiantly.

Dot stood and looked down at him.

'It's the decision of the majority that counts,' she said, with a gloat, 'not just you.'

And with that, she shoved her chair back under the table, turned, and walked away.

'I've never been on strike,' said Charlie, with a perverse hint of excitement.

'She won't have much chance of a strike,' he replied.

'How can you be sure?'

'It's May,' he said, in a tone that implied he knew something, she didn't.

She couldn't figure out the logic.

'What's May got to do with it?'

'We shut down in July, for three weeks. People don't want to be breakin up for their holidays, and havin to stop at home, because they're skint. Holiday money doesn't go that far.'

'So, that's how the politics of a walkout works? Get the timing right, or forget it?'

'It was the same when she called the strike over my dispute,' he continued, 'three weeks before Christmas.'

She could see the sense in his logic, and as she pondered his words he finished with,

'They'll probably go for an overtime ban, to start with. That's bad enough.'

What she wanted to reply with, was something like, 'Well, there you go,' or, 'You don't say,' or maybe even something a bit more philosophical like, 'You learn something new, every day.' She didn't. He was, obviously, opening-up to her.

She noticed, that since his heart to heart about his dad, his thwarted ambition, and his dereliction of career progress, his attitude towards her had begun to change. He was at his most impressive when he wasn't trying to impress. She wasn't terrifically interested in the machinations of engineering a strike but didn't want to insult him with a flippant comment.

A lot of the time it wasn't what he said, but the way he said it, that really caught her attention. His voice: unpretentious, down to earth. His pronunciation, with the inflections being bandied about with abandon when he was excited, and then, the way the silky fluidity would return, as he calmed down, and began once again, to recede into that gentle manly tone: soothing, calming. Sometimes even raising goose bumps on her arms and the back of neck, as his words lazily tumbled out. She looked across at him. He'd shut up shop, for a couple of minutes, and had taken a dark red nectarine from the pocket of his overall, and was looking down at it, as he rubbed it shiny on his lapel. She smiled inside as she watched. Then, he raised it to his mouth and bit into its plump ripeness. His head began to turn in her direction as he chewed, and she glanced down at her spoon, pretending to scratch a blemish of dried food from its surface. As his mouth returned to its prey, she slowly cast her eyes back in his direction. His elbows were resting in front of him on the table, and he was holding the fruit level with his mouth,

'I didn't know you ate fruit,' she said, mischievously.

'Mmn,' he replied, without looking at her, engrossed in his feast.

She watched, as he gently manouevred the plump fruit into position between his fingers, lowered his opened mouth onto it and began to suck its juice. He turned it, slowly, and once again bit into its flesh. His moist lips glistened, as he chewed on its tart succulence, then, having swallowed, he pushed out his tongue and began to lap at the oozing mess, that trickled from its skin onto his fingertips. He continued gently biting, licking, and sucking, until the tender young flesh had been devoured. She averted her gaze as he reached across and dropped the redundant nectarine stone into his pudding bowl. She looked down at the mound of chocolate pudding and custard, that Joan was expecting her to eat. She'd managed to avoid being roped into a main course but succumbed to Joan's thoughtful landslide of pudding. As she sighed with consternation, 'What's up?' he asked, sucking his fingertips.

Charlie didn't hear him. She had things on her mind. As she looked down at the Mini Mont Blanc, in her bowl, she imagined eating it. Wolfing it down - quickly. Then making an excuse, leaving the canteen, and going to the ladies' room. Once there, she could go into a cubicle, lock the door behind her then kneel in front of the lavatory bowl. She could then take out the pudding spoon, she'd secreted into her pocket. She could open her mouth, take the cold steel spoon, and insert it. She could push the spoon backwards and forwards, deep into her throat, inducing herself to vomit. She could then watch with gratification, as the lumps of semi-digested pudding splashed into the water. Then, it would be done. Over with. No need to worry about the hundreds of calories being released into her system. Bloating her. Making her face look porcine. She could press down on the handle of the cistern and watch as the poison was flushed away. Gone. She'd done this many times before, why should today be any different?

'Are y'gonna answer me?'

'Answer what?'

'What's up…? What's the matter with yeh…?'

'I feel sick.'

She looked down at the foul, brown and yellow heap, that stared back up at her from the pudding bowl. Rick watched. She picked up her spoon. She poked the pudding as if expecting a response. No response was forthcoming. It just lay there, pretending to be dead. If she wanted to find an excuse not to eat it, she had to do it by herself. She rescued a minute blob of custard from the summit looked at it and raised it to her mouth. Rick watched. She put the spoon near her lips, then they opened, and her tongue came out and slowly licked the custard off the spoon.

Should she delve in and finish the lot? Dash to the lavatory? Bring it all back up? No. She was determined never to do that again, however strong the desire. She didn't know what to do next. She wouldn't insult Joan by refusing a main course, then leave her pudding. She'd just have to take a deep breath and shovel it down. But what if she couldn't manage it? What if she threw up in the attempt?

'Are y'gonna eat that, then?'

She paused, then guiltily replied, 'Yes.'

'Well, it doesn't look like,' he replied, snootily. 'It's gonna go cold.'

She took a deep breath, and was just about to lower the spoon and decapitate the chocolate pudding, when the clouds parted and a choir of heavenly angels sang, delivering her from eternal damnation, as Rick spoke,

'I'll have it… if you don't wan it.'

She raised her eyes, and they met with Rick's. Of course. How could she have been so stupid? The answer to her dilemma had been sitting opposite her for the last twenty minutes, and she hadn't seen it. She smiled at him. Relenting, he gave her one of his gormless grins. She pushed the bowl across the table to an eagerly awaiting Rick, who grabbed it, scooped up a spoonful of the monstrosity, and shoved it into his mouth, with greedy enthusiasm.

As he enjoyed his feast, she rested her face into her hands, closed her eyes and bit onto her bottom lip, as again she visualised his mouth, gently biting, licking, and sucking, at the juicy orifice of the plump, young nectarine… *I should be so lucky.*

5

Joan excitedly entered her front door then slammed it shut. The big day had arrived. Eric was out, fishing at the canal, and she'd arrived home from work, full of the joys of spring. She'd arranged for him to get back home at half one, when she'd have a special meal prepared. She also had another couple of treats up her sleeve. The amalgamation of all three would, she was sure, culminate in the transformation of the said Eric from a burping, farting fisherman, into a sperm-pumping superstud in the mould of Casanova. She rapidly removed her coat then draped it over the banister, walked down the hall and entered the kitchen. She opened the polythene bag she was carrying, took the oysters out then dropped them into a pan, and held it under the cold tap, to rinse them off. As she watched the gurgling water submerge the thick crusty shells, her mind wandered to her bedroom, the wardrobe, and the brown paper parcel she'd so cunningly hidden, a week ago. She could hardly wait to take it back out from its hiding speck, open it up, take out the basque, stockings and suspenders, and put them on, once again. As she daydreamed, she subconsciously turned off the tap, and the gurgling stopped. She visualised the scene of debauchery that was to follow, and her breathing began to quicken. She thumped the pan down, and the water splashed onto the drain board. She picked out a large lemon from the fruit bowl and condemned it to death. She drew the large knife from its pine block, lay the lemon onto the chopping board, then, without asking if it had any last requests, slid the knife backwards and forwards, until it was sliced neatly into two halves. And, all this time, Gertrude the goldfish had been watching her every move, maybe wondering if she was going to be next?

***

They came flowing out. Gushing like a torrent. A torrent of humanity. Through the main gate. The bell had gone three minutes ago, and for two minutes and fifty seconds it was the lull before the storm. The rivulets raced from each clocking station then made their way down alleyways and passages, converging as they went into bigger stronger flows. Taking shortcuts through locker rooms and machine shops. Gathering pace. Their urgency disproportionate to their final goal. Released from their shackles. They surged, towards the fresh air. The daylight. Elated by freedom. The stink of oil replaced by the mirage of food, playing tricks with their nostrils, as they rushed home. The match tonight. A pint with the mates. Cut the grass. Babysitting. Judo class. A kip on the couch. A clandestine date. The telly. Clean out the pigeon loft. Freedom. Until tomorrow. They came, flowing out. Like a dropped vase, shattering into hundreds of shards. Each one unique. Each one the same. Into the car park. Anxious feet crunching the cinders. Got to be first, onto the scooter. Got to be first, into the car. Got to be first: onto the bike. Got to be first; to cross to the bus stop. Through the main gate. Spewing out. Like a wave of molten humanity, erupting from the mouth of the factory. Gathering pace. Unstoppable. Their urgency disproportionate to their final goal. All... except Dot.

She sat behind the wheel of her Astra, motionless, almost in a trance, as the skewed lines of Vectras, Golfs, Corollas, Mondeos, Fiestas, Clios, Old Uncle Tom Cobley an' all slowly, weaved their snail-like trail towards the exit. She was in no hurry. Let them go. She moved her head backwards and lay it on the headrest. *Repeat a lie often enough and people will start to believe it.* She *deserved* to keep it. Why *shouldn't* she? Yes - she deserved to keep it.

Goebbels was right.

As the lines of cars snaked out onto the road, the space around Dot's became larger and larger. Greater and greater, until she looked at the clock on her dashboard: 5:56.

Right, she thought, *that's it. The stupid bugger. He should take more care of his stuff.*

Her mind was now definitely made up. She was going to treat the kids to a proper meal, each, instead of chips: down to the Bengal Tiger. Nan bread, onion bhajis, tikka masala, mango chutney, Rogan Josh, those big round things that looked like giant crisps. Right - the Bengal Tiger it was, then. Except, little Bobby wouldn't eat Indian food, she'd have to nip up to Mario's Pizza Parlour, and get him a Margherita (and chips). Likewise, Bernie. Her favourite treat was crispy duck and pancakes, with chips, from the Happy House takeaway (a bit of a misnomer there, because Zhou, the owner, never smiled. He was a right, miserable bugger). She racked her brain, and it gradually drifted back, that the last time young Dot had Indian food she turned her nose up, as well. But she did love kebabs. Right. A kebab and chips for young Dot, then. And Francine loved KFC. Job done there. That just left Emma. Emma... What would she eat? Erm... Mmmn... Breast of chicken and chips!

So, it'd be, down to the Bengal Tiger for Dot's curry, over to Mario's Pizza for Bobby's Margherita then, across to KFC for Francine, up to The Happy House for Bernie's crispy duck, round to The Crescent for young Dot's kebab then, on the way home, nip into the chippy for Emma's breast of chicken... *Sod this for a game of soldiers,* she thought, as she realised that the execution of the logistics for 'Operation Get Food' was going to take the best part of an hour and half. And even then, the whole lot would be bloody stone cold, by the time she got home.

By now the car park had emptied. Except for Dot's Astra and of course, the skeleton of the old Lansing Bagnall fork-lift truck, that had stood over by the foundry wall for the last twenty-one years, devoid of as many salvageable spare parts as could be plundered. She reached down under the driver's seat, took hold of the Aldi bag and pulled it out. Putting her hand into it, she drew out the wallet. Opening it, she ran the side of her thumb across the crisp edges of the banknotes, as if for reassurance that they were still there. Within her power. To do with whatever she wished. She paused, then carefully, slowly, began to part the individual leather flaps. It was then that the two photos stared back at her. She hadn't noticed them before, so intent had she been, on checking and counting and counting and checking *all that money*, that the only other thing she'd noticed had been the obvious; his plastics and driver's licence. But the photos had been tucked away, hidden in a long-forgotten, little compartment. It must have been years since they'd last seen the light of day. She took hold of them and lifted them out. They were the little things, the type you get from one of those kiosks. The two separate photos were from the same strip of four. The most rubbish two having probably been binned. They were much alike in their subject. Each one showing the same young couple, with an arm around each other's shoulder, smiling happily as they obeyed the will of the all-seeing eye. They looked about late twenties. He, handsome(ish) in a flattened boxer's nose sort of way, was wearing a Kiss Me Quick hat. She, pretty and with a sparkle in her eyes that revealed the love within her, was holding a stick that bore the pink, wispy remains of a candy floss.

An almost-smile of nostalgia almost spread across Dot's lips, as a hint of something reached out from the photos and touched her. She turned one over to see if there was anything written on the back.

I love you.
Blackpool
1971. xxx

She picked the second photo between her thumb and forefinger and lifted it to the front. She turned it over.

Not as much
as I love you.
Blackpool
1971.

xxxxxxxxxx. X.

She looked again at the two faces. Fifteen seconds passed as she attempted to conjure up a story, behind the photos. Were they young marrieds? She couldn't make out if the girl was wearing a wedding ring, he wasn't. Maybe they were just courting, in the first flush of a relationship.

Their smiles were certainly genuine, not like the forced smiles that evolve with the passage of time. Blackpool. Probably a day trip. What was it in aid of? Maybe he was going to propose to her? Would she accept? Did she accept? Or maybe, she turned him down. Left him broken-hearted, crying into his pint. Maybe they married. Traditional. White dress and big black wedding cars, the type that double for funerals, not taxis. Had kids. Then, a few years down the line, he buggered off, with some floozy. Maybe they didn't marry, just let the relationship run its course then split up. Of course, that's why he's got both of the photos - she give him hers back when she binned him, went their separate ways. He's probably forgot all about them over, the years, even if he did remember them, he'd probably rip them up. She looked at his face. Big, soulful eyes, like a basset hound. Strong cheekbones. A mass of brown hair and a pair of eyebrows that met in the middle, forming the wings of a bird. His face was weather-beaten, rugged. And his flattened nose, a bit like Elvis. She wondered how he'd turned out. Matured. From his day trip to Blackpool, all those years ago. What was he like now? From the boy to the man. Fat, maybe. Forties', probably. As she held him in the palm of her hand, she sighed. A second of his life captured on a photo. Not knowing what lay ahead, the years to come. Just like Dot, all those years ago.

She was glad, she'd found the photos. It made her mind up for her. Forced the decision upon her. She knew it was wrong. She'd always brought her kids up not to steal, to be honest. She knew it was wrong, to keep what didn't belong to you. Even though she didn't had two ha'pennies to knock together, she knew, deep down in her heart, that she couldn't keep the money. She'd been brought up to be honest, and though she'd wandered off the straight and narrow a few times in her life, and still would, she *was* an honest person. That was why, if she could admit it to herself, she hadn't touched the money, in three days. She couldn't bring herself to do it, and all the bravado about having a spending spree, was just a load of bullshit, because she knew it was wrong. She couldn't admit this of course, the rumblings of social conscience lay repressed, deep within her psyche. As her mind went into militant shop steward mode she papered over the cracks with the rumbling of, *Why the Hell did I find these pictures? I'll have t'give him his wallet back, now.*

That was another of her traits; believe one thing but say another. Huffing in exaggerated frustration, she flippantly yanked out the driver's licence from one of the leather flaps. She unfolded it and looked at the address. She decided that she'd take it 'round to the bloke's house, herself.

***

46 Cledwen Close... The Swan... Yeah, she knew The Swan area well. It was one of those just out of town areas on the posh side of the city. Well, it wasn't that posh really, but was mainly private houses as opposed to Dot's normal, council shite. She'd often dropped fares off up there after they'd had a night out on the town. She was up that way a couple of times last week. She couldn't place Cledwen Close, though. Maybe, she'd get a reward out of it. Twenty quid, or a tenner. Knowing her luck - bugger all. Right, the bastard, he's not getting off Scott free. Just to be on the safe side, and of course to cover her petrol money, she thought it somewhat prudent to siphon of a twenty-pound note and stash it away in her purse. That still leaves him

with a hundred and forty-five quid, plus his plastic. Now, that wasn't a bad result for him, was it? Dot wasn't stealing the money, she was just misappropriating it, whatever that meant. She lifted her bag off the front passenger seat and started to root through it for her purse. She found it buried beneath twenty ton of debris, at the bottom. She lifted the purse out, opened it, and shoved the purloined twenty-pound note into it. Just as she was about to drop the purse back, something in the bottom of her bag caught her eye. She reached in and picked it out. The lucky penny that Joan had returned to her. Dot didn't realise this, of course, she just thought it was a run-of-the-mill, 'Not Lucky' penny. She opened the flap of her purse and dropped it in.

* * *

It was all coming back to her, now: the area, the road. She *had* been here, last week. Twice.

But this part she remembered, because just before she was about to turn into the road, the fare told her to drop him off, on the corner. As it was a cul-de-sac, it'd save her having to do a three-point-turn. She thought he was going to do a runner, but he didn't. He gave her a twenty-pound note and said, '*keep the change.*' Then, struggled out of the Mondeo, and stumbled away into the night. She was racking her brain to remember what he looked like. No. She couldn't think. He was about forty-five, maybe fifty, that's all she could recall. But then... it started to return... Her memory began to clear. Yes, it was him - definitely. She remembered his voice,

'*Cledwen Close, The Swan.*'

He'd said it to her, just after he'd got into the car and

said,

'Alright, gorgeous. Any chance of a date...?'

Yes, she remembered the glint of his tears, as they trickled down his cheeks. She glanced into her rearview mirror, and there was a gold Renault Espace following close behind. She slipped her indicator stalk up and the winker began clicking a left turn. Dot took her foot off the accelerator. As the Astra began to slow, the Espace pulled out and drove past, continuing down the road.

It was here. Just here, she was sure... Yes. As the opening to the road revealed itself, the sign, CLEDWEN CLOSE loomed into view. She skipped the gear lever from fourth to second, and the car stumbled to a walking pace. She turned into the road and pulled the car up, at the kerb. As the engine ticked over, she looked down the road. It was the usual middle-class sort of place. Rows of identical fences, guarding rows of identical 1960s' semis. Along both pavements, rows of flowering cherry trees surrendered their pink snowflakes, to the evening breeze. She pushed the gear lever into first, and allowed the car to gently crawl forward, along the gutter. Number forty-six would be quite a way down, on the right. She gently accelerated the car and carried on.

A minute passed, as she took in the sight of how the other half lived, then eventually, she reached the bottom of the cul-de-sac. Number forty-six was standing alone, slightly elevated, at the end of the road. A large, detached bungalow fronted by a low brick wall and a shiny laurel hedge. A row of lavender, running up one side of the drive, was opposite a row of four or five thick-stemmed thorny, rose bushes, just coming into bud. There was a silver Mercedes estate parked on the incline, and the surrounding wet concrete glistening in the sun, told her that the car had not long been washed. Thin trickles of water slowly crept down the drive like *the Beast with Five Fingers*, as Dot rubbed the edge of her thumbnail up and down her front tooth. The garage door was open. She could also see that the television was on in the front room, but there was no sign of anyone. She didn't know what to do. Once again, the best laid plans of mice, men, and Dot had gone awry. It seemed like a good idea at the time. To bring the wallet back. But now that she was there, arrived, and seen the place where *he* lived, the Mercedes, the lovely garden, she felt, well, she felt – scruffy, vulnerable. What would he think of her? Pulling up in a clapped-out, old banger. She nervously sprayed some Intimate Nights on the back of her neck. She steered a three-point turn, drove a few yards further back up the road, stopped the car and began to rehearse her lines. What was his name again? She took the driver's licence from the wallet and unfolded it. As she walked towards the bungalow, her heart began to pound. She pulled her stomach in and fastened her duffle coat toggles. She reached the drive and made her way up the incline, past the car, towards the porch. All her carefully rehearsed words evaporated, in a cloud of apprehension. The door was in front of her. The bell stared at her. She nervously squeezed the wallet in one hand and raised the other hand towards the bell. Her extended forefinger hovered in mid-air... '*I haven't got time for this,*' she berated herself, under her breath, '*the kids need their tea...*' (Believe one thing but say another). She pushed the brass flap of the letterbox open with her thumb, slid the wallet through the gap and, as it dropped onto the coconut mat of the porch, she turned and scurried, like a frightened mouse, back to the car. As she slumped onto the driver's seat, started the engine, and accelerated the car down the road, James Edward Currie rushed down the drive. All he could do was watch, as Dot's rusty Astra disappeared into a swirling mist of cherry blossom snowflakes.

6

Fifty-six redundancies. Fifty-six. There were just over seven hundred workers in the place, and management wanted fifty-six of them to put their hands up for the bullet.

It wasn't just a question of '*Thanks for all your past loyalty and hard work, blah, blah. Here's your thirty pieces of silver, now bugger off.*' It went deeper than that, much deeper. It wasn't just fifty-six jobs, up the Swannee, to be reinstated the next time it got busy. It was fifty-six livelihoods, terminated. Gone.

The meeting had become heated. On one side of the boardroom table sat the three amigos: management. On the other, *Union* Jack Brady, the convener, surrounded by his cohort of Dot and the three other shop stewards. All the usual clichés were rolled out with monotonous sabre rattling regularity, '*We won't be sold down the river, sacrificing our birthright, at this moment in time.*'

Then the management had theirs lined up,

'*A fair day's work for a fair day's pay; survival of the fittest; moving forward, together.*'

After an hour of sweaty armpits, and holding in farts, the cavalry arrived in the form of Petronela, pushing the refreshments trolley with one hand, and carrying a humongous mound of assorted biscuits, on a grey plastic tray, in the other. They broke off for 'fifteen minutes', during which they spoke mainly of watching the telly, and keeping fit, as Dot noted that the seven, stem ginger nuts she had her eye on, had all disappeared with great alacrity, into the gaping gob of Jack. He, who had refined the art of munching on mouths-full of sloppy ginger nuts, in tandem with sucking in gobs-full of sweet, milky tea, while espousing the benefits of health clubs, for '*those who need them.*' Then, after twenty-three and a half minutes, when copious amounts of liquid refreshment had been swallowed down, and all that was left on the biscuit tray was six arrowroots and two halves of a malted milk that someone had picked back up off the carpet, the meeting was reconvened. At which point, two of the shop stewards, Dick Dodd and Ben Swift, decided they needed to empty their bladders, and subsequently, to a chorus of huffing and tutting, mainly from the three amigos, exited to the little boys' room. They didn't really need to go but they always liked to prove to the evil management just who, really, had the whip hand (in more ways than one).

So, as part two accelerated to a crawl, the meeting eventually reached the dizzy heights of a snail's pace, as much going-over old ground, repetition of clichés, and superfluous chuntering, in the finest tradition of irrelevant waffle, was allowed, to take precedent. Jack, and his boys (including Dot), rejected out of hand the idea that they would lie down and allow management to implement a redundancy strategy, whereby deliberate erosion of workforce numbers would be accompanied by an increase in annual company profits. Every job would be bitterly defended. It wasn't the union's place to make profits for the company, but to keep their members in full-time employment. Then the amigos opened fire. Firstly, there would be no compulsory redundancies. Which was a major climbdown even before they'd climbed up. With compulsory redundancies, you can cherry-pick all the shite. The lazy bastards, who won't do a tap, then give them the heave-ho. All gone, bye-bye, goodnight. Result, a cleaner, greener workforce, which runs on a mixture of enthusiasm and conscience. Voluntary redundancy was a different matter entirely. Lazy bastards don't usually volunteer, for suicide. It normally attracts those with a spark of ambition, or those with another job to walk into.

Secondly, the redundancy package 'on the table' was generous, to say the least. So generous in fact, that Jack, was desperately racking his brain to try and tailor it to fit the description *derisory*. It was, divide and rule plain and simple. Jack and the famous four, were having none of it. The proposal would be put to the membership, with the recommendation that the offer be 'rejected out of hand'. There would be no redundancies, voluntary or otherwise. Management would get their reduction in workforce numbers by natural wastage, which sounds like something you flush down the lavatory, but means retirement, death, and people leaving for pastures new. The natural wastage system would, indeed, yield the required fifty-six vacancies that management were asking for, the minor hitch being that management were insisting on the reduction in the workforce taking place within the next three months, not the next twenty years. But that's management for you - intransigent. Dot certainly was wearing her *one out - all out* face, as she traipsed out of the boardroom.

* * *

'At the next roundabout, take the first exit.'
He pushed down on the indicator stalk, then steered the car left.

'After one hundred yards, turn right.'
It was completely mad, of course. Utter lunacy. He couldn't explain, what had made him come to such a decision. He had an appointment with his accountant, on this side of town, so he wasn't travelling too far out of his way, but, well... She obviously wanted no reward or recognition, otherwise, she wouldn't have scampered off, like a frightened mouse. And now...

Why couldn't he just let the woman be? He shouldn't go shoving his nose into other people's lives. Intruding. But sometimes, people do things they don't mean to. Scampering off like a frightened mouse, for example. And now, he's doing something he thought he'd never do. Not to start with. He thought it was an open and shut case. Man loses wallet, containing wedge and plastic. Wallet gone forever. End of. But that was yesterday. Before he heard the *plop* of the wallet hitting the coconut mat. What he didn't expect was: woman finds said wallet, returns it and disappears. Man can't trace woman. Ships that pass, blah, blah. End of. How could he allow it to be the end of this story? Her coat was ragged. She jumped into an old banger. She drove off, not wanting to be seen. Seeking no reward. And as he ran down the path, the only thing he could think to do, after his shouts had fallen on deaf ears, was to memorise the registration number of her car. Then, by the time he'd watched her driving off, and wondered if he should jump into his car to try and catch her up, and decided against it, and turned and ran back up the drive, to get a pen and paper, and found that the front door had slammed, behind him, and ran around, to the back of the bungalow, and through the kitchen door, and pulled open the drawer to find a biro, and dashed around, looking for a piece of paper to write the number down on, and, not finding any, picking up the Daily Mirror, to scribble the registration number onto the border, he'd forgotten the bloody thing. Well, he hadn't exactly forgotten it. He could remember all the right letters and numbers, but not necessarily in the right order, like the great man once said. He jotted them down, as best he thought they went, then rang his nephew. Then, his nephew rang back and said the car was a Citroen belonging to a man, living in Chesterfield. Then, he wrote them down again, and rang his nephew. And his nephew rang back and said the car was a Vauxhall, belonging to a woman in Devises. And he rung his nephew back, two more times, and got similar negative answers. When he realised that the numbers and letters had tossed and turned and tumbled around in his brain so much, that he could no longer remember which order they went in, he rung his nephew again and said to forget the whole stupid idea, and his nephew said, '*Okay, Unc, no probs,*' while thinking, '*Thank fuck, for that*'.

When, at twenty-six minutes past four in the morning, the ache from his bulging bladder woke him to get up, and he clambered out of bed and made his way through the dark, to the lavatory, stood naked in front of the pan and, as he bore down to start his flow, just after he let out an insignificant fart, the registration number appeared in his mind. Clear as day. There it was. And he interrupted his peeing, and raced back into the bedroom, clumsily stubbing his toe on the linen basket, switched on the light, snatched his pen from the bedside table, and wrote it down. Clear. For all to see. Onto the dust cover of Harry Potter and the Philosopher's Stone while wondering what his wife would think, of the desecration of her book.

'*After fifty yards, take the next turning left.*'

The three-pointed star swung to the left, as the car followed its command, and joined the dual carriageway. What should he say? What *could* he say?

'*Hello. I'd just like to thank you for returning...*' No.

'*I happened to notice you, driving off, yesterday and...*' Shite.

'*Are you the lady who...*'

She's obviously the bloody lady or he wouldn't be standing on her doorstep. What if she takes offence? She might think he's some kind of weirdo. Pervert. How big is her husband? What if she sets the dog on him - a Rottweiler, with jaws like a hippo, and teeth like a Great White. He knew it was lunacy. Madness. Maybe, he should just turn the car around and head for the accountant.

'*At the next roundabout, take the third exit.*'

Yeah, that's what he'll do. When he gets to the roundabout, just go right around it and head back down the dual carriageway. It was all nice in fantasy, but not practical in real life. He hasn't wasted the flowers he's still got that old, blue vase under the sink. The one he bought in Oxfam, with the leather jacket. And in the distance, he could see blue, flashing lights. He eased his foot off the accelerator as he saw the brake lights of the cars in front, slowing down to ogle the gory sight ahead, on the opposite carriageway. It must have just happened. An RTA, as his nephew calls them. There was a green Fiesta, looked as if it'd pulled out to overtake something, and been hit up the arse end by the Number 32. A police car was parked across the lanes of the opposite carriageway. The two coppers were out. One was barking into his radio the other was seeing to the driver of the car. He was unconscious. Slumped over the steering wheel.

Weouu, weouu, weouu, weouu.

He could hear it coming from behind, rapidly approaching. The unnerving banshee-like wail. He glanced into his mirror, as the two lines of traffic in front began to part, opening up a passage down the centre of the carriageway.

Weouu, weouu, weouu, weouu.

He steered towards the central reservation and braked. It passed in a flash of blue, skirted the perimeter of the roundabout, and began to head back down the opposite carriageway, towards the crash.

'*Take the third exit.*'

'Sod off, missus,' he mumbled, as he steered the car around the roundabout and ground to a halt, as the traffic began to gridlock. As the paramedics hurried towards the Fiesta, he noticed a diminishing gap in the left-hand lane, and headed through it, carrying on back to where he started.

'*Take the third exit,*' she repeated.

'*Bugger this, for a game of marbles,*' he thought, indicated left, and forced his way between the back end of a Cortina estate and the front end of a Metro.

'*Take the next exit.*'

He squeezed the car towards the requested exit, leaving behind an irate Metro driver, who was now calling him all the arrogant, German bastards under the sun.

So, here he was, sitting in the Mercedes, outside the

woman's house. In spite of his last-minute decision to abort his decision to go there, he *was* there. What could it have been that brought about his change of direction, he wondered? The hand of fate? Destiny? (It was a smashed-up Fiesta, on the dual carriageway). He looked at the house. Thirties'-built. Council. Semi-detached. Fairly large, three-bedrooms, maybe four. As he admired the courses of brickwork, memories of his childhood flooded back. He visualised his dad in the front garden pruning his roses, tending the lavender. Upstairs in the front bedroom, his mam, changing the nets as Gerry and the Pacemakers sang out, courtesy of the Dansette, in the front parlour. He knew this type of house like the back of his hand. He switched off the engine, pulled on the door handle, and pushed with his elbow. The door opened and he stepped out, onto the damp pavement. He picked up the flowers off the back seat, walked past the unkempt mass of privets that masqueraded as a hedge, and through the gaping, wrought-iron gate. The 'front' door was on the side, and as he walked down the path, he had no idea what he was going to say, when he came face to face with her. He raised his hand and pressed the bell push with his middle finger. Nothing happened. He didn't hear anything. He pressed it again, this time listening more intently for any sound of the bell. Nothing happened - twice. Was it God, telling him to turn around and go home? Maybe. But, if it really was God telling him to turn around and go home, why was there a big, brass knocker hanging there right in front of him, waiting to be knocked? He took hold of the knocker and thumped it three times, against the door.

Dum, dum, dum...

He waited. Nothing happened. He took hold of the knocker again and thumped it, this time, more assertively, five times - like a rent collector.

Dum, dum, de, dum, dum...

Nothing happened - twice. It was at this point the thought crossed his mind, that his newly found belief, about the hand of fate guiding him here, could, quite conceivably turn out to be just another, load of sentimental bollocks. Well, at least he'd tried to redress the balance. To give something back in return, as a *thank you*. He wondered about leaving the flowers on the doorstep or slipping two tenners through the letterbox. Sod it. He turned, and as he was about to start walking back up the path,

'Wha, d'you want?'

The voice came from behind him. He turned around, and there, standing in the gap where there used to be a back gate, was a street urchin, about seven, maybe eight, holding a bike wheel in one hand, and two large spoons in the other.

'Is the lady of the house at home?' he said, then smiled, reassuringly.

In the four and a half seconds that passed, the boy stared back at him, as if he had two green heads, and had just descended from the planet *Zog*. Then, tentatively, his young lips parted, and he muttered, almost incoherently,

'We 'aven't got no ladies, in our 'ouse...' he paused, then tacked on, 'On'y me mam.'

'And what's your mam's name, son...?'

After three seconds,

'Dorothea...' slithered out of his lips. 'But her real name's, Dot.'

7

They should have guessed there was an ulterior motive, but no, they didn't see it coming. The opinion was that it was just the age-old ploy by management, to prune down the workforce, then, squeeze the remainder until their pips squeaked. Extricate the last ounce of sweat, and eventually, achieve the same output as before, but now with reduced numbers.

The P word - profit.

Dot came the closest to exposing the tyranny that lay within the blackened heart of the inner sanctum, with her fabricated suggestion of a Japanese takeover. Devised entirely to strike fear into the heart of an earwigging Rick, her notion was not a million miles from the truth. Rick, not a great lover of the Japanese, had carried a life-long grudge against the Land of the Rising Sun because of, *What they did to the British motorbike industry*. Seemingly, oblivious to the fact that it was British motorcycle buyers, not the Japanese, who committed the dastardly act. Dot, an inveterate veteran of twisting the knife into Rick, at every opportunity, concocted the Japanese story, as another form of psychological torment. What she didn't know was that moves *were* afoot for Nelson Engineering to become the object of a buyout. Not by the Japanese, but a phenomenally successful competitor, with a bulging order book and contented workforce.

With a factory Kaykay had now outgrown, the options were, the major financial investment required in larger premises and brand-new plant or, scout around for a mismanaged bloated inefficient, yet reasonably well-equipped, company that could be had for a fraction of its potential future value. Kaykay Engineering had been a thorn in the side of Nelson's for almost eight years. Started toward the end of the sixties, by Sergeant Kenny Kingston, the business had grown through ambition, guts, and sheer hard work in the space of thirty-odd years from a one- man band, operating in a rented lock-up garage, to a multi-million-pound operation.

The death knell for Nelson's sounded ten years ago, when Kenny Kingston retired and handed the business over to his son and daughter. Inheriting their father's flair for cheekily courting customers, ruthlessly reducing costs, treating their workforce like humans, not shit, and producing the right product, on time, at the right price, their reputation as incorrigible mavericks preceded them. But, of course, from the day Kenny Kingston took on his first employee, he already knew that one of the main keys to success was harmony. *Show the men respect and they'll show it back*, was a byword he'd learnt in the Royal Engineers. He chose to run his business along the lines of his military values, and those values were instilled into his son and daughter. By the time Kevin and Karen Kingston had taken over the reins from their father, the number of regular Nelson Engineering customers jumping ship to the greener pastures of Kaykay was reaching alarming proportions. Now, behind closed doors, pulled drapes, in serious tones and hushed solemnity, between bouts of nervous laughter and fractious words, in a large, detached house, standing in two acres, somewhere on the outskirts of town, a deal was struck. Kevin and Karen Kingston, together with turncoat Hardcastle, persuaded the octogenarian brothers, Archibald, and Reginald Nelson, to hang up their hats, for the deal was good - too good - to turn down. Hardcastle almost salivated when he heard what his cut was to be. And so, the overture had ended. The first movement was about to begin.

**

As the rumours of redundancy were confirmed, the repercussions reverberated around the factory, but nowhere greater than within the confines of the rectification area. Dot had come screaming in, like Boadicea on her chariot, sending up clouds of dust and whirlwinds of effing and blinding. All she was short of was a face full of woad and a blood-drenched spear. Divide and conquer was the order of the day, as the cat had been well and truly flung amongst the pigeons. Joan argued that Rick should volunteer, being a single man. Charlie agreed with her. Rick saw red, and barked that Charlie should be the first out, as she was the last in. Dot spat out that it didn't affect the temporary workers, as their contracts weren't being extended anyway.

'They're slimmin us down, prior to a sell off,' said Joan.

Charlie enthused that it could be the best thing that'd ever happened, cutting back the dead wood. Rick accused Charlie of being a management sympathiser. Dot demanded to know whose side Charlie was on.

'You've got to move with the times,' she said.

'I'll show you how much we're gonna move with the times,' shouted Dot, 'We'll bring this place to its friggin knees.'

'Like you did, last time?'

It wasn't the most tactful of replies. But then, for all her high-class education, and intelligence, tact was never one of Charlie's strong points. Familiarity wasn't breeding contempt, in Dot's gut, the contempt had been festering from day one, familiarity was breeding utter loathing. Indubitably. Charlie realised she'd shot herself in the foot, as the guns fell silent. Dot turned and fixed her with a glare, that would give a laser beam a run for its money.

'This time, it's different,' she said, through clenched teeth, 'and when we put the resolution to the membership, *and make them see sense*, this place'll be like a ghost town.'

***

Its nickname was Pork Chop Hill, though it wasn't shaped like a pork chop. An incongruous knoll of grassed-over earth at the head of the car park, adjacent to the main entrance to the factory. Nobody knew where it came from, or what its original purpose was meant to be. It was just there. An enigmatic hump of grass. And lo, as the mackerel cloud did blanket the May sky, the hundreds of Sportyman-clad feet did wend their way crunching across the cinders, from the building of doom, unto the hill of Pork Chop. And a great effing and blinding did sound throughout the land as the populous did share, and exchange, their disgruntled chuntering regarding the imposed need to give up an hour's overtime, to attend the mass meeting.

Jack took pride of place. Standing on top of the hill, he raised the loudhailer to his mouth. After a couple of seconds of high-pitched, squealing feedback raised derogatory comments from the assembled mass of humanity gazing up in disillusioned awe, the words,

'Is this fuckin thing switched on?'

bellowed forth, above the heads of the throng.

Dot stepped forward, took hold of the loudhailer, and did some impressive fondling of the switch before, accompanied by an authoritative *'Yeah,'* handed the contraption back to Jack. Once again, he raised the loudhailer to his mouth.

'Can y'all hear me, at the back?'

'No.'

'IS THAT BETTER?'

'YEAH.'

Now in full swing, Jack went straight for the emotional jugular, 'Brothers…'

'And, sisters,' retorted Big Mary, the main source of her irritation being the pain from her piles.

Having momentarily knocked Jack off course, in his infant steps towards world domination, 'Brothers - *and sisters,'* he grudgingly conceded, before going on to lambaste management's assumption that there would be people stupid enough to sacrifice their birthright for thirty pieces of sliver, or silver, as he quickly corrected himself. Even if the silver took the shape of a golden handshake. And so, as five minutes turned to ten, and ten minutes turned to twenty, what started as a cool May breeze turned into a cold wind, then a biting chill. As Jack's blather transformed into waffle, then meandered gradually into repetition, the coat collars began to rise, and the beanie hats were pulled down over numbed ears. As feet were stamped against the ground, in an effort to warm them up, various members of the mass began to exhibit their displeasure at the length of the meeting by projecting questions to the union convener, such as,

'*Will y' get a fuckin move on? I'm starving.*'

Then, the motion to strike in the event of management's redundancy plan being brought to fruition, was put to the membership.

'All those in favour.'

Almost half of the workforce raised a hand.

'All those against.'

Almost half of the workforce raised a hand.

Jack, and the other five, were perturbed. All the rhetoric, the histrionics, the bullshit, had failed to deliver with the goods - the magic words, '*motion carried.*'

Jack stood in stunned silence for a few seconds, as over in the pallet compound *Ratticus* tucked into the rotting remains of a dead, baby hedgehog. The mutterings of discontent from Dot and the other stewards were drowned out by the grumblings of the mass. Then a huge groan of disapproval rose from the crowd as Tony announced over the loudhailer that the vote was inconclusive and would have to be taken again. He wasn't in the mood,

'Take it for me, would you, Dot?'

Dot lost no time in taking the loudhailer out of his hand. She raised it to her mouth and admonished the angry throng by asking,

'D'you lot realise how important this vote is?'

She then proceeded to cut a short story long, by going over the salient points of Jack's speech, embellishing them with Dottisms, as she went. This was where she was born to be, standing in front of a crowd, loudhailer in hand. Persuading, cajoling, reinforcing the solidarity, praising, flattering, then, reiterating the evil machinations of Management. Using the words that had been passed down from dear Uncle Harry, all those years ago. '*Sold down the river... the thin end of the wedge... management's intransigence...*'

Eventually, Dot's oration ended, to a standing ovation from Jack and the other four, but bearing in mind they had no seats, there wasn't any other type of ovation they could have given her. Nevertheless, it was an impressive show of solidarity in front of the workforce and sent out the right message. Dot then repeated the motion, put forward by Jack, and asked them, again. Her chest swelled with pride, as she heard the mutterings of approval coming from behind her. She raised the loudhailer to her mouth. It was a done deal.

'All those in favour...'

Almost half of the workforce raised their hand. Dot hesitated, to give any waverers one last chance to put their hands up. None. Almost half? She made a rough, mental headcount and - it *did* look like just half.

'All those against...'

Almost half of the workforce raised their hand. Once again, it had to be announced that the vote was still inconclusive, and it would have to be taken, yet again. And throughout the land was heard a great gnashing of teeth, from the rabble. It was then, that Dot remembered a trick, told to her years ago, by beloved Uncle Harry. First, empathise.

'*Look...* do you lot think I like havin freezin, cold feet, as well?' Empathy box ticked, now the threat.

'We can't go home 'til we've decided this, conclusively, one way or the other.'

Go for the jugular. The weakest link. The abstentions. Those who are determined to go on strike, will stick to their guns. Those who are determined to carry on work, will also, stick to their guns. That left the abstainers. That chunk of mediocrity who hide anonymously in the mass, raising their hand neither for nor against a strike. Strike fear into them. Ferret them out. Shine a light on them in order to force them make that quantum leap, from ambiguity into decisiveness.

It was always Uncle Harry's belief that when pushed to the wire, the abstainers will almost certainly give their allegiance to those in favour of a strike. They don't wish to be seen as traitors. This was Dot's gamble. She remembered what she'd been told. Now, she was about to put it to the test.

'Right,' she said, into the loudhailer, 'what we'll have to do is...'

***

The Astra pulled to a halt outside Dot's house. Remembering to leave it in gear as the handbrake was duff, she then elatedly leapt from the car, slammed the door shut, half-skipped past the tangled mass of privets, and through the opened wrought-iron gate.

She'd done it! It worked. She'd crushed the abstainers. Uncle Harry was right. The strike was on. Well, it wasn't *yet* on, but thanks to Dot's cunning stunt, she'd extricated a mandate from the workforce for Jack to take back into the boardroom and throw onto the table. The excitement of her achievement caused her heart to beat almost as fast as if she was having an orgasm. Maybe not. It probably had more to do with her heaving her overweight bulk down the path, and to the front door, at approximately seven miles an hour. Nevertheless, as she inserted her key into the door lock, sprightly entered the hall, skipped past the oversized print of Franz Hals', The Laughing Cavalier (it seemed like a good idea at the car boot sale), and walked into the lounge, there was a certain something that had returned to Dot's life. She dropped heavily onto her throne, flicked the remote at the telly, and a second later the screen burst into life. Without stopping to see which programme was on, she stood, and went into the kitchen. She ran some water into the milk pan (the electric kettle was another casualty waiting to be returned to the front). She opened a cupboard, dropped a teabag into a mug, and shouted, '*Bobby.*' She toyed around with the idea of going out to the shed, and seeing if he was there, but decided against it as she'd have heard him hammering and banging at his bench, if he was. She returned to the lounge, carrying her mug of tea and four Jammie Devils. She sat, gazed at the carpet, and grinned. As the telly blathered on about making something out of sticky-back plastic and three toilet roll tubes, all Dot could hear, wandering through her mind, in slow motion, were the words she'd conquered the abstainers with…

'*All those in favour, move to the left… All those against, move to the right…*'

Dear Uncle Harry had triumphed again… from his urn.

***

He wasn't the kind to do speed dating. He was knocking on fifty, now. He was too old, and it was too new. He wasn't the kind to ring up these new-fangled, voicebox malarkeys, springing up in every paper you pick up. No, he wasn't the kind. He carried his mug of tea into the sitting room and sat. The canary chirped. He didn't fancy Dot, of course not. He'd only had a fleeting glimpse of her, as she rushed back to the car. She was married. Had kids. No. Of course, he didn't fancy her. But every little contact with the opposite sex was appreciated. Especially when they were new. Unknown. Polite chitchat. An exchange of views. Maybe a laugh and a joke. Maybe. He leaned back in the green Chesterfield and closed his eyes. He spoke to Nora, and told her how much he still loved her, and how much he missed her. How there would never be another woman, to take her place: the usual clichés of the bereaved. When Toby licked the fingers of his left hand, he woke, and it was ten to ten. His tea had gone stone cold. The canary sat with its head under its wing. He drew the curtains, then walked into the porch, to get the lead. No, she hadn't rung. Why should she? Still, at least, he'd let her know how much he appreciated her bringing back his wallet. Her honesty. As he walked down the path, with the little Westie straining at the lead, he wondered about whether he should buy the Magnolia he'd seen in the garden centre. It was reduced from nearly fifty pounds, to thirty. A Stellata. Thirty-one minutes later, he was walking back up the path. He went into the kitchen and unclipped the lead off Toby's collar. As he did, Dot kissed Bobby goodnight, and headed back down the stairs. She chivvied the girls to get ready for bed. She sat, picked up the telly mag and looked to see if anything good was on, after the news. As she flicked through the pages, the *'Thank You'* card and the, now wilting, bouquet of flowers were still lying on the bench in the shed, where Bobby had left them.

8

Three days had passed since Dot had acquired her mandate for a strike, and Ted's red roses, pink carnations and spray of Gypsophila had been so ignominiously condemned to death by dehydration. The proposal for a strike had been put before 'Management' and a response had been promised in two weeks' time. The original kafuffle between them regarding who should go and who should stay, had evaporated, and once again, a fragile 'peace', for want of a better word, had been restored amongst the four of them. Charlie and Rick had kissed and made up, after their little spat (well, made up anyway), and had been getting along a lot better as the days had passed, to such an extent that Rick had gradually without intention, managed to garner her interest in his beloved birds, having pointed out to her from the canteen the little recurring, clockwork toy soldier that was the pied wagtail, she'd seen on her first day. Under Rick's guidance she'd now learnt to identify six different species, that were regular visitors to the field. He spoke with such an enthusiasm that it had become contagious, and when he was describing the inhabitants of his aviaries, she suddenly piped up, out of the blue,

'I'd like to see them sometime. Maybe one day you'll let me?'

Rick, was still recovering from the experience he'd had twelve months earlier with the flirtatious Angela. He'd given his heart away only for it to be torn to shreds, then thrown back in his face. He had since, resolutely, vowed to keep his guard up. He kept Charlie at arm's length by making excuses, while subconsciously wanting to take her home, to see his feathered friends. Surreptitiously though, he was falling in love with her, and so, the hand of fate stepped in, on that afternoon, and took control out of Rick's hands.

The emerging throng were dispersing from the factory in their normal, panic-stricken, *let's get the fuck out of here* fashion, and as the streams of cars snaked their way out, one car was resolutely refusing to start - Rick's.

'Bollocks,' he said, as the engine churned and churned again, as he turned the key. The battery finally gave up the ghost, and there sat Rick, watching the last remnants of the snaking lines disappear, out onto the road. He thought it might possibly go with a jump-start if he could manage to push it to the slight decline of the car park, that led to the main exit gate. That notion went for a Burton as soon as he started to push, and after a couple of feet, the front wheels of the rust-speckled, Volvo estate dug into the soft cinders.

'Double bollocks.'

He opened the door and sat in sideways on the driver's seat, gasping to get his breath back, and looking down, disconsolately, at the gap between his feet. Three seconds passed, then he heard a car pull up.

'Rick. What's the matter?' He looked up, and there was Charlie, shouting through the passenger window of Cooper.

'The battery's cream-crackered.'

'I beg your pardon?'

'Donald-Ducked.'

'Would you care to translate?' she said, as she stepped out of the Mini.

'Cream-crackered – knackered,' he said. 'Donald-Ducked...'

'I've got the gist of it, thank you - would you like a lift home?'

Every fibre of his being was screaming '*yes,*' but somehow the translation vocalized itself as a macho,

'No, ta.'

'Right. I'll get going,' she said, making her way back to the Mini. As she opened the door, she cast a last glance at him and said,

'So, you're absolutely, 100% certain, that you definitely do not want a lift home?'

'*Yis,*' he said, curtly, then the words, *please ask me again* stampeded through his mind.

'Yes, you're certain, that you don't – or, yes, you're certain, that you do?' she asked, throwing him a final lifeline, as she sensed he was starting to crack.

Five seconds passed as he gazed back down at the space between his feet, and summoned up the courage to admit defeat and say,

'Yes, I'm certain that I don't... thank you.'

Unfortunately, his macho posturing backfired, as he heard the Mini's door slam shut, and Charlie drove off like a scalded cat, toward the main exit.

'*Triple Bollocks.*'

As he sat huffing in disgust at himself, and his idiotic charade, he watched the Mini approaching the exit gate.

As he huffed once more, the car suddenly turned left, and began to sweep in a large circle around the empty car park, arriving back beside the Volvo. The Mini window descended, and their eyes met as each of them managed, valiantly, not to burst out laughing. Three seconds passed, then Charlie floored the accelerator pedal, and her Mini gave a roar. Rick rose to his feet, locked the Volvo then climbed in beside her.

'Thanks,' he said, quietly, as she drove off.

'Pardon, did you say something…?'

'Thanks,' he said, slightly louder.

'I'm sorry, I can't hear what you're saying.'

'I said… *thank you*,' he said, in a loud clear voice.

'Now, that didn't hurt – did it…?'

He looked out of the side window, and, as the Mini sped on its way, bit his bottom lip, cursing the trembling laughter that was welling within his stomach. Charlie sat, staring dead ahead, as a smile of victory marched across her lips.

How had it come to this? What made it come to this? He turned his gaze to the road, ahead. She was there, sitting beside him. The most beautiful, sexiest, elegant woman he'd ever come across, in his entire life. He wanted her so much, yet it wasn't meant to be. In the silence that followed, he breathed in the aroma of her *No 5*.

Some lucky bugger's gonna end up with her, and it won't be me.

'So,' she said, trying her utmost to sound deadly serious, 'have I remembered this correctly? The black-headed seagull's head…'

'Gull… you don't call them seagulls. They're called gulls.'

'So, the black-headed *gull's* head isn't actually black at all? It's chocolate brown?'

'Yeah - But only in its summer plumage. It's white during the winter.'

'Well… why did they call it the black-headed gull, then…? Surely it would have been more accurate to describe the bird as the *chocolate-brown headed seagull?*'

'*Gull,*' he said with a huff.

'Oh yes, of course – gull,' she said. 'As in… *gull*-ible.'

'Yeah…'

***

The Mini came to a halt, outside Rick's house: a Victorian, end-terraced cottage, with a postage stamp front garden, and a narrow, but quite long, garden at the back. A half-hearted ramshackle, timber garage was propped up against the gable end.

'Thanks for the lift,' he said, not wanting to get out of the car.

'What's on the agenda for tonight?' she asked, also not wanting him to leave.

'The band… We've got a gig at The Omnibus.'

'You never told me you were in a band.'

'It's nothing special – mainly covers. We're a four-piece. Raise a few quid for charity. Pass the hat 'round.'

'What time are you on?'

'Nine o'clock…'

He put his fingers behind the door handle, and, as he pushed the door open, she said,

'So, you're not going to ask me in…? To see your birds…'

How could he refuse, after her kindness in offering him a lift? He looked at her.

***

The back garden had a series of four, medium sized aviaries, running its length. Each aviary contained a pair of different types of finch. The Goldfinches, and the Bullfinches, were breeding, and both had clutches of eggs. As he pointed where, within the tangled bundles of tied-up twigs, the tiny nests could be seen, he subconsciously wrapped his left arm around her waist, drew his head next to hers, and pointed, with his right hand, as he whispered, softly,

'See... there... that's the hen, incubating... She's on five eggs...'

'What kind of bird is it?' she said, in a whisper, hardly daring to breathe.

'A goldfinch...'

Charlie's searching gaze carefully penetrated the gaps between the thorny twigs, until she discovered the tiny nest, smaller than a teacup, hidden within, and beautifully constructed of moss, lichens, and spider webs. And there, peering back at her, over the rim of the nest, was the little red face, and pair of black, beady eyes, of the hen goldfinch.

'She's beautiful...' whispered Charlie, almost mesmerised.

'She's been sittin for ten days,' said Rick, in his soft whisper. 'Another coupla days an they'll start t'hatch.'

As Charlie became entranced, she found within this moment, the relaxing tranquility for which, in the last ten months, she had so desperately searched. Their whispered conversation, the protective feeling of his arm, gently, but innocently, caressing her waist. The secretive delight of his obvious sense of pride, and stifled excitement. She turned her head and looked at him. He turned, and their eyes met. Her lips formed into a smile of gentle appreciation.

'You don't have t'be a nerd, to like birds...' he whispered, with a smile. 'But it helps...'

He gave a cheeky wink, and she stifled a sympathetic chuckle, but, as he continued looking into her eyes, he noticed they had begun to glisten, in a mist of tears.

'What's wrong...?' he asked, quietly, as her bottom lip began to quiver.

She shook her head, gently.

'Nothing...' she whispered, then, through a smile, 'absolutely nothing...'

* * *

'Daddy, where's your bird book?'

'Which one, dear?'

'I don't know. The one with a goldfinch in.'

'*Garden Birds* - I daresay, it will be in one of the bookcases.'

'It isn't, I've looked.'

'It's in the conservatory,' said Charlie's mother, entering the room. 'On the chair, near the doors.'

Charlie crossed the hall, passed through the dining room then through the French doors, leading into the conservatory. She found the book, moved the binoculars off the chair, sat, and began to scan the index. Her mother silently entered.

Page 52.

She flicked through the pages until she reached, The

Goldfinch.

'Carduelis carduelis. One of the most colourful and distinctive of all the British finches.'

Her mother approached.

'The goldfinch is known as the 'thistle finch.'

'What's caused this sudden interest in birds, darling? You've never taken any notice of them before.'

Charlie knew exactly where this conversation was heading. She hesitated as she prepared one of her usual, submissive replies. As the inoffensive words were about to leave her lips, she imagined Dot, giving her oppressive, domineering mother both barrels. She veered onto another tack, as she said nonchalantly,

'A friend of mine, from the factory, breeds them. A good, friend. A particularly good friend.'

'From the factory…?'

'Yes, his name's Rick. He's rough, working-class, he drives a fork-lift, and pulls a pallet truck for a living, owns a rusty old Volvo, and lives in a house that's not much bigger than a sentry box…'

'I knew this sort of thing would happen. The second you came up with this ridiculous idea. I knew exactly what was going to happen. I said to your father…'

'And tonight, I'm going to see him perform with his rock band, at The Omnibus pub.'

'The Omnibus pub?'

'Yes… it's one of those spit and sawdust pubs, were big, tattooed people with broken noses drink gallons of cheap beer – and that's just the women.'

'And, no doubt, they take drugs.'

'And afterwards, I'm going to have sex with him, on the back seat of his rusty old Volvo, as his friends watch.'

Charlie stormed out of the conservatory, and it was all she could do to stem the flood of hysterical laughter that was welling up, in the back of her throat. As she ran up the stairs, firmly pressing her palm against her mouth, she made a vow to herself that, from then onward, a tiny part of her would remain forever *Dot*. Her mother, stunned by Charlie's newly found, defensiveness, stood, walked out onto the patio, and, as a great tit flew off the peanut basket, she gazed dispiritedly toward the oak trees, and heaved a sigh of disbelief.

It was Charlie's mother, more so than her father, who had been dead against this crackpot scheme of hers, ever since she announced it. Even though the psychologist had agreed with Charlie, that the ensuing lack of responsibility and commitment, could possibly have a beneficial effect on her rehabilitation. But, according to her mother, at least, all she had to do was have six weeks rest, at their villa in Corsica, then come back, right as rain, and rejoin the law college to complete her studies. They'd been very understanding and had said that her place would be held open indefinitely. So, why, for goodness sake, did she have to pursue this ridiculous avenue of self-destructive plebeianism? But, the one thing that Charlie's mother couldn't learn to accept, was that her daughter never again wanted to be wrapped in cotton wool. Mollycoddled, and hidden away on Corsica. That's how she'd allowed herself to be led down the road that finally culminated with her stay, in that dreadful unit. Being too weak to say 'NO'. Allowing her politeness to become her Achilles heel. All her life, she'd been intimidated, pressured, and bullied into compromising and submitting. Bending her will. Accepting what was unacceptable. Well, not anymore - enough was enough. She was determined to become her own person. One, of the real world. Whatever mistakes she might make, whatever self-inflicted tears she might shed, she was prepared to take the risks, because they would be the results of her own decisions, nobody else's – hers. So, that was it. She'd made up her mind; she'd lie on the bed for another twenty minutes, reading *Garden Birds*, then shower, get dressed, and she was going to *The Omnibus* for nine o'clock, to see Rick and his band. Although, she'd only thrown in the bit about shagging him, to annoy her mother.

It is appropriate that the collective noun for this attractive bird is 'charm.'

9

Dot's house at breakfast time was like a Star Wars battle, The Charge of The Light Brigade, and a Marx Brothers movie, rolled into one. To call it a chaotic, disorganised shambles would be an insult to a chaotic, disorganised shambles. Such was the frenetic comings, and goings, of her numerous progenies, in various states of dress, and mastication, searching for numerous mislaid items of various apparel, that had all mysteriously decided to play musical chairs, during the night, and swap bedrooms. Socks gone astray, mixed up knickers, blouses needing ironing, lost underpants. Some kids even woke up in a different bedroom to the one in which they fell asleep. Oh! and the milk's run out, too. But, somehow through all of this, eventually, the panicking would begin to subside, and be gradually replaced with the mutual assistance of a discernible pecking order, and Bernie would burst through the front door, clutching another bottle of milk, from Patel's, and vanished socks would begin to reappear, and knickers begin to find their rightful owners, and a semblance of calm would once again begin to emerge from the chaos. Dot would traipse upstairs to the bathroom, to put her lippy on, and wish she had another face as she looked at her reflection, in the mirror. The kids would be sat on the couch, like a string of sparrows on a washing line, finishing off their bowls of various cereal or crunching the crusts of the last of their toast, in silence, watching the telly. All this, and it still wasn't yet half past seven.

It was when Dot came thumping back down the stairs, and went into the front room to say, *'Tara,'* to the row of zombies, glued to the telly screen, that the pronouncement was made.

'Make sure they all get out on time, Bernie,' said Dot to her eldest daughter, as she bent down to kiss little Bobby. And, as an almost indiscernible grunt came from the opposite end of the couch, Dot kissed her youngest, on his toast-crummed lips.

'Bye-bye, son. See y' tonight. Be a good boy in school.'

Dot turned, and walked towards the hall door, and just as she reached it,

'They're in d'shed…'

She turned and looked back, at Bobby.

'What did y'say, son…?'

Without shifting his gaze from the gogglebox, Bobby repeated robotically,

'They're in d'shed.'

'What's in the shed?'

'D'flowers.'

'What flowers…?'

'Will you two shurrup. I'm watchin the telly.'

'Off d'man…'

'What man?'

'D'man with d'big, silver car… He come 'ere… de other day, when I was fixin me puncture... I put dem in d'shed for yeh...'

***

The shed door creaked open, and Dot walked in. There, lying on the bench, amongst the detritus of long-forgotten broken tools, discarded household paraphernalia, various assortments of junk, and Bobby's bike tyre inner-tubes and bent spoons, lay a gift-wrapped bunch of dried-up flowers, with a small card stapled to their wrapping. As if she was seeing an apparition, Dot slowly moved toward them.

D'man with d'big silver car...

She stood, transfixed, for a few seconds, as she stared at them, then reached down, picked them up, and read the card.

To the kind and honest lady. Thank you, for returning my wallet. Ted. xx

As she read his phone number, she raised the flowers to her face, and sniffed them.

The kind and honest lady.

Seven seconds passed, as this simple gesture found its way into Dot's heart. She slowly, carefully manouevred the card, from the cellophane.

The kind and honest lady.

Dead or not, they were the most beautiful bunch of flowers she'd ever been given. They were the *only* bunch of flowers she'd ever been given.

***

'Where is she?' said Joan, holding a mug of Yorkshire tea, and four Chocolate Chip Cookies. 'It's not like her, to be late.'

'I haven't seen her,' said Charlie, as she began to brush the floor of the area. 'Maybe, she has overslept?'

'Overslept? With that lot? A corpse couldn't oversleep in that house.'

Joan put the tea and biscuits down, onto Dot's work bench.

'I'll leave them ere. If she doesn't turn up, get them down your neck.'

Joan turned to head back to the canteen, as Dot sat in her Astra, in the car park. The flowers lay on the passenger seat beside her. She took the card from her pocket, and looked, forlornly, at it, once more. She placed her head back onto the headrest, closed her eyes, and sighed. She could see his face, once again. Young, smiling, a boxer's nose, and eyebrows that joined in the middle. His words kept piercing her feelings, like well-aimed darts,

The kind and honest lady.

She felt a surge within her. She couldn't describe it. A surge of what? She didn't know what had happened to her. She'd gone to bed last night. Got up this morning. The usual breakfast-time chaos. The usual dread of another shite day, in that shite factory. Trying to make nothing sound a lot. Trying to justify the unjustifiable. Another day of hauling Charlie and Rick over the coals. But then, as she'd kissed little Bobby *Tara*... her world had been turned upside down - by a bunch of dead flowers. And a man. A man, she didn't know, but couldn't stop thinking about. She slipped her fingers behind the door handle and pushed her shoulder against the door. As it opened, a gush of cold, damp air invaded the cold, damp air inside her clapped-out Astra (the heater and door seals were also knackered). She sucked it into her mouth and felt cold. She stepped out. Short. Dumpy. She reached back into the car and took her duffle coat off the back seat. She pulled the baggy coat on. It did nothing to complement her plump figure. She raised the hood around her head and fastened the toggles. She reached back in, took her Aldi carrier bag off the passenger seat, then removed the key from the ignition. She looked at her car. She wished someone would rob it. Behind, she could hear the symphony of her life: presses stamping, hydraulics hissing, drills screeching, voices shouting. She put the key in the door and locked the car (the remote fob was also knackered). She turned. The factory stood before her. Huge. Grey. Imposing. From the foundry chimney, a pall of acrid, black smoke lazily searched its way toward the clouds. As her eyes took in the scene, she couldn't see it. All she could see was *his* face. She'd felt that gush within her again, and all she could think of was... Ted.

As her Hush Puppies crunched their way across the wet, black cinders of the car park, she began to sing quietly, to herself. On the same day, for the first time in her life, she'd been given a bunch of flowers, and, also, for the first time in her life, although she didn't yet realise it, Dot had fallen in love.

* * *

She walked into the area. There was no sign of Charlie. She walked across to her locker and opened the door.

How did he know where I lived?

She took her coat off, then took her overall out of the locker, and put it on.

How could he know where I lived?

Her initial elation was beginning to evaporate, as she began to bombard herself with doubt. She sat at the workbench and took a sip of her tea. It was just about drinkable. She devoured two of the cookies. How could he know where she lived? Maybe, he was some kind, of stalker. A sex maniac. She shoved another of the cookies into her mouth, then went back to her locker, opened it, and rooted through the chaos of her coat pockets, until she found the card. She returned to her chair, and slurped a mouthful of the lukewarm tea, as she, once again, read the neatly, written message.

But the flowers were lovely, though... A sex maniac wouldn't send such a lovely bunch of flowers... but he might... How could he know me address...? Unless he really was a sex maniac. But why would a sex maniac be interested in a bag like me? What if he was just a sensitive, kind-hearted bloke... but, there are no sensitive, kind-hearted blokes – they're all shite... Except for me Uncle Harry... dear Uncle Harry... I wish he was 'ere, now... instead of bein stuck in that urn, on me aunty Vera's sideboard.

She looked at the phone number on the card. Should she ring him? Why should she ring him? Let sleeping dogs lie. Mind you, it'd been a few days since he came to the house with the flowers, and she'd not rung him back. He must think she's a right ungrateful sod. Dilemma.

'Good morning, Dot,' said Charlie, as she returned from the toilet, and made her way to the work bench. Dot grunted an acknowledgement, as, with the speed and sleight of hand of a card sharp, she surreptitiously shoved Ted's card securely into her overall pocket. Or, thought she'd done so. Charlie picked up the brush and continued to brush the floor. Dot watched her and huffed.

Then thought of Ted.

She swallowed the last mouthful of cold tea, from the mug.

And thought of Ted.

Then, slowly but surely, the novelty started to wear off. She realised she was behaving like a love-struck schoolgirl, swept up in the romance of it all. Handsome stranger seeks his Cinderella. And the rest. No, she's just acting stupid. He was just some bloke who said *thanks*. That's all.

'You're quiet, this morning?' said Charlie, as she brushed some muck, and tiny bits of swarf, onto the shovel, then threw it into the crisp box.

'Yis,' said Dot, as she thought of Ted, then pushed her hand into her overall pocket, and clumsily fumbled around under her hankie, and mobile, as her fingers rooted for the remainder of yesterday's chocolate fudge. Absent-mindedly, forgetting the precious card, she pulled out the crumpled-up cellophane bag, Ted's card slipped out, over the edge of her pocket, and floated to the floor. Dot shoved a chunk of the sticky fudge into her mouth. She picked up her empty Simpsons' mug,

'I'll take this back to Joan,' she said, as she made her way out of the area.

'Okay.'

Ted's card lay on the floor. Abandoned. Lost. Alone. Once again ignored by all

humanity. There wasn't even the chance of Charlie finding it, with her diligent sweeping, for she'd already swept that section. As Rick entered the area pulling his pallet truck with a stock bin of reworks on the forks, she turned and smiled at him.

'Hi, Rick.'

'Alright, Silk Knickers. How's it goin?'

Now, his voice had a warmth to it. She'd noticed it yesterday, as they were watching the goldfinches, together. She could sense that he was beginning to thaw, lower his guard. This made her happy because she genuinely liked Rick – a lot. As they continued to talk, he pulled the pallet truck towards the bench, pressed the release lever with his foot, and the forks lowered.

'What did y'think of me birds, then?'

'There's a lot more to this bird-watching than meets the eye.'

He pushed the bin of reworks onto the floor, with his foot, and it came to rest on top of Ted's card. As they continued to chatter, Rick felt the urge to say to her, *I thought y'might have come to the gig, last night?* but he didn't want to show his hand. OK, she's lovely, and they're starting to get on well together, but, at the end of the day, she's just a workmate. That's it. Don't get involved. She's joinin the army, anyway, Joan told him. As their chemistry proceeded along its narrow, precarious path, Charlie had the urge to tell him, that she really wanted to go to the gig, but fell asleep on the bed, and woke up at ten past ten. Now, wouldn't that have gone down well?

Yes, Rick, I really wanted to see you last night, but to be honest, I couldn't give a toss. I'd rather have a kip instead.

He turned, and was about to start walking off when,

'Rick...'

He looked back at her. Three seconds passed, as they looked at each other.

'I wanted to go to the gig, last night...'

Cautious relief washed over her, and stifled elation

welled within Rick, as they played facial poker, each not prepared to show their hand. Should he give her a cheeky wink, then walk away? Play it cool? Or just walk away, and ignore her? What to do?

'Why didn't you, then?' came out of nowhere.

A cheeky smile crept across her lips.

'What are you smirkin at?' he said, feigning annoyance. This made her smile grow larger, and it turned into a giggle.

'I'm sorry... I'm so sorry,' she said, with a chuckle... 'I fell asleep...'

It was then that it happened. As he stood there, looking at her, shrieking and giggling as if a naughty schoolgirl, all his cool, calm, calculated reticence disappeared, like frost in the morning sun. The last vestige of his armour evaporated, as her arrow sank deeply into his heart. He felt himself moving towards her, glowering at her, with feigned anger.

'Y'fell asleep...? Y'fell asleep...? The biggest band since The Beatles, and *YOU fell a bleedin sleep?*'

He grabbed her around the waist, and gently dug his fingertips into her sides, as he began to vigorously tickle her.

'How dare you fall asleep... D'you hear me, Silk Knickers... How dare you fall asleep.'

Eventually, the nonsensical banter began to subside. Between convulsive gasps for breath, she managed to spill out,

'I couldn't help it. I was reading a bird book, and I dozed off.'

Rick also, had calmed down.

SHITE.

He'd done it now. Shown his hand. Made a right dickhead of himself. All the things he'd sworn not to do –

he'd just done, in the space of a few seconds. But he couldn't help himself. She was like a drug, and he was hooked. How could he get out of this one? Get her out of his system? Ten minutes later it would all have calmed down and gone back to normal. She'd have forgotten all about this little episode by tonight, when she'd be back in her big house, in the suburbs. Having supper with mummy and daddy. He was just a novelty. A bit of rough. How wrong he was. As their eyes met, she did *that* smile again. *That friggin smile.* With the sexiest mouth on earth.

'I better get goin,' he muttered, sheepishly. 'I've got an appointment at the doctor's... I'll be back, this afternoon.'

'What's the matter? Is anything wrong?'

'No... I'm fine.'

'Why are you going to the doctor's, then, if you're fine...?'

There was a pause, as she looked into his eyes.

'It's, er – just a male, bloke thing, you know?'

She felt that there was something wrong. His reluctance to answer. The way he'd momentarily, broken eye contact with her. She could feel that he was hiding something. He wasn't telling the truth.

'Yeah – it's just a checkup. Nothing to worry about.'

Her intuition told her that, indeed, there *was* something to worry about. She could tell.

'I'll see you this afternoon, then?' she said.

'Yeah, OK.'

'Good luck.'

He turned and started walking toward the alleyway. As she watched him go, a tiny seed began to take root within her heart.

10

The lounge of The Queens Arms had been roped off, and a sign saying, Private Function had been strategically placed to stop ignorant stragglers entering the area, until the main funeral party arrived back from the graveyard. There was no point really, because everyone within two miles of the pub knew what had happened, and most of them had crowded into the church. Pew after pew, filled with the blank expressions of disbelieving faces. The respect and love of the close-knit community had formed an invisible shield, around them both.

She'd watched as her husband, standing in the grave, was handed the small, white coffin of their little son. She had no tears left to cry. He looked up at her and forced a supportive half-smile. '*Goodbye, sweetheart,*' she mouthed silently, '*I love you,*' as John laid Thomas to rest. The crowd were numbed into silence.

***

The front door opened. She walked into the hall, followed by John. She stood, silenced by grief, as he removed the key and closed the door. She couldn't move. He put his arm around her then, gently, guided her toward the front room.

'I'll put the kettle on,' he said, in a hushed tone.

As he walked toward the kitchen, she entered the parlour, moved to an armchair and sat. Resting her head back onto the chair, she closed her eyes. The sound of the kettle being filled broke the deafening silence of the house. She heaved a sigh, and felt empty inside: a shell, her emotions destroyed. All that remained within her was the undying love in her heart of a mother, for her child. She opened her eyes and gazed through the window, into the street. Her gaze gradually lowered, and it was then that she noticed them; the smudges of his fingerprints, left on the windowpane. It was three months before she could bring herself to wipe them off.

*** * ***

She sat on her stool, behind the serving counter, the middle fingers of her right hand threaded through the handle of the mug, her left hand curved around the warm porcelain. She gazed down into the tea, the overhead strip light reflecting on its surface. She could see no tea... no mug... no reflection.

The silence of the empty canteen was intermittently broken by the clattering and pinging of pans plates cutlery, and the idle chatter and laughing from *her girls*, in the back area. Her girls... Sandra, Sue, Lesley, Lauren... and Petronela.

She closed her eyes, to be with him... To see his smile once more.

11

He was a slimy bastard in more ways than one. A deceiving, manipulative parasite, who only had one aim in life - to feather his own nest with the plunder of lives he'd wrecked. He'd done it three times before, three years, five years, and six years ago. Another three vulnerable, lonely women, consigned, once again, to the Broken-Hearts Club. Left to pick up the pieces and try to start again. He was a Class One, serial TWAT, skilled in the art of tugging on heartstrings. A master of deception and guile. So, when he met her, she had no idea that she was just the next gullible fly to enter his web. The next one in line, ready to be taken to the cleaners.

This time was different, but the end result was, inevitably, going to be the same. Unlike the last three, he didn't meet her through lonely hearts clubs. No, it was his lucky day, or should I say night. She was out with a group of her friends. They'd jumped a cab, into town. It was Beryl's birthday, and as it was the big Three-0, they'd decided to push the boat out. Give her a night to remember. Dressed as if out on a hen-night, they trawled through pub after pub, and eventually, her fate was sealed when they decided to go to The Queen's Head. One small, seemingly innocuous decision that was destined to change the course of her life.

By this time, they were the usual, rowdy though harmless, bunch of pissed-up, laugh-out-loud women, enjoying a Saturday night out. The five of them had plonked themselves down at a table. Forty minutes into the lagers and Chardonnays, he walked through the pub doors and turned left, into the lounge. He was on the prowl. Five foot-eleven, dark-haired, muscular, smartly dressed in blue jeans and a white, linen shirt, and wearing a pair of brown, suede shoes, he carried his jacket over his shoulder. His eager eyes took stock of the situation, immediately. He ordered a pint of Carling, then settled down at the next table. It wasn't long, before the hunters became the hunted. He took his phone out and pretended to be engrossed as he periodically took a mouthful of lager. He sat and waited for them to take the bait. It wasn't long.

'Come an sit with us - if you know what's good for yeh,' shrieked Maureen, and a gale of laughter rose from the table.

He looked across at them and smiled politely, scanning the various faces. There was one that caught his eye. Dusky blond, slim, pretty, about early thirties. She glanced back and they made eye contact. The remnant of laughter eased away from her face and was replaced with a look of 'if only' intent. He held his gaze for two seconds longer than he should have, smiled at her. She smiled back, as he finished off his pint.

'Where should we go after ere?' shouted Kathleen, through the din of the pub.

'The Millstone,' shouted Betty, and they agreed. 'C'mon then, sup up.'

He finished his pint, stood, then casually walked

towards the exit. Once outside, his pace quickened, as he made his way toward The Millstone. Never was a pub more appropriately named.

***

Dot's ambling down the alleyway drew her closer and closer to the canteen doors. Nonchalantly swinging her Simpsons' mug, in a non-Dot manner, she saw the canteen doors getting closer and closer. Within seconds, she'd be through them, and into the canteen. *No.* She couldn't do it. She couldn't go into the canteen, without having one more read of Ted's card. It was Dot's secret, and she wasn't prepared to share it with anyone. She pushed her left hand into her overall pocket and confidently groped around. She couldn't feel the card. Nervously, her fingers began to probe, under her hankie, around her phone. It was there, somewhere. She put it there... She stopped. She pulled the hankie out of her pocket. As the concern swelled within her, she took out the phone. She plunged her hand back into her pocket, pushed the few, dried up pieces of tangerine peel to one side – and still couldn't feel it. It must be there... It wasn't - it was gone.

She turned and looked back up the alleyway, toward the Rectification Area. Her eyes scanned the floor, as she made her way quickly back.

'I thought you'd gone to the canteen?'

Without answering, Dot's eyes clawed at the ground, around her bench.

'Have you brushed anythink up?'

'Just some muck and swarf. Have you lost something?' Charlie continued, as Dot's eyes feverishly scanned the area.

'I thought I had a fiver - I must've dropped it.'

She couldn't understand where it had gone. As she stood, near the bin of reworks that Rick had recently brought, she had no idea that her foot was inches away from her beloved Ted card. As a last hope glanced through her mind, she walked over to the crisp box, thinking she might have absent-mindedly thrown it in. As she approached it, the rim of the box drew closer. She hoped against hope, that she'd cast her glance over the rim, into the smelly box, and there it would be – smiling back at her. She did. It didn't. She'd lost it. It was gone. She was gutted.

***

Nineteen fifty-nine was an eventful year for Richard Edwards. Within the space of eight months, he'd bought a second-hand, Morris quarter ton van, put a deposit down on a two-bedroom, terraced house, and, during August, had finally married his childhood sweetheart, Winifred. The wedding was a simple, quiet affair – Friday afternoon, straight in then straight out of the Register Office, into The Bluebell pub, next door, for drinks and sandwiches with a few close friends and family then it was off on a two-day honeymoon to Cemaes Bay, Anglesey.

They arrived back at their little love-nest on the following Monday, which he'd taken as a day's holiday.

A lorry driver by trade, Richard was an 'entrepreneur' before the word became trendy, common parlance. He loved his job. He loved driving. He loved the freedom of the road. He loved the stranded hitchhikers he picked up on a regular basis. But it wasn't enough. If he was working for someone else, he'd never be free to be his own man.

To control his own destiny. He drove a seven-ton Thames Trader for Walkers Haulage, but now that he was a married man with commitments, he wasn't fussed on the various nights he had to spend away from home. Neither was Winifred. As a stepping-stone to self-employment, Richard bought the little, olive green van from a local auction house that was selling off twenty of them, on behalf of the General Post Office. He kept his job for as long as possible, while building up a regular clientele of customers, who wanted small boxes and parcels shifted around quickly. What we call today, a 'courier'. His business thrived to such an extent that within eighteen months he'd swapped the little Morris in, for one of its bigger brothers – a fifteen hundredweight J2. At that point, Richard took the plunge. He handed his notice in and started working fourteen-hour days, six days a week. Winifred, although completely pissed-off at hardly ever seeing him, was one hundred percent supportive of her husband, and took over running the office side of the business. A further fourteen months down the line, the business was growing faster than Richard could cope with. He asked his brother, Chris, who'd had it up to the back teeth with being a butcher, to join them. Richard then bought another J2, to take on the extra workload. And so, it went. Twenty- four years later, Falcon Haulage had grown to become a nationwide haulage company, with a fleet of forty-two, consisting of box, curtain-siders, and flatbeds, together with numerous vans. Yet, for all the achievement, all the success, all the accoutrements of wealth, nothing made him happier than that day back in 1962, when, tired and irritable, he stormed into the hall of their little terraced house,

'What a day I've had. That bleeding A6 is doing my

head in.'

Winifred was standing halfway down the hall. She began to smile.

'What are you smiling at?'

She began to titter as the anger left his voice.

'I said, what are you smiling at?' he said, trying hard to conceal his own smile.

He moved toward her and gently placed his hands onto her hips.

'Will you answer...?'

She pressed a forefinger against his lips,

'Shhh...'

She took hold of his hand and placed it onto her stomach. There was a few seconds pause, as the realisation washed over him.

'Sweetheart,' he said quietly, as she bit her bottom lip, 'sweetheart...'

Baby James Kenneth Edwards was born seven months later.

12

Joan's great gift was for finding the comedic view of life, even in some of the most serious circumstances. Sometimes, she was funny when she didn't mean to be. It was her default setting, Her relief valve. Her safety mechanism. It took her mind off thinking about her dead child. Even now, that was still the psychological cross she had to bear. She was an actor. She had to be. It stopped her from thinking of suicide. When she reached the point of no return, beneath her comical smokescreen, lay dread. Sheer, utter dread. If there was a God, in Heaven, surely, he wouldn't turn His back on her? This could be her last chance to have the child she so desperately needed. She'd started by giving herself the injections, one a day for two weeks, to suppress her menstrual cycle. When that occurred, she had to give herself another twelve-day course of fertility hormone injections, to increase the number of eggs that her ovaries produced. Little wonder then, she referred to her bum as being like a pin cushion. The clinic where with her every step of the way, keeping an efficient, professional eye on her. There were vaginal, ultrasound scans, to monitor her ovaries, blood tests. Then, thirty-six hours before the eggs would be collected, she had to give herself a final hormone injection, to help them mature. When that point was reached, she and Eric had to visit the clinic, Joan carrying her hopes and dreams, Eric carrying his sample. She was taken into the side ward, sedated, then with ultrasound guidance, a needle was carefully passed through her vagina, then into each ovary. After twenty minutes, the precious harvest had been gathered in. The nurse then inserted a pessary, to help prepare the lining of her womb to receive the embryo, should fertilization be successful a few days later. And that was it. Joan could do no more. The outcome was in the lap of the Gods. She dressed, and Eric drove her back to the house. Throughout the journey home, they both remained silent.

The front door opened. Joan walked into the hall, followed by Eric. She stood, silenced, as he removed the key and closed the door. She could hardly move, so overwhelmed with nervous anticipation. As he walked toward the kitchen, she gradually entered the parlour, moved to an armchair and sat. She rested her head back onto the chair and closed her eyes. The sound of the kettle being filled broke the silence. She heaved a sigh, as she thought of her eggs, mixed with his sperm, now resting in some anonymous laboratory.

Please, God... please, please God, let it work. Please, let it work.

As Joan sat in the parlour, Eric stood in the kitchen. He gazed ruefully at the kettle as he waited for the water to boil, thinking,

How did I get myself into this fuckin mess? I don't want no fuckin kid... I should've just bled her dry, then fucked off, like I did with the others.

Chapter 12

***

Kevin and Karen Kingston had been receiving regular updates from Nelson Engineering, from Hardcastle, regarding the state of play with the voluntary redundancy situation. Despite the sabre rattling from the union, the whispers had been spreading throughout the company. The silent majority had caught wind of the salient points of the informal talks, between Nelson's and the union, thanks to Hardcastle, surreptitiously drip-feeding selected information into his reliable grapevine. Linking up and discussing amongst themselves the forthcoming *derisory* redundancy package from Nelson's, they, too, were struggling more and more, to justify the label *derisory*. Hardcastle was like a dog with a bone. Providing the takeover went without a hitch, the Kingston's had earmarked him to take over HR at KayKay as well as running Nelson's, as their current HR director would be retiring shortly. Big pay increase + Jaguar company car = happy days. It was easy to see why KayKay Engineering wanted Nelson's, and had made an offer, which, on the face of it, was deemed ridiculously generous. The two plants were just twenty miles apart, separated by the M6 motorway, making inter-plant logistics perfect. Apart from this, Nelson's had five acres of adjacent land going spare. More than enough to construct a sizeable extension to the existing premises, should the need ever arise. Failing that, the land could be sold off. This idea had never entered the heads of Archibald and Reginald Nelson. They'd settled into the quiet life, and hardly ever visited the factory, let alone licked it into shape. Such was the state of its neglect that it was well and truly on the slide. In true-to-form, swashbuckling, maverick manner, Kevin and Karen made their next audacious move.

Such was the size of the KayKay order book, that they were struggling in some departments to keep up with demand. A recruitment drive had already been planned, and now with the advent of a Nelson's takeover, the timing was perfect. Hardcastle had been approached by KayKay's, and the suggestion was made that he, via his reliable grapevine, release the information, that twenty-eight vacancies would be appearing soon at KayKay's, and preference would be given to people with previous engineering experience and a glowing reference from Nelson's. The idea being, that under a cloak of darkness, Hardcastle could hand-pick twenty-eight, of his coterie and give them a job at KayKay's. All they had to do then was wait for the volunteer redundancy package to be announced and apply for it straight away; have their cake and eat it. Twenty-eight down, twenty-eight to go.

* * *

Dot was gutted. I don't mean ordinary gutted, like someone who sees a cashmere sweater, half-price in a sale, dithers about buying it, only to go back later and discover that someone else has snatched it from under their nose. I mean gutted almost to the point of despair. How could she have lost it? Where did she lose it? It was in her overall pocket – where did it go? She was so gutted that she couldn't summon up the will to give Charlie and Rick their normal daily doses of grief. She couldn't stop thinking of Ted. Kept seeing his face smiling at her, out of the photo. She'd just have to write it off to experience. Be more careful next time. What next time? What she didn't know, was that the card was staring her in the face, and she was oblivious to its presence.

The day after Rick had put the box of reworks onto the card, as he was passing, on his way to the canteen, he saw that Charlie's bench was ready for more work, he detoured, picked the box up and thumped it onto her bench to save her the effort. Dot and Charlie were already in the canteen, and, as Rick turned to join them, the tip of his boot clipped the edge of the card, sending it flying a foot in front of him. He picked it up and read it,

To the kind and honest lady. Thank you for returning my wallet. Ted xx

Without a second thought, he threw it into the crisp box, as he passed.

***

'Where's Joan…?' asked Charlie, nibbling the skin off her apple. 'Dot…?'

'What?' said Dot, gruffly, performing what looked like a blowjob, on a six-inch Cumberland sausage.

'Where's Joan…?'

'She's norrin.'

'I know, but where is she? Is everything okay?'

'For Chissake. What is this, twenty questions…? She's gone to the c - l - i - n - i - c.'

'Is everything alright?' said Charlie, concerned.

'Jesus wept. Can I have me dinner in peace? She's gone,' lowering her voice, 'to have, the you-know-what, put in her you-know-where.'

'What?'

'The - *you know what,*' Dot said in a whisper.

'Which?'

'The friggin embryo - up her how's your father.'

Charlie gasped.

'Is it today? Already?'

'Yis. Now, look – don't dare ask me one more question, or you'll get this friggin sausage up your hole…'

'Are you alright, Dot? Is there something wrong?'

'I said don't ask me one more question!'

'That was two questions.'

'*Jesus wept.*' Dot exhaled in exasperation, sounding like a cross between a foghorn and a long, drawn out fart.

'Where's Joan, Dot?' Rick said, chirpily, as he approached.

Dot stood and pushed the half-eaten sausage into her overall pocket.

'If anyone wants me, I'll be sittin in me car, listenin t'the radio.'

She turned.

'If I can get the bleedin thing t'work.'

She ambled off toward the rubber doors. Halfway there, she took the half-eaten sausage out of her pocket, took another bite of it, then shoved it back in.

***

Joan lay on the bed. Smiles were exchanged between her and the doctor, together with some predictable, friendly banter and professional words of reassurance. There was no need for sedation. There was no feeling of embarrassment. Over the years, Joan had learned to leave her dignity at the front door, when visiting the hospital as a patient. The doctor gently, gradually, inserted the catheter, and with the help and guidance of an ultrasound scan, she lay and watched the screen as the embryo was passed into her womb.

Her heart swelled with pride and happiness as she realized that for the second time in her life, she'd become a mum. For how long she would remain a mum, this time around, she didn't know. She only hoped and prayed that it would be for the rest of her life.

13

'*Ladies and gentlemen, please put your hands together for Rick & Roll...*'

The crowded Omnibus pub erupted into cheering, whistling, and screaming, as Rick and his band took over the stage, and burst into, Long Tall Sally. It was one of the live music nights that were regularly held at Rick's local pub. It was normally a case of three songs and then off, but tonight, the second band due on had to cancel at the last minute, and Rick & Roll had been asked to do six songs, to fill the gap. As Long Tall Sally ended, it brought the house down. After a short pause for breath, the band burst into, I Saw Her Standing There. This was a particular favourite of the pub regulars, and the response was deafening. As Rick began the intro to the third song, and the crowd got wilder and wilder, a metallic blue, Mini Cooper pulled up outside. Charlie stepped out of the car to be greeted by a thunderous, thumping beat coming from the pub. As she pushed on the door, it would hardly move open, such was the crowd inside. Once inside it was no easier to move around than it was to gain access. She managed to progress about six feet into the pub, before she gave it up as a bad job and decided to stay put, where she was. Her eyes moved to the stage. Above the bouncing heads, she caught momentary glimpses of Rick, dressed in a black shirt and black leather jeans, hammering out, Johnny B. Goode. A huge smile bounded across her mouth, as she watched him giving it his all. She could hardly believe the transformation of the quiet, unassuming Rick she knew from work.

The pounding beat, the deafening music, the enthusiasm of the crowd, combined, and gradually began to soak into her pores, and she began to bounce up and down, clenching and shaking her fists as she became enthralled. It was her first experience of raw, unadulterated, classic rock & roll, and she loved it. Johnny B. Goode came to an end, followed by an immediate explosion of cheering. Charlie was screaming at the top of her voice, and still couldn't hear herself.

'D'you want some more?'

'*Yeah.*'

'I can't hear yeh.'

'*YEAH!*'

'You don't have t'shout.'

The crowd roared with laughter, at Rick's quip.

Now changing the tempo, he began to sing, Love Me Tender. As he did, the crowd fell silent. Charlie became entranced with each word, each line. The crowd began to disappear, the band began to disappear, until all that remained in her mind was Rick, standing alone on the stage, sending the plaintive declaration of his love to her. As she stood listening to the emotive ballad, gently, gradually, without realising it, she was falling deeply in love with him. As the last few chords brought the song to an end, a rousing cheer went up from the crowd. Three Steps to Heaven came next, with the set coming to a full-on, deafening finale with, Get Back.

She'd arrived unannounced. It was a spur of the moment decision that she'd made, after another quarrel with her mother. Rick had no idea that she'd been there. He was making his way to the bar when he caught a glimpse of her, attempting to make her way to the exit.

'Charlie...! Charlie!'

He pushed his way through the crowd, desperately trying to reach the door, before she drove off.

She slammed the Mini door shut and started the engine. As she put the steering on lock to pull out into the road, Rick came bounding out of the pub.

'Charlie...!'

He ran to the front of the car to stop her. With a massive smile on her face, she stopped the car and opened the window.

'What are y'doin, here?'

'Waiting for a bus.'

He persuaded her to go back into the pub, and amid the hullabaloo they tried to hold a conversation.

* * *

Charlie's Mini pulled up outside Rick's cottage. He invited her in for a coffee.

'Do you have any decaff?'

He burst into laughter.

'What are you laughing at?'

'Do I look like the sort of bloke, who has decaff coffee in his cupboard?

'I just wondered.'

'I drink proper coffee, what puts hairs on y'spit.'

A moment passed as they shared a smile. The time to part had arrived. She didn't want to go. He didn't want her to go, but what next? She was obviously out of his league. Why would she want anything to do with the like of him, other than as her workmate? She looked at him: the kind of man she'd always wanted to find, but always managed to end up with players, the leg-

over brigade. Rick was different. No, she didn't want him to go.

'Right, silk knickers, I'll be off, then. G'night.'

As he put his fingers on the door handle,

'Rick…'

'Wha…?'

She leaned across and took his face into her hand. He felt her lips press against his, gently, softly.

***

The key turned in the lock, and Rick ushered her into the tiny hall. The stairs were straight ahead, and he turned her left, into the living room. He switched on the light to expose the detritus of a bachelor life. Gravy-stained plate and two, tea-stained mugs on the coffee table, Various magazines strewn about on the furniture. Tee-shirt, socks, and underpants in all their finery, draped over the radiator. A scale model of a Triumph Bonneville 650 took pride of place on the oak-beamed mantelpiece of the stone fireplace. And in the far corner, almost hidden from view behind a chair, a Spanish guitar was propped up against the wall.

'Take a seat,' he said, 'I'll put the kettle on…'

She sat, on the small, cottage suite couch, as he began

to remove his jacket.

'Right, then, what d'you want, proper coffee, or tea?'

He sat, momentarily, opposite her, and waited for her reply.

'I don't suppose you have any Chamomile?' she asked, teasing him, mercilessly.

'Correct.'

Her eyes gave her away, and he warmed, realising, once again, that he'd been duped.

'One of these day – one of these days, silk knickers,' he threatened, waving his forefinger in her direction, 'you're goin over me knee...'

'That's a beautiful guitar,' she said, changing the subject. 'It's Spanish, isn't it?'

'Yeah. Nylon strings blah, blah.'

'Do you play classical?'

'Nah. Me nana and granddad bought it f'me eighteenth. Paid for a course of lessons, an all, but I couldn't get the hang of it. Me fingers kept gettin tongue-tied. I give up after five lessons. I just wanted t'play rock and roll.'

He stood.

'Right, what are we havin?'

'I'll have...'

'Go on, live dangerously for once.'

'A cup of proper coffee – no, make that a mug. Black, no sugar.'

'You sure know how t'push the boat out,' he said, then gave a large yawn.

'Am I keeping you up...?'

He smiled, then crossed the room, and entered the tiny kitchen, which was complete with a prehistoric range, a halogen oven perched on the top. He picked up the kettle, half-filled it, and switched it on. He reached into the cupboard and took out two mugs, spooned coffee into each, then, as he was about to pour the milk, music began to play from the living room. He listened to the haunting, evocative melody. He put the jar of coffee down onto the worktop, turned and slowly moved back to the kitchen door, he stood in the doorway, and looked into the living room. Charlie had taken the Spanish guitar and was playing it. In a relaxed yet confident manner, her fingers moved up and down the chords as she continued, oblivious to his presence. For three minutes, he watched, and became mesmerized at her skill. He knew that melody. He'd heard it somewhere before. She finished the tune then stood, to replace the guitar. He moved quickly back into the kitchen.

'Is the coffee ready?' she called.

'Yeah,' he shouted back, pouring the water into the mugs.

He picked up the mugs and turned. She was there, standing beside him. Their eyes met.

'I've got a few custard creams, knockin about somewhere, if you fancy one…?'

'Will you turn out to be another bastard, Rick?'

'What are you talkin about?'

A pause ensued during which, he could see the sadness in her eyes. He put the mugs down onto the worktop,

'What's the matter…?'

A smile crept across her mouth and she gazed, dispiritedly.

'Charlie…? What's the matter…?'

Her words gradually began to emerge.

'I didn't deserve it. What he did to me… It was wrong. I didn't deserve it…'

'Who did what t'you? What are you on about...?'

Tears flooded into her eyes.

'I didn't deserve it...'

He wrapped his arms around her. Her body began to tremble, as the anxiety and panic once again, began to take a grip. A flashback started to thunder through her mind, as she visualised him, again, drawing up outside her gran's house, in the Healey. She stood, a face at the window, gazing down onto the road; and him, high as a kite on drugs and alcohol, shouting and calling her all the bitches, whores, cunts under the sun. Blaring the car horn, screaming obscenities like a maniac.

She broke down completely and again began to sob.

Rick wrapped his arms around her tightly.

'It's okay, Charlie. C'mon... It's okay. No-one's gonna hurt you again.'

She felt safe in his arms. Her breathing began to relax. The panic and anxiety began to dissipate.

'I'll have to go.'

'You're not goin anywhere, the state you're in.'

'I've got to go.'

'I'm not lettin you. Be told.'

Once again, the hint of an appreciative smile crept across her lips. She felt safe in his presence. She felt she could trust him.

'Get y'coffee down y'neck, before it goes cold.'

For two seconds, they looked into each other's eyes, then he began rummaging through the cupboard. He extricated his biscuit tin from its hiding place and flipped the lid off.

'Here y'are, I've got... four custard creams... two Bourbons, and 1-2-3-4-5- six Hobnobs. Well, they're like real Hobnobs, but they're not, 'What d'you want?'

She looked at him.

'There he goes again, with that smile. The bloody sexiest smile on earth.'

***

The bedroom door opened. Rick entered and switched on the light. She followed him in.

'We'll have to be up handy in the mornin, for work.'

He opened a cupboard door, reached in, and pulled out a large, black tee shirt, with Norton Motorcycles emblazoned across the chest.

'Y'can use this for pyjamas.'

'Thank you.'

'Right. I'll be off, then. I'm cream-crackered.'

He moved to the door and turned.

'Goodnight,' he said, quietly.

'Sweet dreams…'

He walked onto the landing, closing the door behind him. She listened as his footsteps disappeared into his room. She began to undress. When she was down to her briefs, she pulled on the tee shirt, and opened the curtains wide, then the window as far as it would go. She switched the light out, climbed into bed and lay looking at the various shadows that were cast around the room. Outside, she heard the screech of a barn owl. She fancied Rick so much. She had so much love to give him. Rick lay naked in his bed. He fancied Charlie so much. He had so much love to give to her, but how could he ever hope of having a relationship with her once she'd found out his secret? *Beware - your sins will find you out*, once again, guiltily, rumbled through his mind. He rested his head back, onto the pillow. After a day's work, and his full-on performance at *The Boilermaker's,* he was desperately tired. Seconds later, his lids struggled to stay open. A languorous mist enveloped him, and his eyes slowly closed as he sank deeply into the oblivion of sleep...

Three minutes passed.

'Rick... Rick... *RICK.'*

He woke with a start. He could have sworn he'd heard a woman's voice calling his name. It then dawned on him that he was in the wrong bed. Just as he was about to put two and two together...

'RICK!'

He threw back the duvet, climbed out of bed and, blearily annoyed, walked out onto the landing.

'Wha?'

He pressed down on the handle and pushed the door open.

'I don't want to be alone...'

'Hang on...'

He went back to his room, pulled his boxers on, came back, climbed into the bed and lay beside her. He wrapped his arms around her, and she snuggled into his chest. He lay his head back onto the pillow and wondered about the upset he'd witnessed, downstairs. He didn't know who this fella was, he just knew that he wanted to tear his fucking head off his neck. He decided not to pry. It was none of his business. It was her world, and he knew that he'd never be a part of it. They were just work colleagues, bordering on good friends. He just felt a massive surge within him, to protect her. They lay in the silence of the darkened room. Words were superfluous. A minute later, he was struggling valiantly, to keep his eyes from closing. For the first time in years, she felt safe, secure. As if, at last, she'd found someone who genuinely cared for her. As he began to quietly snore, she smiled, kissed him on the chest, then closed her eyes. As the barn owl screeched again, she joined him in sleep.

* * *

At eighteen minutes to seven the following morning, Rick was woken by the raucous rattle of a passing tractor, hauling an even rattlier muck-spreader. He eased his eyes open, and for two seconds, in a state of torpor, gazed at the ceiling. As his mind kicked into gear, the realisation washed over him. Hardly daring to breathe, he slowly turned his head sideways, and there she was. The beauty that was Charlotte was sleeping soundly, beside him. He delicately eased back the duvet, then slid silently out of the bed. He tip-toed toward the door, pressed gently down on the handle and let himself out of the room. He began to breathe heavily with sexual anticipation, as the vision of her, lying there, her pert, nipples pressing through his tee-shirt, re-entered his mind. He looked down at his rigid, nine-inch pole, jutting out from the front of his boxers.

* * *

He placed his hand onto the handle and gently pushed it down. The door opened and he walked, fully dressed, into the bedroom,

'Charlie…? Charlie…?' he said, gently.

Her eyes slowly opened, and she saw him, holding a mug of tea, standing at the side of the bed.

She stretched her arms and smiled.

'I haven't slept like that for ages.'

He put the mug onto the cabinet.

'Get that down yeh, we'll have t'be off soon. It's gettin late.'

'I don't want to go to work.'

'At least, it's Friday.'

'I'll have to go home and get changed,' she said, picking up the mug.

'D'you want some breakfast?'

'I don't do breakfast.'

'You'll have to have somethin. You can't be goin t'work on an empty stomach.'

'What have you got?' she said, then took a sip of tea.

'Erm... a banana.'

'A piece of toast would be nice.'

'I've got no bread...'

'I *haven't any* bread,' she said, mischievously.

'Neither, have I,' he replied, cheekily.

'You certainly know how to treat a woman.'

'I wasn't expectin visitors.'

'So - it's a banana, or nothing...?'

'Well, er... yeah.'

A tiny smile crept across her mind, then began its journey down to her lips.

14

After having gone home and got changed into her working gear, Charlie clocked on at 7.52.

She made her way to the area. There was no sign of Dot. She put her overall on, then sat at her workbench waiting for the start bell to sound, feeling like one of Pavlov's dogs. She'd have felt guilty at depriving Rick of his last banana, so she'd passed on his kind offer. She was now, though, hearing rumblings from her stomach. Normally, she'd persevere until break, however hungry, but Rick's words kept running through her mind. *You can't be goin t'work on an empty stomach.* She smiled at his turn of phrase. She'd had the most enjoyable evening, and night, with him. In honesty, if they hadn't had to get up for work, she'd have quite happily stayed in bed with him all morning, laughing, joking, talking, making love. Especially making love. But she'd accepted the fact now, that, incontrovertibly, he didn't want to get involved with her. He couldn't have. It was obvious, last night, when she invited him into her bed – and he fell asleep. She needed him so much. To enter her. To cast out her demons of the past. To make slow, gentle love to her, building up a passionate climax. But it wasn't meant to be. He fell asleep. She was just a workmate. Pity.

She flipped open the lid of her lunchbox, took out a tangerine, sank her thumbnails in and undressed it. Carefully peeling off the spidery remnants of pith, she dissected the segments and began popping them into her mouth, one by one. The start bell rang. She scooped up the detritus of her feast, then made her way to the crisp box. As she let go of the peelings, she noticed the half-hidden Ted card. She picked it out of the bin and read it. She remembered Dot, days earlier, frantically searching the area for her 'lost fiver'. She read the message on the card.

I wonder... She glanced up and saw Dot in the distance, approaching down the alleyway. She turned, quickly walked over to Dot's workbench, and frantically scanned the floor. Where to place it – nowhere obvious – Dot was getting closer – nowhere too obscure – Dot was approaching... She bent down, placed the card near the workbench, just managing to half-cover it with an empty, small stock bin, then rush back to her own bench, as Dot entered.

'Morning, Dot...'

No reply.

'When is Joan coming back...?'

There was a pause of three seconds, then,

'She's got to have two weeks off,' said Dot, opening her locker, and taking out her overall. 'She's got t'take it easy,' she continued, slipping her arms into the sleeves.

Charlie kept glancing at the half-visible card, as she wondered if Dot would notice it.

'Mornin', girls, how's it goin'?'

Lesley, Joan's Scouse number two from the canteen, walked into the area, carrying Dot's beloved chipped Simpsons' mug. Charlie smiled and said, 'Hello,' as she sat, diligently, with great enthusiasm, assembling nut and bolt fixtures. From a stock bin of nuts and a stock bin of bolts, she had to marry each with each, then put them into a third stock bin. When the third stock bin was full of the completed fixtures, she had to weigh one fixture on the scales, in a fourth bin, to determine its weight on the calibrator, then pour the contents of the third bin into the fourth bin, until the screen showed that she'd poured in 150 pieces. These would then be ticketed and, eventually taken by Rick, to Herman the German, in the stores. *Oh! The thrill of factory work!*

'I don't know what the fuck's wrong with her,' said Dot, grumpily, to Lesley, as she stared at Charlie. 'She makes a shite job look interestin.'

Lesley smiled to herself, *Get a life, you, cranky, old bastard.*

'Right, I'm off,' said Lesley, placing the mug onto Dot's bench. Then, she turned and headed back to the canteen. As Dot plonked her arse onto the tiny seat of her stool, Charlie surreptitiously glanced across to see if there was any movement on the Ted's card front: no. Dot remained oblivious. as she took the first sip of her tea and started flicking through the pages of something that looked like a small diary. Charlie decided to assist matters, so walked over to her, then, in her best working-class accent,

'I'll shift this out y'way, Dot,' she said, picking up the stock bin, leaving the card fully exposed. She turned and walked back to her bench, intermittently glancing across until... *Bingo!* Dot cast her glance to the floor and saw the card. She quickly raised her head a split-second after Charlie had quickly turned hers back to her job. Dot was trembling inside with excitement. She kept clocking Charlie to make sure she hadn't noticed, her eyes darted from side to side, checking the alleyway, back to Charlie, back to the alleyway. Her face took on an expression that looked like someone had shoved a red-hot poker up her arsehole, and she was trying not to scream. Charlie decided to mischievously play cat and mouse.

'What did you do last night, Dot?'

'Nothink.'

'How are the children?'

'Orright.'

'How is the car going?'

Under normal circumstances, Dot would have replied, by now *'What is this, friggin twenty questions?'* But such were the fraught meanderings in her mind, regarding how she could pick up the card without being seen, that the best she could come up with was, 'Orright.'

Then, she had a light-bulb moment. Dot didn't get where she was today without having light-bulb moments.

'Charlie, y'couldn't do us a favour, could yeh?'

Charlie had turned her back to Dot. A huge beam spread across her face as she stifled a titter, before becoming serious and turning,

'Sure...'

Lesley's forgot me biscuits. Could you nip down t'the canteen an ask her for a few?'

'Right-oh,' said Charlie, peeling off her latex gloves. 'I'll be right back.'

'Take y'time, there's no hurry – Don't get me no Arrowroots – I *hate* Arrowroots.'

Charlie had to rush past Dot and head for the alleyway, clenching her lips together, to stop herself from bursting into laughter. Dot's eyes furtively followed her every move, then, when she was assured that she was out of the danger area, and well on her way down the alley toward the canteen, she slid sideways off the stool. Keeping an eye out for any sudden appearance of an intruder, she heaved a stretch down toward the floor and her fingernails clawed up Ted's card. She read his phone number. Then read it again. Then again. Her inside began to tremble with excitement. Her breathing got heavier and quicker. She was going to do it. She *was* going to do it. She took her mobile out of her overall pocket. She looked at the card. She looked at the phone. She looked back at the card, as her thumb began to press, 0 - 1 - 7 - 4 – 4… she finished pressing the remainder of the numbers. The call rang out on his landline. A second ring… her breathing got heavier… three times… she started biting her lip… four times… She was almost panting… five times… she felt like she was going to faint… six times…

'*Hello, we are not at home at present. Please leave your message after the tone and we'll get back to you…*' BEEP.

'*Shit.*'

She had no intention of saying anything. She just wanted to hear his voice, and then she was going to hang up. Now, this robot's fucked everything up, by him not being in.

What should I say? What should I say? stampeded through her mind. *Don't say nothink. Don't say nothink – just hang up. Hurry up, the time's runnin out. You've gorra say somethink – you can't say nothink.*

She poised her finger over the cut-off button, and was just about to end the call, when Charlie came walking back into the area, carrying a saucer of biscuits.

'*Thanksformeflowers,*' spurted out of her mouth, in a fevered whisper, as her heart pounded in her chest. She pushed the button and ended the call, then almost slumped onto her workbench, such was the feeling of relief mixed with shock. As Dot's left forearm and hand propped up her head, Charlie approached.

'There you are, Dot. Your favourites,' said Charlie, placing the saucer onto Dot's bench.

Dot gazed down at the saucer, and the six Arrowroot biscuits, staring back at her.

'Dot...? Are you alright? You look like you've seen a ghost.'

She turned and looked at Charlie, then back at the Arrowroots. The wind had completely left her sails. It was all she could do to remember what day of the week it was, never mind if she'd seen a ghost or not. She picked one of the biscuits up, bit it in half, and slowly started to chew it, like a cow chewing the cud, as the word 'yeah' squeaked quietly, out of her mouth.

As Dot was undergoing the terror, torture, and trauma of newly found, middle-age love, the object of her affection was passing through passport control at Liverpool John Lennon Airport, about to jet off to The Algarve for a week's holiday.

* * *

By the end of the following Friday, what had started out, a week earlier, as Dot's glittering Yellow Brick Road had, as usual, over the course of the week, gradually disintegrated into a pothole-strewn, dirt track, littered with broken bottles, fag-ends, and used Johnnies. She didn't even have a Toto to, at least, make her feel useful for something, by pissing on her leg. Over the Rainbow – my arse. Her dream of ever meeting Ted remained just that. And even then, the dream had already begun to untangle – disappear beneath a shroud of *Did he ave a moustache...? Was his air dark or fair...? It was Blackpool wasn't it? Or was it Morecambe? Oh, sod it.*

It was with great disappointment and sadness, that Dot found herself, on the Thursday morning, tearing Ted's card into four pieces and pushing them into the crisp bin, carefully burrowing them to the bottom of the smelly mound. Condemned to languish forever in oblivion, it was goodbye Ted's card four pieces. Amen.

Charlie and Rick had now accepted the inevitable – they were just work buddies. The elation of their clandestine night together had, like Dot's Yellow Brick Road, been brought down to earth by the reality of the smelly, noisy, industrial shithole that was Nelson Engineering.

However much the appeal of another romantic liaison that each of them felt, there was still the awkwardness of how, where, why, when. Charlie thinking Rick had no interest, Rick thinking Charlie was intrinsically out of his league. Rick had the gun Charlie had the bullets – but the bullets didn't fit the gun. Stalemate. Mid-afternoon on the Friday, Management had called an extraordinary meeting with the union for the following Monday, to make an announcement.

Joan had remained uncharacteristically quiet for the past week, hardly daring to breathe. She was determined to take her pregnancy to full-term. Spending most of her time in bed, reading magazines, or watching daytime telly, The Parasite had shown a token effort of caring by bringing her up the odd cup of tea, or plate of food. He'd remained quiet all week. Conversations between them had been strained.

At last, Joan's penny had dropped. She had the inkling that the initial excitement and euphoria he'd demonstrated was just that – a demonstration. Suffering from cabin fever, she eventually persuaded herself to get out of bed, shower, put her make up on and do her hair. As it was a mild, sunny Saturday, she asked him to give her a lift into town. Not to go shopping, but just to sit alone on a bench for a couple of hours, flicking through a magazine and, intermittently people watching, catching snippets of conversation, getting some fresh air, maybe enjoy a choc-ice: ME time. They'd arranged that he'd return at 4 o'clock, to pick her up. He didn't arrive. She never saw him again. But it wasn't with a feeling of devastation that she walked back into her house, at 6 o'clock that evening. It was with a feeling of relief. A weight had been lifted off her shoulders - one which she'd never realised was there, such was the hectic pace of her life. It was only now, as she saw her home stripped of his belongings, that she experienced the feeling of freedom, washing over her. The only thing he left behind were his maggots, in the fridge. She flushed them down the lavatory. He'd gone. And, being the coward he was, without so much as a farewell note. Good riddance.

* * *

'I'll tear his bollocks off,' was Dot's reaction, on finding out the news. She'd come round, Sunday teatime, with a box of cream cakes, to see her sister, and enjoy a mug of tea and a chinwag. She'd let herself in with her own key, and not finding Joan downstairs, had made her way up to the bedroom. Joan was lying asleep on the bed, clutching a silver frame which held a photo of her son, Thomas. He'd died at the age of two, having contracted meningitis. Dot walked into the room and stood at the bottom of the bed, gazing down at her sleeping sister.

'Sweetheart...' she said, gently, in a rarely seen show of tenderness. Joan opened her eyes, and after a few minutes of quiet conversation, the two women made their way downstairs. Over four mugs of Yorkshire tea, two chocolate eclairs and two cream doughnuts, the beans were well and truly spilled, in both directions. In what started off as a heart-to-heart to enable Joan to come to terms with her 'desertion', it finished up as an outpouring of wailing, and groaning, from Dot, regarding the state of her shite life, prospect of no prospects, and her fear for the futures of her offspring. It got to the stage where Joan couldn't take anymore and, after a valiant attempt to stop herself laughing, by biting her bottom lip, went off on one, howling with convulsions of laughter at Dot's misfortunes. Now, anyone else who had the temerity to portray such an unashamed display of irreverence, would have, well and truly, verbally at least, had their head separated from their neck. But, after Joan gulped and gasped, through her howling laughter, 'Look on the bright side – there's always someone else worse off.' Dot replied: 'There might be, someone else worse off – but if there is I don't know where the fuck they are.' As the pair collapsed into uncontrollable guffaws, a simultaneous trickle of pee found its way into their gussets. After another mug of tea each, Dot, fired with enthusiasm, left her sister's house with a new battle to fight. OK, it was a shite life for her, but that didn't stop Dot wanting to do her utmost to help others, and her divine crusade now, was to help bring Joan's pregnancy to full term. She saw in her vulnerable sister, a cause to fight, and when the need arose,

Dot was the one to have on your side. As she clambered onto her huge white stallion, her breastplate glistening in the sun, the down-trodden mass waved, and cheered, as she slowly rode up Orleans Road, towards St. Ossie's Street, her sovereign standard curling in the breeze. '*Honny swa key molly pants,*' she shouted, to the adoring throng. She didn't know what the fuck it meant, but it sounded dead good – she'd heard it on the pictures, donkeys years ago. By the time she got to the top of the road, the adoring throng had gone, Dot's breastplate had disappeared, and the huge white stallion had transformed back into her clapped-out Astra, with the dodgy clutch, but the spirit of *Jeanne d'Arc* still raged, within her bosom.

15

Monday morning came in with a bang. The meeting with management was scheduled for 11 o'clock and Jack Brady together with his cohort of shop stewards, had arranged their own meeting for 10 o'clock to finalise their plan of attack. No matter what management offered, there was no way they were going to accept thirty pieces of silver and sacrifice the jobs of their membership with compulsory redundancies. The Rectification Area was waiting on work, and, as Dot stood daubing woad on her face, and sharpening the blade of her spear, she mumbled to Charlie, 'Shove a brush round ere, will yeh? Tidy it up a bit, but not too much, or they'll think we've got nothink to do.'

We haven't, thought Charlie, as she replied, 'Right-oh.'

At ten to eleven, Dot left, and ambled down the alleyway on route to the meeting with her beloved Fuehrer. Charlie began to diligently brush the area, under the work benches, around the perimeter, behind the lockers. The various brushings had begun to have a therapeutic effect on her. Slowly, but surely, the repetitious banality of mundane tasks such as this, had over the period she'd been there, started to reduce the trauma in her mind. The flashbacks were now coming fewer and farther between. What she'd hoped for, for so long, had begun to appear on her horizon. Now that her mother had come to terms with the fact that she'd turned into a strong-willed young woman of steel, who was capable of determining her own future, it gave her an inner strength, upon which she intended to build. It began to glean in her mind, that much of this new-found obstinacy, and independence, had evolved as a direct result of knowing Dot, and the examples she'd set, in certain ways. She brushed a load of dirt and swarf, onto the shovel, walked over to the crisp box and threw it in. The box was almost full, so she picked it up. then made her way to the skip. As she swung the box upward toward the edge, the soggy bottom collapsed, sending banana peelings, tea bags, stale remnants of butties, tangerine peelings and other smelly articles of rubbish all over Charlie's feet. '*Shit*,' she said with a hiss, as she gazed down at the mound of crap, now waiting to be cleared up, once more. She returned with the brush and the shovel and began to scoop the offending articles up. As she did, she noticed one of the pieces of Ted's card. She picked it up and realised what it was. She carefully picked her way through the rest of the rubbish until she'd recovered all four pieces, putting them into her pocket, she finished off clearing up the mess.

***

At 10.55 Jack Brady, and his disciples, trooped into the Boardroom for the meeting. The management were sitting down one side of the table, Jack and his band sat opposite. The Plant Manager, Arthur Rothwell, declared the meeting open, and Jack, a firm believer of *attack is the best means of defence* fired the opening shot, repeating the fact that the union would not countenance any move by management to impose compulsory redundancies. Unfortunately, the opening shot that he fired happened to go straight through his own foot. After management had let him offload his tripe for a full ten minutes, he finally ran out of steam. As Jack bathed in the glow of approving comments from his cohort, Hardcastle reached down under the table, lifted a loaded Bazooka and took aim straight at Jack. He gently squeezed the trigger and sent the shell exploding towards his chest as he announced that management agreed with the union – there would be no compulsory redundancies. There was no need for compulsory redundancies, as the request from management for voluntary ones had been hugely over-subscribed. As Jack struggled to come back with a response, Hardcastle rubbed salt into his wounds by stating that the management were in view of the demand, currently re-evaluating various positions within the company, to see if any further redundancies could be offered. The Nelson/Kingston conspiracy had worked to an even greater success than was first anticipated. The cunning manouevre had paid off with dividends. Via Hardcastle, and a selection of hard to resist offers - payoffs, plus new jobs in KayKay Engineering for those who wanted them, or generous redundancy packages for those who preferred to leave or were coming up for retirement - it was easy to see why the redundancy number was over-subscribed. After another half hour had passed, during which Rothwell had magnanimously allowed Jack, and his crew, to save face by offering to assist in the completion of the redundancy procedures '*if such is the desire of our members*', the meeting ended at 11. 52. As a defeated, deflated Jack and his followers spilled back out onto the shop floor, looking a like Jesus and His disciples might have looked, having discovered that someone had just pinched their fishing boat, a great howling of delight emanated from behind the door of the boardroom.

Dot was devastated, feeling like Napoleon when he first cast eyes on St Helena. After a few minutes of licking each other's wounds, the group broke up and threaded their spidery paths between the machines, back to their workstations, inside the factory.

'Just my friggin luck,' Dot said with a hiss, under her breath, as she trundled along the alley. The first, and only, time in her working life that she'd been instrumental in engineering a 'yes' vote for a strike, and now the bastard management had thrown, with their underhanded tactics, defeat into the jaws of her victory. As she continued to amble along, staring into space, she thought of Uncle Harry. Dear Uncle Harry. What would he do in the same situation? How would he handle this? But try as she may, however hard she racked her brains, no answer, no solution, to the problem was forthcoming. As the realisation of imminent endgame approached, her thought turned in anger to the traitors – the backstabbers - who'd applied for their thirty pieces of silver. Her mind was working like a computer. The passage of time would reveal who these renegades were, but in the meantime, she began to wonder, exactly what their thirty pieces of silver amounted to. Each application would be dealt with on an individual basis, the package being based mainly around the length of service. For someone who'd worked there a considerable length of time, Dot, for example, the payout would be hefty. Hmm... Not that she'd ever apply for redundancy, of course she wouldn't, but that creeping little question had worked its way into her mind, and she was having trouble dispelling it. Just exactly what would her redundancy package amount to? She wondered, also, what sort of jobs were on offer at KayKay Engineering. 'What the fuck am I thinkin of?' she admonished herself, for having the gall to allow this traitorous thought to infiltrate her mind.

As she continued along the alleyway, an Easyjet A320 completing its descent, was flying over the Runcorn-Widnes bridge, as the pilot levelled the plane then lined it up for its landing, at Liverpool John Lennon airport. As the cabin crew and passengers were strapped in, and preparing for the thud and vibration, as the tyres hit the runway, a young mum, with a little daughter, turned to the bloke reading his magazine, sitting next to her,

'Oh, God, I hate this bit,' she said, in a voice that trembled with fear.

The bloke glanced up from his magazine and smiled reassuringly at her, 'Not to worry, lass - we'll be fine.' Then, Ted Currie turned back and carried on reading his *Classic Cars* magazine.

As the tyres of the plane touched down, Dot, complete with fifty-six, blood-drenched daggers sticking out of her back, turned right into the canteen.

Two hours later, a blue Peugeot taxi pulled up outside 46 Cledwen Close, and Ted got out, paid the driver, then pulled his suitcase up the drive, and made his way into the bungalow. He went into the kitchen and put the kettle on, then went to the phone, picked it up and dialled 1571. There was one message, but he couldn't hear clearly, what was being said. Being hard of hearing, he repeated the message, but still couldn't make it out. It sounded, he thought, like a woman's voice, but he wasn't sure. The voice was quick, muffled, and seemed to be coming from a noisy workshop of some description. Third time lucky, maybe. He pressed the repeat button and listened intently,

'Thanksformeflowers'

No, he had no idea what was being said. He pressed number 3 and deleted the message then went into the kitchen, made a mug of tea, and sat down in the living room. After half an hour he backed the Mercedes out of the drive and drove off, to collect Toby and Colin.

16

As rumour, counter rumour, supposition, and half-truths were rife throughout the factory regarding the redundancies, Jack Brady had called a mass meeting for four o'clock the following afternoon to make the formal announcement to the workforce, regarding the situation. This time, as there would be no show of hands, and this would be a cursory reporting back of the details, the meeting would be held in the canteen.

'Brothers and sisters…' said Jack, precariously balanced on one of the canteen chairs, 'as you all know, management and your union, held a meeting yesterday, to formalise an outcome to the redundancy situation.'

The meeting was over in fifteen minutes. The workforce dispersed back to their machines, to see out the rest of the day. When the time to clock off arrived, Dot couldn't wait to get out of the dump, and go home. She sighed, as she walked down the path. Could anything else go wrong? She just needed a piece of good news – for Chrissake. Just once in her life, was anything going to go right? As she approached the door and raised her key, she suddenly remembered Joan and the baby. A smile crossed her mind.

As she walked down the hall, the Laughing Cavalier was still laughing at her. She walked into the kitchen, picked up the milk pan and poured some water into it, lighting it on the gas. As she was throwing a teabag into a mug, her eldest daughter, Bernie, fifteen, walked into the kitchen.

'Me dad's been 'round.'

'Your dad...?'

'Half an hour ago...'

'What did he want?'

'He's comin back t'night, at eight o'clock. He wants a word with yeh.'

'Worrabout? Did he say?'

'He just said he wanted a word with yeh... in private.'

'What kind of mood was he in?'

'He was alright. Laughin. He said how much he missed us all.'

As Bernie left the kitchen, the words drifted through Dot's mind like old friends returning home,

'...*how much he missed us all...*'

She added a splash of milk to her drink, then took it into the front room. She was in such a state of distraction that she'd forgotten her usual handful of biscuits. She plonked onto the couch, and her stomach began to tremble with excitement. She looked at her *Rolex*, it was knackered again, and had stopped at ten past five. She scampered into the back room, where the only clock in the house that worked was guarded by two, pot dogs, left to her six years ago by her grandmother, May. *Five past six*. Her breath gently trembled out of her mouth, 'Maybe there is a God, after all.' Without another thought to her mug of tea, she hurried up the stairs, went into the bathroom, and started running the bath. She began to search feverishly for those pink and peach bath cube things, that the kids had bought her for Christmas, two years ago. She suddenly remembered she'd given them to the charity shop, the day she bought the Hush Puppies. *Imperial Leather!* – of course. She had a carton of the talcum powder, somewhere. She rooted through the overstuffed wall cabinet, various bits and pieces dropping into the sink in the process, searching in vain for the red carton. It was there somewhere, she only used it the other day to sprinkle into her gusset, when she'd run out of clean knickers. *'Bollocks'* It was gone. But she knew exactly where it'd be. *'Suffering shite'* she said angrily, as she thundered down the stairs, half-ran out, through the kitchen door, then out into the shed. There it sat, like a little red coated sentry, outside Buckingham Palace, guarding the makeshift tools and debris on the work bench. Little Bobby had been fixing yet another puncture. On her way back through the kitchen, she snatched the washing up liquid off the worktop. Six minutes later, a naked Dot clambered in and, looking like an ocean-going liner sliding down the slipway, having just been launched by The Queen, slowly sank into the massive mound of froth, that swelled over the edge of the bath. She rested her head back and closed her eyes: bliss. Her troubles were relocated to the back her mind. For these precious, few minutes, she became – just... Dot. She wasn't the deserted wife, the fat woman, the hostile shop-steward. Just Dot. In this warm cocoon of tranquility, she began to catch sight of true herself, once again. She raised her knees, and her body sank slowly beneath the water.

Thirty minutes later she was rummaging through the wardrobe for that nice, black dress she got from the car boot sale, last Easter. She fished it out. It smelled a bit, so she sprayed a tiny squirt of *Intimate Nights* onto each of the armpits. After another forty minutes, the finished product was unveiled to the world. As she stood in front of the bedroom mirror, she thought she didn't look half-bad: the hair nicely done, the restrained make-up, Aunty Anne's earrings and necklace, the high heels. The only thing that stood out like a sore thumb on this vision of understated elegance, was the gaudy oversized, shite *Rolex*. She snatched it from her wrist and condemned it to a life of loneliness, in the cabinet drawer. As she stood and gazed at herself, she wanted Liam Neeson to walk through the door, sweep her up in his arms, lay her down on the bed and make passionate love to her for the next two hours. But it didn't *have* to be Liam Neeson, anyone would have done, as long as he had half a pulse, didn't pick his nose in public, and fart in bed.

Having plundered the 'holiday fund' of its contents, £38.78, Dot had charged young Bernie with the authority to shepherd her younger siblings to the local McDonald's, for a cornucopia of splendiferous treats – providing they stayed out until at least 9.30. She now sat in the back room, intermittently glancing at the clock. At 7.46, it suddenly dawned on her that she hadn't brushed her teeth. '*Balls,*' spattered out over the banister, as she hurried up the stairs. She entered the bathroom, snatched the toothbrush, squirted some paste onto it and plunged it into her gob. As she began to vigorously brush, a knock came at the front door. '*Uckin ell*' was spat out of her mouth into the sink, together with the toothpaste.

She opened the door, and there he stood: five foot eight, broad, overweight, dirty hair, two dark slits for eyes, and a face that looked like the crust of a lumpy, meat and potato pie. There was no semblance about his appearance to suggest he'd made the slightest effort to tidy himself up. Her heart sank slightly at the realisation, but she put on a brave smile.

'Hello, Dave...'

He cast an eye over her appearance, and came back with the smirking, 'gentlemanly' compliment, of, '*Who the fuck got you ready?*'

Dot smiled, even though her heart had sunk another notch.

'Well, are you lettin me in or wha?'

Smelling of ale and cigarette smoke, he entered the house, and they went into the front room. Sitting opposite him, Dot's negotiating skills, masterful oratory, and abrasive edge were all consigned to the coal shed, as she realized that *this* could be her only chance to win him back.

In an unexpected attempt at diplomacy, he asked how she was keeping, talked about the kids, things at Nelson's. Laid bare for all to see, he was just beating about the bush – but to Dot, eager to believe the unbelievable, he was showing an interest in her and her life, laying the foundations for a return.

After another ten minutes of idle waffle, 'Would you like a cuppa tea?'

'Have y'got nothin stronger?'

'No.'

'Go on, then.'

She filled the milk pan with water and put it onto the lit gas ring. He entered the kitchen and sat at the table. As Dot rooted through the cupboard for the biscuit tin, she realised that this wasn't going how she'd hoped it would. Another minute of inconsequential exchanges followed, then a short pause ensued, during which, he gave a low, nasty laugh.

'What's funny...?'

'I heard about Joan, gettin dumped.'

The words landed like darts, on Dot's feelings. Before she had time to reply, he came back with, 'I was with him, the other night – havin a pint.' He continued to laugh, this time louder, and more nastily. 'Fishin... gone fishin...'

'What d'you mean...?'

'If she was stupid enough to believe that one, she deserved to get dumped.'

Dot looked into his eyes, as a broad smile cracked across his pock-marked face. 'He's been bangin that red-haired one, outa your place. The one with the spikey nose and the glasses. He said she fucks like a bunny. I wouldn't mind a bit of that meself. I wonder if she'd be up for a threesome... I'm not surprised he left borin, old Mother Hen Joan.'

By now, the anger was bubbling up inside Dot. She realised that getting back together was the last thing on his mind. And now, all that *absence makes the heart grow fonder,* was just a load of bollocks. The clouds parted and Dot saw the light of day. How could she possibly want such an evil, nasty-minded bastard back into her life?

'I think you better go, Dave, don't you?'

'I'll go when I'm good an ready. I haven't finished yet.'

'Well, say what you've got to say, an be on your way, please.'

She was being as polite and courteous as possible, trying not to inflame the situation.

'Who the fuck are you talkin to... eh? You, fat, ugly cow. I'll do what the fuck I like in my own house.'

The words, *It's not your house* were fighting to escape

from Dot's lips, but she managed to keep them in check.

'I want yeh to divorce me... and I want half of everythin you've got. So, you better get it sorted... If you know what's good for yeh,' he said in a sinister tone.

By then, she'd had enough. She knew from previous experience, that the best course of action would be to cower submissively and agree with everything he said. But that was previous experience, this was now. Her lips parted and she suddenly felt the words, 'But how could I find grounds to divorce such a perfect husband?' spilling from her mouth. His eyes narrowed, as he looked at her. Clenching his teeth, then rising to his feet, he approached her and grabbed her by the throat, yanking her to her feet.

'Feelin brave, are yeh? Feelin fuckin brave? I'll soon knock that out of yeh.'

Dot crumpled. She knew what was coming next. 'No, Dave... please.'

She screamed, as he swerved her across the room. His clenched fist crashed into her stomach, and she doubled over in pain. He brought his knee up into her face with such a force that it sent her reeling back, into the wall.

'No, Dave, please. No more...' she said, painfully.

'No more? I haven't started on yeh, yet. Yeh fat, ugly twat.'

'Please, Dave. Please don't hit me again...'

His face distorted with maniacal, psychopathic laughter, as he approached, then grabbed her with both hands by her chest. As she looked into his bulging eyes, she opened her mouth to scream, but all that came out was a pathetic yelp, like that of an injured animal caught in a trap. He drew his head back and was about to butt her in the face when, *CLANG...!* His mouth slowly drooped open. His eyes rolled in his head as his grip relaxed on her. His hands fell from her chest and, as if drunk, he staggered backwards. As he moved from Dot, Joan, holding the frying pan, came into sight. *'Get out now,'* she hissed like a cobra, about to strike. 'You pathetic excuse for a man. Go on – *FUCK OFF!'* she roared into his face. He staggered backwards, holding his head in both hands, toward the door. Dot and Joan stood, looking at him. As he began to regain his senses, he made a noise that sounded like a cross between a growl and a groan.

'Dave, just go… Please, just go…' trembled from Dot's lips.

He was standing ten feet from Joan, and they squared up to each other, like a pair of gunfighters.

'Go…? Go…?' he uttered, almost incoherently. 'After what she's just done to me…?

I'LL KILL THE CUNT'

Dot screamed, as he sprang toward Joan. She knew he was too close to get another swing at him with the frying pan so, with the reflexes of a cat, she threw it down, snatched the milk pan off the gas ring and lashed a wave of boiling water over his face and chest. His screams of agony sent shudders of fright through Dot and Joan. Five seconds passed then Joan, recovering her courage, decided to finish off the job. As he stood howling and screaming, she boldly marched up to him and grabbed him by one of his ears, making sure that she dug her sharp thumbnail as deeply as possible into its flesh, she swung him 'round, toward the back door: 'What part of *fuck off* don't you understand?' She said, in a quietly evil tone, through clenched teeth, her eyes glaring. She pushed him through the door, as she shouted, 'You *ever* lay another finger on my sister, an I know someone very big, an very vicious, who'll tear your bollocks off an stuff them down y' throat. She raised her leg, then kicked him with her full foot in his arse, '*NOW, FUCK OFF*' she roared, as she sent him sprawling onto his face into the back garden. She slammed the door shut and bolted it. Dot was trembling with shock and sobbing uncontrollably, as tears flooded down her face and dripped off her cheeks. The front of her dress was ripped open and her precious Aunty Anne's necklace scattered in broken pieces around the floor. She slumped onto the kitchen chair and completely broke down. Joan wrapped her arm around her sister's shoulders and gently kissed her hair. Dot sobbed for a full two minutes, then slowly, gradually, she began to calm down. She cradled her head in her hands, bowed forward, and rested her elbows onto her knees. Heaving a tremulous sigh, she gazed into the void, that was her nonexistent future. Her spirit now broken, she spoke in a low, defeated voice, that was resigned to her fate,

'I might as well be dead… I've got nothink to live for… nothink to live for…'

There was a pause, then a timid voice could be heard, coming from the direction of the hall.

'You've got *us*…'

Dot raised her head and standing in the doorway were her children. Her heart swelled with love for them, and a gentle smile graced her lips as she stretched out her arms. They surged forward and began to smother her with kisses. Little Bobby clambered onto her lap, wrapped his arms around her neck and hugged her tightly, as he whispered, 'I luv you, mam…'

* * *

The following morning Charlie was putting on her overall, about to start work. There was no sign of Dot. As she pulled the overall on, she slid her hand inside the pocket and felt something. She took it out and it was the four pieces of Ted's card. Surreptitiously glancing around to make sure there was no sign of an approaching Oberreichfueherin Dot, she placed the four pieces onto her workbench and arranged them like a jigsaw to read them, once again,

'To the kind and honest lady. Thank you, for returning my wallet. Ted. xx'

She glanced at the phone number and smiled, mischievously. Should she? Shouldn't she? Should she? No, it was none of her business. Besides, the card mightn't have belonged to Dot. The kind and honest lady? It certainly wasn't a description that hung comfortably on the Dot that she knew. Foul-mouthed, hostile bully – now *that*, she could have believed. She walked over and threw the pieces into the fresh crisp box, that she'd replaced yesterday. As she looked up, Rick came walking into the area. He looked concerned about something. 'What's the matter?' she asked.

'Have you not heard about Dot?'

'What?'

'Joan rang me, last night. That bastard beat her up again, that's why she's not in.

He laid into her, good style. If Joan hadn't walked in, he might've killed her.'

Charlie's stomach became twisted with shock and revulsion. She still hadn't conquered the knack of liking Dot, but no woman deserves to be abused, physically or mentally. She became silent.

'Charlie…?'

'I'm going to visit her tonight,' she said, determinedly.

Chapter 16

'Do you have her address?'

Rick told her Dot's address.

'Do you want to come with me...?'

'No... I can't... Not tonight.'

'It won't take long - just on the way home from work.'

'No, I can't, honest. I've got t'be somewhere, at five o'clock.'

'Where?' she inquired, tactlessly.

Rick felt like saying to her, '*Mind your own bleedin business,*' but, Rick being Rick, he said, 'The doctor.'

'Again...? Rick, what's wrong? Tell me...'

'Just, tell Dot I'm thinkin about her, an... whatever...'

He began to walk away.

'Rick... *RICK...!*'

17

Never in her life, had Charlie been so intent on checking the time on her watch, over, and over again. She realised that without Dot's sarcasm, huffing and puffing, and intermittent appearances and disappearances, the Rectification Area seemed a lonely place. She had to admit it to herself – she missed Dot. She'd had her dinner with Rick, but the conversation was subdued, restrained. Their friendship was just that. As soon as the clocking-off bell went at 4.30, she'd be away.

At 5.04, the Mini Cooper pulled up outside. Charlie got out and lifted a bunch of Sainsbury's best, and a card, off the passenger seat. She walked down the path, and rang the bell, which didn't work. She waited... then, rang it again... then,

DUM, DUM, DUM...

After a few seconds, the figure of a small child could be seen through the frosted glass, reaching for the knob. The door opened, and there stood little Bobby. He looked, silently, at her, as if she was the second alien visitation he'd had in the last few weeks. Then, the silence was broken by Charlie, saying, 'Hello... who are you...?'

Eventually, he replied, 'Bobby...'

'Well, Bobby, is mummy at home...?'

'D'you mean me mam?'

Before he had time to answer, Dot shouted from the front room, 'Who is it, son?'

'Some, posh woman... wiv a bunch of flowers.'

Before Dot had time to reply, Charlie shouted, *'It's me, Dot. May I come in...?'*

'Oh, bollocks,' groaned quietly, from the front room, then, she shouted, 'As long as y' don't mind the place lookin like a shithole.'

Charlie walked down the hall, glancing at The Laughing Cavalier, and into the front room.

'I came to see *you*, not the house... I brought you these...' she said, handing Dot the flowers and card, while trying not to notice the bruising on her face. Dot was touched by the gesture, and put the card, unopened, onto the mantlepiece. The conversation started off stilted and clumsily, but as the minutes ticked away, both women, stripped of the formality and rigidity of their workplace environment, began to thaw.

'I berra put these in some water,' said Dot, painfully rising to her feet. 'Would y'like a mugga tea?'

'That would be nice. Thank you.'

Charlie followed Dot into the kitchen, determined not to mention what had happened the previous evening.

'These are lovely...' said Dot, as she arranged the large, yellow flowers in a vase. 'What are they?'

'Globe Chrysanthemums.'

'Better than the last bunch, I got give – they were shrivelled up,' said Dot, tutting and rolling her eyes, comically. 'The story of my life – everythin a man gives to me is shrivelled up.'

'Who, on earth, gave you a bunch of shrivelled-up flowers?' said Charlie, with a giggle.

'Some bloke. He give them to Bobby, when I was out. He put them in the shed with his bike stuff, an forgot t'tell me. I don't know who the bloke was.'

'Very romantic.'

'Wouldn't be my luck,' said Dot, absent-mindedly, as she stripped leaves from the stalks.

'I've never met him... I found his wallet in me cab, an pushed it through his letterbox.'

Charlie's penny dropped.

'Hey, missus, would y' like t' see me new bike...?'

She turned, and little Bobby was standing beside her. She looked down into the cute face that stared back.

'He's gorra *new* bike, in the shed. Been workin on it for the past month,' said Dot.

'Would y'like t' see it, missus?'

Charlie caved; how could she resist those eyes?

'I certainly would,' she said, with an eagerness that was genuine.

* * *

The shed door creaked open, and Bobby entered, followed by Charlie. On the workbench stood his *new* bike, precariously propped up against a small tower of breeze blocks.

'I rubbed all de ol' paint off, wiv some em'ry paper off Mr Parsons, next door - den I painted it wiv some primer paint off ol' George, over de road - den I painted it wiv dis blue stuff wha' me mam had under de stairs.'

Charlie cast her eyes on the result of little Bobby's magnificent effort. *Jesus Christ.* It was shite. An abomination.

'It's the most beautiful bike I've ever seen,' she said, with a convincing gasp.

'I know,' said Bobby, proudly admiring his handiwork. 'It's me birfday bike f'nex week.'

'What do you mean?'

'It's me birfday, next Fridey, but me mam said she's skint... so I can't have a new bike, so I'm makin' me own one, instead...'

Charlie's heart melted, as she gazed down at the cheeky, industrious, little tyke, with the smudged face, and tousled hair. He looked like one of *Fagin's* gang.

'I might get one for Chrissmas,' he said, downheartedly. 'If they've got dem left.'

'They'll have plenty, left,' said Charlie, attempting to cheer him up.

'No... not dees ones, de won't.'

'What do you mean?'

'They've only got three... in 'alfords.'

'Three what?'

'Carrington Gurkhas,' he said in a mumble, that was almost incoherent.

'What's the name of it?'

'A Carrington Gurkha...' he said. 'It's me fav'rite bike, in all of de world.'

* * *

As Charlie drove home, there was nothing she could do to stop thinking about Dot, and the despicable situation she was in. In the forty minutes they'd spent, over a mug of tea, the two women had grown closer. With her thoughtful kindness and genuine, caring nature, Charlie had eventually, inadvertently, been allowed to squeeze through a chink in the armour that was Dot's inverted snobbery. And, coming in the opposite direction, she'd discovered in Dot, a warm tenderness, that three weeks ago, she'd have sworn would have been impossible to exist. She also, of course, could feel nothing but empathy with her, for the catalogue of abuse she'd been subjected to, over the years. Whether physical or mental, Charlie knew from her own personal experience, that they were opposite sides of the same, evil coin.

Later that evening, Dot remembered the card. She walked into the front room, took the envelope off the mantlepiece and opened it, *'Dear Dot, hurry back, soon. Charlie xx'* It was accompanied by two twenty-pound notes. Dot inhaled, pursed her lips and closed her eyes. Her mouth began to quiver.

* * *

Her Mini Cooper swerved into the drive, proceeded twenty yards, then came to rest next to a black Audi. Charlie got out, pressed the remote, and entered the house. She met her mum in the hall, who whispered, 'Uncle Bill's here.' 'I've just seen his car,' she replied, then went into the cloakroom, hung up her metallic, olive green, Sportyman puffer jacket, then proceeded toward the living room. As she entered, Uncle Bill and her dad were standing with their backs to her, chatting, as they looked out into the back garden.

'Uncle Bill,' she said, with a smile, as she strode toward him.

William Gregory Hardcastle turned. 'Charlie,' he said,

beaming. 'How are things at the coal face?' he added, with a chuckle. She pecked him on the cheek.

'I'll leave you two to get on with it, then,' said her dad. 'Whatever it is that you, industrial types get on with,' then, feigning a flummoxed smile, he left the room, closing the door. Hardcastle sat in one of the armchairs as Charlie crashed onto the couch, kicking off her Sportyman trainers.

'What is it you wanted to talk to me about? You sounded quite concerned.'

'It's Dot... I am concerned.'

'I trust, she's been behaving herself?'

'Er... well, yes – to all intents and purposes – Dot, being Dot.' She sprang to her feet.

'Would you like a drink?'

She carried on talking, as she fixed a Campari and soda for herself, and a Jura with ice for Hardcastle, who, was taken aback by the news of Dot's brute of a husband, and the way he'd recently beaten her up, and had regularly beaten her up, during most of their marriage.

As the story unfolded, he became genuinely concerned about her welfare. They'd never really got on over the years, rooted as they were on opposite sides of the industrial, labour track, but there was a glimmer of admiration within him, for her devotion to any cause that she, however misguided, thought deserved her support. As one drink led to another, Charlie had been sounding out if there was any way that Dot could be offered a generous redundancy payout. This, she thought, could help relieve the pressure on her to be constantly on the go, just to stay afloat, financially. Even better if she could be offered a job at KayKay. This was all unexpected by Hardcastle, and when he left fifty minutes later, it was on the promise to Charlie that he'd look into the pros and cons, of such an offer.

As the Audi turned out of the drive then accelerated into the road, Charlie's mother entered the room.

'What did Uncle Bill want?'

After a pause, Charlie answered, 'Work business.'

'So... you have done it, then...?'

'Done what...?'

'Handed your notice in...'

'No... and I've no intention of doing so.'

'How long must this madness go on? Can you not see you're making a complete fool of yourself? You need to be back at law college. *What's the matter with you...?*'

Charlie could feel her stomach beginning to knot. She was doing all she could to stop herself, from exploding with anger. Gone forever, were the *cower, cower, yes, mummy, no, mummy, three bags full, mummy,* days.

'For goodness sake mother, will you be quiet. This is my bed I'll lie in it.'

'With one of your rough and ready types, no doubt...'

'Will you please...' she sprang to her feet and yelled, 'just leave me, *alone...*'

Her mother was taken aback by this outburst.

'How dare you shout at me.'

'It's not the same, anymore... Why can't you get it into your head? This world is different from the one that you grew up in. I don't care that you and dad were consultants, *I don't care.* I don't want to follow, subserviently, in your professional footsteps. Can't you see, *I don't want to be a fucking solicitor – I never did. It was you – It was always you.*'

'How dare you use that language in this house. After all I've done for you... the life I've provided you with...'

Chapter 17

'Oh, for God's sake, mother, *give it a rest.*'

She stood and approached Charlie.

'You are an ungrateful, common slut...'

She slapped Charlie hard across her face. Unwilling to show any remorse, she glared at her mother in silence. Her dad entered the room.

'What's going on...?'

Charlie, her eye and cheek screaming with pain, walked calmly and serenely, out of the room. Leaving the babble behind, she ran up the stairs two at a time, went into her bedroom, closed the door, and lay on the bed. As she rubbed her palm slowly up and down the side of her face, she was determined not to cry, although her eyes were beginning to mist over. How she wished this bed could be Rick's. She closed her eyes and could see his face: his cheeky wink and that *bloody* smile. His smile became contagious, the more she thought of how he made her laugh. She realised that she was now only happy when she was in his company. Dear Rick – the only man, apart from Sir Reginald Fortescue Bogpipe, she'd ever known, who'd treated her with kindness, courtesy and respect. She thought back to one of the highlights of her life; the day she felt his gentle arm around her waist, hardly daring to breathe, as they watched the hen goldfinch incubating her eggs. And here she is, now, miserable, in a seven-bedroomed, mock-Tudor house, in an affluent suburb of the city, as happily, he tends to his birds in his postage stamp, farmworker's cottage. How she wished she could be with him. She prayed, that whatever it was, he'd gone to see the doctor about, wasn't serious... She reached across and picked up her Spanish guitar. Quietly, gently, she began to pick out the tune she'd played that night, at Rick's: Cavatina.

* * *

Rick had sat in silence that afternoon, as the news had been broken to him, then,

'There must be some mistake,' he said, stunned.

'There's no mistake…'

'So, what happens now, then…?'

'Just sign, where indicated, and we'll contact you, when we need you to come back in…'

'When will that be?'

'About two weeks.'

He signed the form, said, 'Thank you,' and left the room. In a daze, he walked down the corridor, out into the sunshine, and got into the Volvo. He slammed the driver's door shut, leant back onto the seat, and gazed out through the windscreen. He heaved a sigh as he watched two pigeons' squabble over the remnants of a crust, then he put the key into the ignition, and started the engine.

* * *

He entered the cottage, made himself a mug of tea, then sat on the coach. His mind could not take in the enormity of the news he'd just been given. He leaned back, rested his head on the couch, and stared at the wall. Eventually, his eyes came to rest on his Spanish guitar. He reached across, picked it up and began to play, remembering how beautiful the music sounded, the night Charlie had played. After a few minutes, he stopped playing, gazed at the guitar, raised it to his lips, and kissed it.

18

At seven minutes past six, the following evening, Wednesday, James Edward Currie was clearing the left-over debris, from his tidying-up in the garden. He brushed the rose clippings and deadheads onto the shovel, and threw them into the green wheelie bin, as he watched a huge bumble bee lethargically ambling its way from bloom to bloom, on the lavender.

I could murder a cuppa tea... jogged through his mind, as he licked his dry lips.

He walked into the bungalow, washed his hands, and put the kettle on. As he stood in the kitchen looking out of the window, he pondered whether to have sprouts or peas, with his breaded haddock and oven chips. He wouldn't normally have sprouts with fish and chips, but the large bags were *two for the price of one,* in Morrisons, and he had to get rid of them somehow. As he struggled to find an answer to the esoteric dilemma in which he found himself, the phone rang. It *was* the phone because he distinctly remembered the sound it made, the last time it rang; a sales call about two weeks ago. He moved into the living room as, *Oh, Christ, I hope no-one's died,* tumbled through his mind.

'Hello…?'

'Hello - am I speaking to Ted…?'

'Aye… who is it?'

'Hi, Ted… I hardly know how to start this conversation, but please bear with me.'

'You're not trying to sell me summat, are you, lass? 'Cause if y'are – I'm putting the phone down, now.'

'*No*, please don't. I'm phoning on behalf of a friend. She's asked me to contact you, and apologise.'

'What are you talking about?'

'The flowers.'

'Flowers? I haven't ordered no flowers. Right, I'm putting the phone down…'

'*Your wallet.* She pushed your wallet through the letterbox, and you took her, some flowers.'

And lo, the clouds parted, and the sunlight flooded down, clearing up his confusion.

'Oh! them flowers. I'm with you now, duck. Aye, that's right. That lovely, kind lady. I went 'round and saw her nipper. Told him t'give them to his mam.'

'Well, Ted, you don't mind me calling you Ted, do you?'

'I've been called worse.'

'Well, Ted, therein lies the problem. You see, the nipper, Bobby, took them into the shed, and…'

The phone call lasted for almost an hour, but Ted didn't mind. It was a rare treat to be the centre of someone's attention. As the call progressed, they gelled. But the more she talked, a twinge of guilt entered Charlie's mind when she realized that this was, in fact, a sales call, she was selling Dot. But the good news was – she wouldn't be a two for the price of one – one Dot was quite enough for anyone to contend with, thank you very much. By the time Charlie hung up she'd had a potted history of Ted's life. But most of it had been innocently coaxed out of him; he wasn't a bragger. Nor did he whinge or whine about the state of his life like some lonely, isolated people do. He was a widower, liked to travel, had some friends, but they were all still-married couples getting on with their busy lives, rarely giving a thought to him. Months would pass without a word. He didn't say it of course, but Charlie got the impression that he felt, since the death of his wife four years ago, he'd been shunted into a siding and left – had grass growing up his wheels. He was fifty-nine, and had built up, over many years, a successful, building company, which, after the death of his wife, he'd completely lost interest in, and now, just takes a back seat as it's run by his two sons. He had a brilliant business mind and a knack for making money, but his Achilles heel was that he couldn't resist a 'bargain'. Hence the sprouts.

'Aye, lass, that's all I do nowadays, potter around me garden, rub some Turtle Wax on the old banger, now and again, and look after Toby and Kenny.'

'Are they your sons?'

'Nay, Toby's me Westie and Kenny's me canary.'

'*Kenny?*' she said, stifling a titter. 'You have a canary, named Kenny?'

'Aye. I named him after me brother. He's a right good singer, an all.'

'Your brother?'

'*Nay,* the canary...'

Charlie was biting her lip.

* * *

As Thursday dawned, since his ground-breaking conversation with Charlie, Ted felt as if he'd had a huge weight lifted off his shoulders. Someone had phoned *him* - shown an interest in *him*, and the two of them had hit the ground running, sharing a cheery, intelligent, informative conversation. He thought Charlie spoke with a beautiful accent, and felt he'd, out of the blue, inherited a surrogate granddaughter. It was as if a tank-engine had shunted into the siding, hooked him up, and slowly reversed out pulling him, if not yet back onto the main line, then, at least, out of the shadows. He was so enamoured with the whole experience that was kicked off by the simple sound of a of a ringing phone, he (almost) forgot he was eating sprouts mixed in with his lamb Rogan Josh and pilau rice, ready meal. Similarly, Charlie felt as if she'd made a new friend. She thought his working-class, northern accent, which possibly originated from somewhere in Yorkshire, was endearing, and his sharp, witty sense of humour had made her laugh out loud, a few times. She kept imagining Dot and Ted as a couple and couldn't find anything to dissuade her from the initial inkling that what was needed was a nudge in the right direction, to set off a trail of conspiracy to engineer a meeting of them both. But how could she achieve that end…?

***

She sat in the conservatory, and as she sipped a vodka and tonic, and nibbled a sour cream and onion *Pringle*, began to peruse the list of bullet points she'd randomly jotted down. She just had to rearrange them into some semblance of a plan. She'd already discovered, from Dot, that she wouldn't be out on the taxi, on Saturday. She couldn't face it. Hmm... it all hung on Ted, now. She picked up the phone.

Ted was sipping a glass of India Pale Ale, engrossed in a documentary on the telly, about narrow gauge, steam engines, and the part they played in the slate quarries of Snowdonia.

'Ee, I wouldn't mind going there and having a look at them, sometime. What d'you reckon, Toby?'

Toby suddenly stirred, thinking he was being offered the chance of a walk, but when Ted carried on watching the telly without another word, he rested his head back onto his paws, huffed and closed his eyes again. The phone rang.

'Hello...?'

'Hi, Ted, it's Charlie.'

'Charlie, lass. How are yeh?' he said, cheerily.

'Fine, thanks - Ted, do you remember we spoke yesterday about Dot, and how you said it would be nice to see her again?'

'Aye, it would, lass.'

'Well... I *might* be going out with her, and a couple of friends, on Saturday, and – it would have to appear by accident of course, because she'd hit the roof if she found out...'

'What are you saying...?'

'Are you doing anything, Saturday night – eight o'clockish?'

'Can y'just ang on a minute an I'll consult me Filofax: No!'

They shared a laugh.

***

It wasn't as detailed, or as intricate, as the combined Allied genius that went into the planning of D-Day, but in its own naïve way, Charlie's Operation Dotted (Dot + Ted), was a smart piece of engineering, in its own right. And now, having Ted on board, it was almost a goer, and just a case of rallying the troops, and enlisting whoever was available to join in the conspiracy, Guy Fawkes eat your heart out. She ended up with three additional volunteers: Joan, who fancied a couple of hours out, Zeta, who'd had a nark with her boyfriend, and was temporarily off men, and Petronela, who was trying her utmost to overcome the vagaries and eccentricities of the British way of life. All three of them shared Charlie's determination to do whatever they could to help get Dot's life into some semblance of normality, instead of the continuous chaos it had descended into. Of course, the villain of the piece, Dot, must not bear the slightest inkling that Operation Dotted was being planned behind her back, and was about to be sprung. The task lay on Joan's shoulders to entice the prey into its trap; talk Dot into going out for a drink.

After Charlie had phoned Joan, Thursday teatime, Joan immediately phoned young Bernie's mobile, and bribed her with the promise of a tenner to volunteer to babysit, after Joan, two hours later, would phone Dot *out of the blue* and suggest a night out. When she did speak to Dot, she found out that she had nothing else planned for Saturday night, apart from, thanks to Charlie's forty quid, a nice bottle of Chardonnay, a large box of Maltesers and hopefully, a decent film, on the telly. As Dot had regaled Joan with all this riveting info, down the telling bone, the thought had crossed her mind that next time she was in the charity shop, to keep an eye open for a couple of nice wine glasses, as the wine, she thought, never seemed to last as long, being drunk from a mug.

'*Do you fancy a drink on Saturday, then? I know you were plannin on stoppin in, but… I need t'get out an see some humans. I'm goin up the wall, stayin in, talkin to the bleedin goldfish.*'

'*Of course, I'll come out with yeh? Where d'you wanna go?*'

'*The Red House'll do. I'll see if I can get a couple of the girls to come with us – cheer us up, you know. We'll have a laugh. I just need to get out for an orange juice and a bag of crisps.*'

And so, the stage was set, the performance was about to begin.

***

Friday morning, seven o'clock, Dot shouted up the stairs, '*Bobby! - get yourself down ere, now, an open y'birthday cards.*' Seconds later, little Bobby, still in his pyjamas, came thundering down the stairs, like a panic-stricken baby elephant. He leapt from the third stair straight into the hall and landed amid the seven birthday cards that were scattered on the doormat. Scooping them up, he shot into the front room, lurched onto the couch and began to open them. Three of them had a fiver in each, one had a postal order, a couple had nothing in them, but one, that he opened, had written on the card, *To Bobby, wishing you a VERY HAPPY BIRTHDAY xx*. But it wasn't signed. It contained no money – but a small, metal key sellotaped to the back of it.

'Wot's dis key for?' he asked Dot.

'I don't know,' she said, genuinely baffled, as she

arranged his cards on the mantlepiece.

He separated the key from the card, and then, as Dot had an inkling, she said, 'Maybe it's for somethink outside?' He was off like a shot, straight into the hall, past the Laughing Cavalier, feverishly undoing the security chain, he threw open the front door and sprang out onto the path. *'Come in, you'll catch your death!'* shouted Dot, as she followed him. By the time she stepped onto the path, he'd run the length of the house to the drainpipe, near the corner. He stood, mesmerized, looking at the large parcel that was wrapped in blue birthday paper, and chained to the pipe. As Dot approached, he began tearing at the paper, feverishly ripping it to shreds. The more he ripped off, the more it came into view: a bike. But not just *any* bike, a fabulous, *brand new* bike, *exactly* the one he wanted, the one he'd been drooling over, in *'alfords'*, for the last, six months: a *Carrington Gurkha*.

Fingers trembling with excitement, he couldn't wait to get the key into the lock and unchain the bike from the drainpipe. It was a beefy-looking mountain bike, with big, knobbly tyres, a dual suspension frame, six-speed gears, power-dual V-brakes and... it was Satin black, with **Carrington Gurkha** picked out in gold, red and white, along the crossbar. Before Dot had time to say, 'Right let's get back in, for your breakfast,' he was on it, up the path, and out into the street. As Dot ran gasping after him, onto the pavement, she couldn't help shrieking with laughter as she watched him, pyjamas and bare feet, peddling furiously in a circle around the large grassy patch, opposite the house, as he screamed at the top of his voice:

'I've gorra new bike! I've gorra new bike, for me birfday! It's a Carrington Gurkha!'

19

Dot-Day, Saturday, June 6th, The Red House. Field Marshall Charlie had done a top-hole job, chaps, of inspiring the troops to respond positively to her call to arms, and now, as 18.30 hours approached, the said troops were in their various billets, preparing to go into battle.

Charlie was facing a minor dilemma – how to dress? Usually, her innate sense of tasteful style, and understated elegance, would produce a look that was exceptionally attractive – but no, not tonight. She wasn't going to risk jeopardising her tentative friendship with Dot, by turning up looking like a *friggin model*. She walked into the wardrobe and began to root around in various shoe boxes, and along rows of hangers. 'That should be OK,' she kept repeating, as she flung various items of casual clothing out, onto the bed. After showering, she dried off and looked at herself, naked, in the mirror. As she noticed she could no longer see her ribs, a slight smile of defiance crossed her lips. Joan's burgeoning mounds of sustenance had finally started to kick in, and erase traces of her dominated past. When clothed, she stood in front of the mirror again, to judge her dressed down, night out with the girls' look.

Great she thought, *I look ordinary.* (she still looked like a friggin model.) In fairness, however, she decided to top the look off by wearing her metallic olive green, puffer jacket. It was only two weeks old and looked tidy enough. At the opposite end of the city where they play 'tick' with hatchets, Dot was going through the same ritual. After her bath, doing her hair, and putting her make-up on, she stood in front of the mirror and looked at the finished article: the blue-flowered, Oxfam blouse was a perfect accompaniment to the British Heart Foundation, A-line, Navy skirt, and the pair of Save the Children, open toe, nude heels added a pleasing touch of contrast. She pulled on her camel duffle coat, fastened the three toggles, the fourth one had gone west donkeys years ago, then, she was ready for the off. Bring it on.

***

Built on the site of a pub known as, The Three Swans, originally, a coaching house, The Red House, was a redbrick pub, built in 1892. It was run by Big Aggie, a widow with a penchant for gaudy tattoos, and piercings, whose husband was murdered two years ago. Big Aggie was the only woman that Dot wouldn't dare pick a fight with. Quite a large pub, its design stuck to the traditional layout of public bar, incorporating dart board, pool table, and fruit machine, and a carpeted lounge, still nostalgically referred to by the locals as 'the best room'. It was an archetypal inner-city, working-class, watering hole, frequented by a mixture of unemployed, employed, and retired patrons. It wasn't a 'wipe your feet on the way out' type of pub, but on the other hand, there was very little class about the place, apart from the faded glory of its Victorian mahogany features, and the mock-crystal chandeliers, all of which, passing eyes had long-since remained oblivious to. If the pub was footwear it could best be described as a pair of shabby, but comfy, slippers. This was the location, where the dastardly crime was about to be carried out: Operation Dotted.

***

Joan was the first to arrive, turning up for duty at 19.28, to collar her favourite spot in the lounge - the corner table, next to the window, overlooking the street. She gathered enough chairs and lay them out around the table before ordering an orange juice. She sat and people-watched for a few minutes. Sitting diagonally opposite, was one of her favourites, Van Gogh – a well-preserved, Scottish bloke of seventy-six, who for many years, had been one of the shabbily-dressed stalwarts – part of the furniture. Saturday night was *his* night out, early doors. He was a kindly, unassuming widower, who kept himself to himself, the sort of bloke that nobody would notice, until he died, then the church would be packed out at his funeral, saying how much they'd miss him. As he sat, quietly sipping periodically, from his half of draught Guinness, a cheeky smile, graced Joan's lips. It was Dot who'd nicknamed old Tommy, Van Gogh. Looking serious, she shouted over, 'Would you like a drink, Tommy?'

'I've got one ere,' Tommy's broad, Glaswegian accent bellowed back, which tickled Joan, although, she didn't show it.

'Thanks, anywe.'

As eight o'clock turned to five past the door swished

open, and Zeta, dolled up to the eyeballs, gushed in. She spotted Joan and took a seat opposite her. No sooner had they began chatting than Charlie arrived and sat next to Zeta. Seconds later, as if someone had turned on a conveyor belt, Dot walked in. As soon as Dot had plonked down on the plush couch, next to Joan, the door opened again, and in walked a completely transformed, if looking a bit confused and embarrassed, Petronela. Charlie sprang to her feet and went to her aid, as Zeta began to take the order for the drinks.

Now, all with a drink in front of them, their atmosphere warmed and conversations between the women began to flow. Charlie complimented Zeta on her slacks and biker jacket. Petronela, or Petra as she wanted to be called, wore a long, Bohemian-style, floral print dress, and her shoulder-length, auburn hair was in small plaits, up, speckled with tiny flowers, reminiscent of the sixties' flower children. She was thirty-two, a strong, independent woman and, apart from still grappling to come to terms with perfecting a foreign language, plus struggling to get to grips with the hurly-burly atmosphere of a factory canteen, she was enjoying her new country. She'd lived in Britain for just on four months and had come from Krakow. Her striking beauty matched her natural elegance. She was cultured and, in her own country, had been a primary school teacher, until she was made redundant. She spoke in a gentle voice, with a broken accent that was appealing. Her talent was wasted, working in a canteen. She hoped one day to return to teaching, not least because she found the needs of a class of boisterous five-year-olds much easier to cater for than the insatiable British appetite for the like of jam roly-poly, toad in the hole – and the inexplicably named, spotted dick.

Joan was happy to turn up looking casual in a pair of grey, baggy jeans and a purple jumper (both a la C&A's closing-down sale), but the surprise attraction of the evening came when Dot suddenly declared in her usual, ladylike, tone, 'It's bleedin roastin in ere. I'm sweatin like a pig. I'll have t'take me coat off,' as she stood, undid her toggles and, as all their eyes turned to her, removed her duffle coat. The sight was greeted with a wave of compliments, enquiring as to where her wardrobe had been acquired.

'That'd be tellin' she replied, coyly, as a wry smile crossed Joan's lips.

When Petra reached across, took hold of Dot's skirt, and felt it between her thumb and fingers, saying, 'I have sin thees dress in Marek and Spencerr - I nearly did buy it, but was much egspensif,' Dot could have kissed her.

The pub was starting to fill up and a convivial atmosphere filled the lounge. The only fly in the ointment was two uncouth dickheads, already well-pissed, standing at the bar. The pair, aged early twenties, weren't locals, and had probably wandered in to get tanked up, on their way to a club in town. They became rowdier and cruder, as the minutes ticked away. Big Aggie was serving in the bar, and the two barmaids were too busy to take any notice. As some witticism shot out from Joan, the group laughed out loud, attracting the attention of the two scumbags. They went walking over and started to paw Zeta and Petra.

'*Hey,*' said Dot, with a bark. 'Behave yourselves, you two.'

'Why? Worra you gonna do about it, fatty?' and the two, burst into derogatory laughter.

'Why do not you two, young gentlemen pliz go 'way, pliz?' said Petra.

'Hey, Terry, a foreigner,' said the taller of the two. 'A fuckin foreigner... tellin us, wha t'do, in our own country.'

'We don't want the like of you in our country. So why don't y'fuck off back t'where you come from?' said Terry.

'Alright now, lads, that's enough. Knock it off,' said Dot, sternly.

'Shut y'gob, fat arse.'

The anger was raging throughout the group, but there was nothing they could do, other than wait for the incident to pass.

'I'm goin for a lash,' said the tall one. 'D'you wanna come and hold it for me?' he leered at Petra, 'See how big an 'ard you can gerrit t'go,' as he simulated masturbation, with his hand.

'An' I'm goin for a dump. Y'can come an wipe me arse, if y'want.'

'Don't go away, girls, we'll be back in a couple of minutes.'

'Form a cock-sucking queue.'

'With fatty at the back...'

Laughing out loud, the pair walked off toward the lavatory. Petra was almost in tears, and the rest of them started to reassure and console her.

The two scumbags were in the lavatory. The tall one at the urinal, the other one, in the cubicle.

'Tell you wha,' said the tall one, 'foreign or not, I wouldn't 'alf fuck her. wouldn't you?'

'Yeah.'

'She's fuckin gorgeous. We could treat her to a bit of English cock.' The two of them burst into laughter. As they were calming down, the lavatory door squealed open and a man walked in. He slowly approached the tall one, as he

190

stood at the urinal.

'Hey, u - Jimme,' said a broad, Glaswegian accent.

'Wha…?'

'U – an ur fockin lowlife oppo, fock off, noo - an dinne cum back. Know wha'm sayin?'

'You wha?' he said, as he glared at old Tommy.

'Ar u deaf - as well as fockin stupid…?'

He stared at Tommy, then, having overcome the intrusion, he said, 'Who the fuckin 'ell are you talkin to? You, fuckin, old has-been. I'll put you on your fuckin back… Don't you talk to me like tha. Old or no old,' he began to prod Tommy in the chest, 'I'll fuckin kill yeh.'

With a lightning reflex, Tommy grabbed his thumb, swung him 'round, rammed his arm up his back, grabbed the hair on the back of his head, and smashed his nose into the lavatory door.

'What's goin on?' shouted the other one, from inside the cubicle.

'Let go, you're breakin me thumb,' the tall one screamed, in pain. Tommy pushed his mouth next to the scumbag's ear and, eyes bulging, whispered eerily, 'U… ever cum back te this pub, an it winna be yeh thumb, I'll be breakin… it'll be ur *FOCKIN NECK!*'

As the blood from his nose gushed down over his shirt, the other one came walking out of the cubicle.

'What the fuck's goin…'

Tommy grabbed his mate by the throat, in a chokehold and crashed his head against the tiled wall. As he stood, dazed, his skull screaming with pain, Tommy whispered, 'I ope u two scumbags like ospital fud – cause if y'ever cum back ere, yull be eatin loads o the stuff – *THROUGH A FOCKIN DRIP.*' Then, he turned and walked out of the lavatory, leaving the two, shell-shocked unfortunates, gazing at each other, trying to comprehend what had just happened.

Old Tommy calmly walked back to his table, sat, and stared at the last inch of his Guinness. Dot and Zeta were on their way to the bar for the next round, as Petra was now regaining her composure, and had managed, with the help and encouragement of the others, to try and laugh the incident off. As Dot passed Van Gogh, she said, mischievously, 'Would you like a drink, Tommy?' The reply wasn't what she expected, 'Aye... I wud, Dottie. Thank yeh very much, I'll ave alf a Guinness, please, no, make it a biggun, seein as you're a bit flush.' As Dot feigned a smile, his face spread into a broad grin. *Gotcha.*

'*Shit*' Dot whispered to Zeta, 'he's called me bluff.' As the two of them laughed, then carried on walking toward the bar, she continued, 'But he's a lovely, old bloke... wouldn't harm a fly.' As Dot tried to attract the barmaid's attention, Sergeant Tommy Fitzsimons, SAS (retd.), gazed at the table and, pinching his bristly chin, tried to remember if he'd turned the oven off.

As Dot and Zeta stood at the bar waiting to be served, Dot had no idea that she'd been led up the garden path, and it was all part of Charlie's elaborate plan to position her in the right place at the right time. Ted, waiting in the Mercedes outside around the corner, had been briefed by Field Marshall Charlie, and told to expect a call at round about 8.30. Bang on the button, Ted's phone rang:

'Hello?'

'Hi, Ted, Charlie. She's standing at the bar in the lounge, now. Blue, flowered blouse, Navy skirt and beige shoes (she didn't like using the word *nude*, to Ted). *Go! Go! Go!*'

Charlie was enjoying the thrill of her role as spymaster, and at one point had toyed with the idea of the message being, *the rat is in the trap*, until it dawned on her that she'd be referring to Dot as a rat. It's not as easy as Bond makes it look, this spy rigmarole.

'He's coming in now,' said Charlie, quietly, to Joan and Petra, 'small daffodil in lapel.'

Charlie had never met Ted, and had no idea what he looked like, but they'd agreed for him to be wearing one of those small charity daffodils. The three of them looked toward the door, all bursting with anticipation.

'Wish me luck, sweetheart,' he whispered tremulously, to his beloved wife, as he approached the pub door.

The door opened, and in he walked. They weren't disappointed: five-eleven, late fifties', rugged facial features which couldn't be described as handsome, in the traditional sense, but ruggedly attractive; a slightly flat nose and eyebrows that met in the middle, forming the wings of a bird. He had the tanned rustic complexion of a man who'd see much outside work, in his life.

I'll only get one chance at this, so I better not cock it up, he'd thought to himself, earlier in the day, as he'd shopped for new clothes. Forking out the thick end of four hundred quid on a waxed Barbour jacket, small-check shirt, lambswool V-neck, chinos, and pair of leather Chukka boots, he was a man on a mission. He saw Dot standing at the bar, as she placed the drinks onto a tray. Bewildered and embarrassed, he was about to turn and walk out, when, 'Go to it, tiger,' whispered Charlie into his ear, as she pushed him into Dot's elbow. A couple of the drinks sloshed onto the tray, as Dot glanced behind with a ratty,

'Will y'watch what you're doin, mate?'

Their eyes met for a second, then…

'Ee, I'm right sorry, lass.'

A moment, then she said, her voice softening, 'It's alright… just be a bit more careful, in future.'

'Aye, you're right. Can I treat you to a bag of crisps, to make amends?'

'I bet you say that to all the girls,' said Dot, with a cheeky smile.

As Charlie carried on to the lavatory, Dot and Zeta walked back with the drinks, Ted ordered a pint of Lancaster Bomber. As Dot started to dish out the drinks to the rest of them, it was Joan's turn to come into play,

'Who's the nice bloke, you were talkin to, at the bar?'

'Y'know,' said Dot thoughtfully, as she sat, 'I'm sure I know his face from somewhere.'

She glanced over at him, as he paid for his bitter.

'He's a bit of alright, him. You wanna stake your claim before I do,' said Joan.

Ted picked up his pint then turned, as Charlie was on her way back from the lavatory.

'That's a nice daffodil you're wearing, Ted,' she said quietly, as she approached. They glanced at each other, and their eyes traded a secret smile, as they passed like ships in the night.

'Who was that nice bloke you were talking to?' she said to Dot, as she sat.

'Oh, for Christ sake, what is this, twenty bleedin questions?'

'He's a nice bit of stuff, him,' added Zeta. 'A proper man, not like the plank I'm engaged to.'

'When you are get married?' asked Petra.

'When Mr Right comes along,' and they all laughed,

except Petra, who tumbled the words around in her mind for two seconds, then asked, 'Who is Mister Wright?'

'The man of my dreams.'

'Until he turns into a bleedin nightmare,' chipped in Dot, which set them off laughing again, the alcohol now taking affect.

Ted was wandering around like a lost sheep, looking for somewhere to sit in the crowded pub. He meandered his way in the direction of the group, when a broad Glaswegian accent spoke out,

'Hey, Jimme, plonk y'arse down there, if yeh luckin fe sumwear t'sit.'

'Ta, lad,' said Ted, taking a seat opposite Tommy.

'I've nat seen y'in ere, before,' said Tommy.

'No, I just fancied a pint on me way home,'

'All dressed up an nowhere t'go,' said Tommy, in a friendly manner, which raised a smile from Ted, as he glanced over at Dot, noticing her popularity with the rest of them; mother hen with her chicks. He liked that idea. As Ted turned to Tommy, Dot's head turned to Ted.

'I can't think where I know him from, but he definitely rings a bell.'

'So did the other fella,' Joan quipped.

'Who?'

'Quasimodo.'

More laughter, except from Petra, as she wondered why people would find a deaf, hunch-backed bellringer a figure of fun. She really must, she thought, concentrate more on becoming accustomed to the British sense of humour.

Dot looked over once again, at Ted - something which hadn't escaped Tommy's notice. He covered his mouth with his hand and said quietly,

'Hey, Jimme, dinne luk noo, bu' I think you migh 'ave an admirer, over the way. Big woman, on the right. Name's Dot. Keeps lookin atcha.'

'Ted's me name.'

'I'm Tommy. Well, Ted, y'could do a lot worse than Dottie... Luvly woman. Puts on this big, ard show, but... inside... Never forget ow she looked after me, when I lost my Alice. Thirty years, roughin it in the army, then, I just crumbled... Didne wanna live na more. Was Dottie what pulled me through. Made me see sense. I'waz all for killin mesel. Aye, like a daughter, she is. Y'could do a lot worse than Dottie... Think the world of er, I do. Anyone upsets her, theve got me to answer to.

Ted smiled, as he thought, *Nice, old bloke. His heart's in the right place.*

'So next time you fine yoursel on the sniff, y'now where to go.' Then, the two men shared a chuckle.

'What mob were you in, Tommy?'

'Ach... one mob's the same as the next. Y'take y'orders an do the job.'

Tommy looked at the clock: 8.50pm.

'Right, I'm off.' He necked the remainder of his Guinness. 'There's a picture on I fancy watchin, at nine o'clock.

'What's that?'

'*Who Dares Wins.*'

'That's about the SAS,' said Ted.

'Is it?'

'Aye, that's their motto. Y'know, the winged dagger: *Who Dares Wins.*

'Well, y'learn somethin new, ev'ry dey,' said Ted.

'Rough gang of lads, them.'

'Bunch o'pansies.'

And the two men laughed as they parted.

'G'night, Ted. Nice meetin yeh.'

'G'night, Tommy. Look after yourself, mate.'

'An dinna f'get wha I said about Dottie. There's a good woman there, goin t'waste.

Ted had a couple of mouthfuls left in his glass. *Another false alarm*, he thought. Everything had ground to a halt. A couple of times he'd surreptitiously glanced over at Dot, and a couple of times Dot had surreptitiously glanced over at him. Unfortunately, none of these glances had coincided with each other. He heaved a sigh, took out his mobile and pretended to be checking it. Five more minutes, then he'd be gone. Charlie now realised that things weren't going according to plan, so decided to launch *Operation Krakow*.

'Why don't y'just go over an ask who he is?' said Joan.

'Behave,' said Dot. 'He'll think I'm desperate.'

'But y'are aren't yeh?' came the reply, causing much hilarity among of the Band of Sisters.

'He is nice, though, isn't he?' whispered Dot, through stiffened lips.

'Nice? He's bleedin gorgeous.'

'At least, he's not a plank.'

Each of them had a part to play in the deception, and this was Petra's, the ace up Charlie's sleeve: Operation Krakow. Petra had on and off, been glancing at Charlie, for the last few minutes, waiting for the signal. She glanced at Charlie once more, and this time her glance was returned with a subtle wink.

'I will go and see de man,' said Petra, excitedly standing, her time to shine having arrived.

'*Petra! Sit down!*' said Dot, with restrained panic.

'No, no, I ask de man.'

'Oh, for Christ sake. What's she doin?'

Ted's attention was drawn, and he looked up, as Petra came bounding toward him.

'Excuse me, pliz, sir...'

'*Petra! Will yeh come back!*' Dot said, in embarrassment, as the others fought to keep their laughter at bay.

'My friend is there, is Dot. She thing you look like Quasimodo...'

'*Jesus Christ!*' Dot said with a gasp, plunging her head into her hand.

'No, sorry, I make mistake. You not Quasimodo. She thing you are not a plank.'

Luckily enough, Ted saw the funny side, and burst into laughter. Charlie's gamble had paid off. Petra's naivety, charm, and thoughtfulness had won everyone over, and gales of laughter ensued, a lot of it coming from Dot.

Right. This is it. Shit or bust, thought Ted.

'Well, thank you very much, young lass,' he said to Petra, 'for relaying that luvly message. An tell Dot, I'm very pleased to know she doesn't think I'm a plank. In fact, I'll tell her meself.' He stood.

'He's coming over,' said Zeta, in a panic-stricken whisper.

Charlie's heart was pounding with excitement.

'I wonder how big his cock is,' whispered Joan, behind her hand, trying to set Dot off.

'*Shut it, you!*' said Dot, stifling a roar of laughter.

Petra came walking back, as proud as proud could be. Ted was close behind.

'Dot,' said Petra, the wine beginning to take effect as she began to slur her words, 'here is the Mister Wright. The man of your dreams and nightmares.'

Much hilarity from all, as Charlie sprang to her feet and, grabbing a chair for Ted, then placed it down, next to Dot.

'Petra,' said Charlie, 'come on, it's our turn to get the drinks.'

'I'll pay for these,' said Ted.

'No,' said Charlie. 'You don't have to buy us drinks.'

'It's the least I can do, after knockin them sideways, before.'

Ted took out his wallet, Dot looked at it, and as he picked out two twenty-pound notes...

A moment.

'Tha wallet...?' she said.

There was a pause, then Ted looked at her.

'Aye, lass...' he said, slowly, with a gentle smile. 'It's the one y'shoved through me letterbox...'

Silence...

She looked at his face: the flattened nose, the eyebrows, the smile... Her mouth opened slightly, and her breathing began to tremble, as she hardly dared to ask the question. Then, it slowly, gently, emerged from her lips, in almost a whisper,

'Ted...?'

'Aye... Dot... that's me...'

Charlie smiled: mission accomplished.

20

Monday morning, Charlie was elated as she walked across the car park. She couldn't wait to see Rick and tell him about her night out 'with the girls'. They'd not spoken much lately, and she thought this would be the perfect opportunity to rekindle their friendship.

If Charlie was elated, then Dot was on cloud nine. Things on the Ted front had progressed rapidly since Saturday night, and they'd swapped phone numbers before parting, not before he'd given her a gentle kiss on the cheek. Sunday morning he'd phoned, and they'd talked, for over an hour. He'd wanted to come round and see her, but she thought, even though she wanted to, it best not to rush things. Then again, the house was a shitheap. They'd arranged to meet for a drink on Wednesday evening.

Charlie's elation was soon brought down in flames at approximately eleven o'clock, when she queried with Dot where Rick was.

'Maybe he's off sick?' she said, hoping he'd had no bad news from the doctor.

'He's off this week,' said Dot. 'Isle of Man. He's gone to the TT, with his mates.'

Charlie's heart sank. She loved motorbikes and, yes, she knew now, she loved Rick, and there he was, the man of her *dreams and nightmares*, at the world-renowned, road-race event.

Dot had, since Charlie's flowers, and Saturday night, began to look at her in a different light. Maybe she was wrong? Maybe the girl was just that: someone with no axe to grind, someone who just wanted to get along peacefully, with her life. But the main thaw in Dot's iceberg demeanour toward her came on Sunday, when she'd discovered after much prying of Joan, that her *coincidental* meeting with Ted had all been the work of Charlie's intricate planning. A few weeks ago, she'd have torn Charlie's head off for interfering in her private life, but now, she didn't know how to thank her enough. But her thanks had to remain under wraps, having promised Joan she'd keep schtum.

Apart from Charlie, Dot had also started to see herself in a different light. She began to wonder when, and where, she'd wandered off life's path, and descended into this embittered, cantankerous bitch of a woman, with a dozen axes to grind. What happened to that happy-go-lucky kid of twenty-five years ago: the lover of acting, instilling in her the dream of one day joining the RSC, then there was the animal-lover, who hoped to become a vet, followed by the nursing ambition, which, also, amounted to sweet FA. All her hopes, and dreams, relentlessly crushed under a hundred tons of life. All she had left were the words of dear Uncle Harry, mentoring her, channelling her in his direction, a puppet to reproduce his ambitions. She had so much to give but there'd never been anyone who wanted to receive it. So, like water, she found herself taking the course of least resistance; fuck hopes and dreams, there's bills to be paid.

As she sipped her tea, she looked at Charlie, busy at her work bench. She'd recognized the look of disappointment on her face, and heard the tone of apathy in her voice, upon finding out about Rick. Mug in hand, she slowly ambled across.

'Y'like Rick, don't yeh?'

'Yes.'

There was a pause.

'You just be careful... Don't be taken in.'

'What do you mean...?'

'Just be careful, that's all.'

Dot walked back to her work bench. Charlie put down the air gun then approached her.

'Dot... what do you mean...? Please. Why should I be careful? Careful of what? I like Rick a lot, he's kind, honest, and respectful.'

'They all are when y'first meet them. It doesn't last... Ted'll turn out the same way.

They build you up, then knock y'down.'

'Ted's a lovely man, Dot... Don't shut him out. I know you've suffered in the past, but... try and see the good in people.'

There was a pause as Charlie's words began to sink into Dot's mind. Then, Charlie continued,

'I've suffered in the past, as well... more than you could imagine, but it doesn't stop me wanting to find happiness in the future. I know life is a gamble, but unless you're prepared to take it, you'll never win.'

'You just be careful with Rick.'

'What is it, Dot? What do I need to know about him...?'

'Don't let him hurt yeh.'

It was on the tip of Dot's tongue to divulge what she was thinking, but the moment passed, and when Zeta came walking up, that was the end of it.

'Morning, ladies,' Zeta said, with her usual Monday morning chirp, and after an exchange of pleasantries, regarding their Band of Sisters night out, she said to Dot, 'Dot, Mr Hardcastle said, if you've got a minute to spare could you nip down an see him.'

'Warrabout?'

'He didn't say.'

Dot placed the mug down, and she and Zeta walked out of the area then down the alley. Charlie walked back to her workbench, gazed at it, then picked up the air gun. She hesitated, before she started work and thought of Rick. As she did, ninety miles away at Hillberry, the superbikes were roaring at 180 mph down the long straight, braking, down to 120 mph, as the riders keeled them over, to take the sweeping left-hander. Behind the wall on the left, amongst the rapturous crowd, Rick and his mates stood within touching distance of these screaming leviathans, as they streaked past. He thought of Charlie, and how much he wished she could be there with him. That was it. He made his mind up. When he got back into work next Monday, he'd booked the morning off, because he had to go and pick it up, but, in the afternoon, as soon as his appointment was over, he was going to lay his cards on the table and tell her how he felt about her. He couldn't bear being in this No Man's Land any longer. If she told him to 'do one', then so be it. At least she'd have put him out of his misery then he could get back on with his life.

***

As Joan sat, reading a dog-eared copy of Cosmopolitan, a little girl came curiously wandering toward her, stopped, and looked up at her. Joan looked down into the little face,

'Hello, sweetheart…'

'Lucy… come here. Don't be disturbing the lady,' said the young mum, as she approached and collected her daughter.

'She's beautiful. How old is she?'

'Two, next month.'

'Bye, bye, Lucy,' said Joan, with a child's wave, as the girl was carried back to the other side of the waiting room.

A nurse appeared from around a corner, *'Joan Smith.'* They exchanged smiles of acknowledgement. Joan dropped the magazine back onto the coffee table, then stood. They entered the treatment room and sat. After the usual social pleasantries were exchanged, 'Small scratch…'

Joan averted her gaze as the needle went in.

A moment.

'When will they have the results?'

'Three days,' said the nurse, as she taped a small blob of cotton wool over the miniscule spot of blood. 'Phone after eleven o'clock.'

* * *

Dot and Zeta entered the HR office. Zeta knocked on Hardcastle's door then opened it,

'Here she is, Mr Hardcastle…'

Dot entered his office.

'Dorothea.'

'Mr *Hardcastle.'*

'Let's cut the shit,' he said, with a smile, 'it's Dot and

Bill.'

Dot smiled and said, cheekily, 'Alright, *Bill*? how's it goin?'

She took the seat opposite him.

'Dot,' he said, becoming serious, 'Now, don't read anything into this, I'm not trying to get rid of you, push you out, so to speak...'

Dot looked sternly at him, *'But...'*

'Well,' he said, hesitantly, 'I've been doing an evaluation study, on certain long-standing, loyal employees...'

'If we're long-standin an loyal, why are you tryin t'get rid of us. *Bill.*'

'Dot... whether you stay or go, is of no consequence to me, but I think there's something you need to be aware of...' He turned Dot's file around to face her then placed it down on the desk. 'That's what your redundancy package would amount to, should you decide to accept it.'

'Is that how you managed to persuade all the Judases to accept their thirty pieces of silver?' As the words left her mouth, she realised that they weren't her words, they were the words of an embittered, cantankerous witch. 'I'm sorry, Mister *H*ardcastle,' she said, timidly, 'I shouldn't have said that.'

'Bill.'

'Sorry, Bill...' she replied, as she leaned over to look at the piddling sum of betrayal. Her eyes focused on the writing. She scanned down to the bottom, and they came to rest on her redundancy amount. She gazed at it, as Hardcastle concealed a cheeky smile with his hand. She became dumbstruck as he said, 'On top of that, I've had a word in the right ears, and there'd be an additional *personal* gift from Archibald and Reginald. In spite, of your differences over the years, Dot, they'd be sorry to see you go.' She looked at Hardcastle, then back down at the sum and cleared her throat nervously, to break her silence. She swallowed.

'Wh-when d'you need to know by Bill?'

'There's no hurry, Dot, whenever suits you.'

('IT SUITS ME, FRIGGIN NOW.')

She was trembling inside. It was as if she was in a dream. She heaved a tremulous sigh.

'OK... Does Zeta know what this is about?'

'She has an inkling, but nothing personal. None of the details.'

'I wonder if you can do me a great favour... which I'd very much appreciate...?'

'Of course. What's that, Dot...?'

Zeta had been straining to listen since Dot entered his office, but gave up in the end, hearing nothing but muffled mumbles from the pair. Dot voice began to rise and become clearer. She saw her reflection through the frosted glass of the door, as she rose to her feet then slammed her clenched fist onto Hardcastle's desk. She began to shout. Zeta was taken aback. The door suddenly flew open and Dot, snarling like a harridan, shouted back into his office,

'Think y'can bribe me with y'thirty pieces of silver? I'm no Judas.'

Then, she slammed the door and strode brusquely across Zeta's office, snarling and muttering as she went. Zeta sat open-mouthed, in a state of mild shock. Hardcastle shook his head and chuckled quietly, at Dot's RSC performance. Dot on the other hand, was walking slowly, down the alley, her legs having turned to jelly, giving the casual onlooker the impression that she'd shit herself. As she went, she was trying to make some sense of the stampede of words that were battering through her mind, '*Twenty-six thousand quid... twenty-six thousand quid...* her mind had frozen into a tangle of knots, with shock. She couldn't get it to function.

Within two hours, the story of how Dot had stood up to the evil machinations of management betrayal, had spread throughout the factory. Her name was carved with pride in the hallowed annals of the long-running Nelson Engineering v The Workers saga. Now all she had to do was figure out a way she could accept the redundancy offer and leave, betraying her comrades into the bargain, in a blaze of adulation.

***

During the following two days, Dot felt as if a hand had come down from the heavens, picked her up, and put her back down into someone else's life. Within the space of four days, she'd begun to take the tentative steps of a relationship with Ted, there was a huge amount of money waiting for her, and all she had to do was blow the whistle, then it would come galloping into her bank account, and Joan would have her blood test result, on Thursday. *Please God, let it be positive.*

***

They'd arranged to meet at eight o'clock, in the car park of The Peacock: a large, Edwardian-built pub of past distinction, now passed into oblivion. Two or three cuts above The Red House in the pub hierarchy, unfortunately it was now owned by one of those 'sizzling platter' type groups, that catered for the appetites of the middle-class masses, providing pub grub at reasonable prices, with the additional joy of screaming kids, and white-haired pensioners, on a Sunday lunchtime. Dot arrived first, driving her banger as far away from the car park entrance as she could, yet still remain within sight of the road. She remembered Ted's silver Mercedes estate, and was sitting with bated breath, eyes glued on the entrance. As soon as his car appeared, her plan was to get out of hers then nonchalantly stroll toward his – the true reason being, that she didn't want him to see the state of her wreck. At eleven minutes to eight, his silver Mercedes turned in, and began to prowl the lines, looking for a space. She got out of her car and made her way to his.

'Ted,' she said with a tempered smile, having suddenly realised she'd forgotten, in her hurry to leave the house, to put on some clean knickers. His face lit up as he stepped out of his car, and with a peck on her cheek and a cheery 'Hello, have y'been here, long?' they set forth on their great adventure, through the pub door (he held it open for her), straight into the mangled, pungent whiffs of spaghetti Bolognese, battered cod and chips, and barbecued ribs. Dot's nostrils drew the knife and stabbed her in the back, sending a gush of golly into her mouth.

'Would you like to eat...?' he said, eager to please.

'I'm fine, thanks, I've already eaten,' she said politely, as the image of her rapidly consumed two boiled eggs and soldiers, appeared in her mind.

Dot sat, as Ted went to the bar and ordered a pint of *Black Sheep* for himself and a half of *Amstel*; she didn't want to give the impression of being a gold-digger. Three minutes later, they were chatting away, as if they'd known each other for years. Ted wasn't a bragger. Neither did he bombard her with unsolicited, boring trivia. He was a talker, but one who knew how to stop for breath, giving Dot chance to add her two-penneth. As the time ticked on they became engrossed in each other. Each felt that this was right. The relationship had legs. She was saddened to learn of his wife, Nora, and how she'd collapsed and died in front of him one evening, having suffered a brain haemorrhage. 'She went down like a sack of spuds,' where his exact words, and words which Dot thought didn't suit the pathos of the story. But that was one of the things she liked about him, he was down-to-earth, unpretentious. He relayed the tale without a hint of sympathy-seeking. That's how it was and that's how he told it. There was much talk about little Bobby and the impact Ted had had on him when they first met. Not to mention the bunch of flowers debacle, the whole episode, reducing both of them to laughter. By the end of the evening Ted had invited Dot, and little Bobby, acting as her chaperone, to his bungalow, the following Sunday. He'd offered to take them for a day out,

'We can go for a trip out, somewhere. Warm the old banger up.'

It was hard for Dot to believe that three hours had passed since she saw his car turning into the car park. As they stood outside at the end of the evening, both nervously fumbling with awkward words on how to part, he looked longingly at her.

'What...? Ted... what...?'

'Well...' he said, hesitantly, 'd'you want to see me again...?'

She looked into his large, soulful eyes, weather-beaten

face, and the gentle smile that betrayed a hint of anticipation.

You, daft bugger, o'course I wanna see you again, she thought.

She took his face in both her hands then gently placed her lips against his. Her kiss was soft and lasted just two seconds – but that was long enough. She drew back with a hint of a smile.

'Maybe that'll give you a clue.'

He looked at her, then pushed his hand around her waist and the other around the nape of her neck. He pressed his mouth against hers then gave her a lingering kiss. As she felt his lips, passionately kissing hers, a torrent of desire was unleashed from within her soul. As the kiss went on, it was broken only by the encouraging cheers from a good-natured group of young men, coming out of the pub. Ted and Dot laughed, then she encouraged him to get into his car (she didn't want to risk him seeing her rust bucket). As he drove off, he shouted, 'Ave you still got the Astra?' She chuckled, as she climbed into it. The chuckle didn't last long. As she turned the key, the engine churned over continuously and wouldn't start. '*Bollocks.*'

The young men came strolling over.

'Y'alright, luv?'

'It won't start.'

'D'you wanna push?'

Before she had time to reply, the tall, handsome lad was barking instructions at her.

'Turn your ignition on and put it in second… keep the clutch down until I bang on the roof.'

They began to push, and when it reached a fast, walking pace, he hit the roof with his hand. Dot let the clutch up then after a couple of seconds of kangaroo touch and go, the engine fired. She blew the horn, turned out onto the road, and headed for home. As the old, misfiring Astra gradually coughed and spluttered its way to 40mph, Dot couldn't have been happier if she'd have been sitting in the back of a chauffeur-driven Rolls-Royce.

* * *

'Hello, health centre…?'

'Oh, hello, I'm ringin up for a blood test result, please.'

'What's the name?'

'Joan Smith.'

'What's your address?'

'44 Woodhall Road.'

'Just hold on…'

She stared blankly at the kitchen wall. It was negative… it was bound to be negative. Why should anything decide to go right, in her life?

'Hello, Mrs Smith, what's your date of birth?'

Her breathing became heavier as the date of birth tumbled out of her mouth.

'The test was positive, Mrs Smith.'

'Pardon…?' she said, in disbelief.

'The blood test - it was positive.'

'Positive…? The test – was positive? Not negative?'

'Your test result was *positive*.'

'You've not got me mixed up with another Smith, have yeh? It's happened before, y'know.'

'No - Mrs Joan Smith, 44 Woodhall Road, Greenbank?'

'Yeah, that's me.'

'Your test was positive…'

'Thank you…'

She slowly placed the phone onto the work top, then walked into the parlour. She moved to the armchair and sat. Leaning forward, she placed her elbows onto her knees then rested her face in her palms. Her stomach began to tremble, which worked its way up through her chest and manifested its way from her mouth, in the form of uncontrollable panting. She began to gasp and whimper as the full realization washed over her. She leaned back in the chair, rested her head on the cushion and closed her eyes. Her face distorted with unadulterated joy, as her whimpering grew louder. She placed a hand on her stomach and began to rub it slowly, gently. Tears overflowed from her eyes, and began to trickle down her cheeks.

21

Dot and Bobby couldn't wait for Sunday.

As the Astra pulled up outside Ted's bungalow, Bobby's eyes exploded when he saw the Mercedes parked on the drive, 'Aw. Look at tha. Are we goin in tha car, mam?' Dot tried to let him down gently by saying, 'No, not that one, son. That's his new car. He wouldn't want us, messin it up, would he?' Then, the embittered witch began to rise to the surface once more, as she thought, *We're not good enough, to go in his new car.*

Ted let them in, then after introducing Bobby to Toby and Kenny said, 'Would you like to see my model collection?' Bobby nodded, not having a clue what Ted was going on about. Ted led them to one of his spare bedrooms, opened the door, and shepherded Bobby in, winking at Dot as he did. Bobby walked into the room, and his mouth relaxed open as he took in the scene, every wall from floor to ceiling, was lined with glass cabinets – each one filled with expensive, limited edition, model cars. Over two thousand. The interrogation began.

'Wooaaaww… What's da one?'

'That's a 1937 Jensen 3.5 S-Type.'

'What's da one?'

'That's a 1949 Humber Super Snipe Mk III...'

After another couple of questions, 'We're gonna be here all day, at this rate,' said Dot, with a smile.

'Well, just before we push off,' said Ted 'come and have a look at these...'

He walked out of the room then into the next one, followed by Bobby and Dot.

'Woooaaawww...'

Once again, Bobby's jaw dropped as he took in the scene: the same as the previous room, but this time it was motorbike models.

'I've gorra Carrington Gurkha,' he said, proudly, to Ted. 'When I grow up, I'm gonna get a motorbike.'

There was a pause as Bobby gazed at the model.

'My dad's rubbish at cars and motorbikes... all he does is drink beer and hit me mam.'

'Right,' said Ted. 'We best be off... I'll just move the car off the drive and get the banger out.'

With the Mercedes parked on the road, Ted had gone back into the house, then through to the garage. Dot and Bobby stood near the gate. The electric garage door began to rise vertically, and when it reached the end of its travel, a car slowly emerged from the shadows.

'*Bloody ell...*' Dot muttered silently to herself, as the car crept silently into the sunshine.

'*WOOOAAAWW...!*'

The metallic Sand over Sable, 1965 Rolls-Royce Silver Cloud III moved silently down the drive then came to a halt, a few feet from Dot. Ted got out. 'Right, are we ready for the off?' he said, in a tone as if he'd just got out of a van.

'Who wants to sit in the front?'

'*ME! ME!*' screeched Bobby, as Dot shook her head and smiled.

Bobby clambered into the front passenger side, as Ted opened one of the rear doors, 'Your carriage awaits, m'lady.'

Dot stepped into the back of the car then settled down onto the tan leather seat.

'What kind of carpets are these?'

'They're not carpets, they're lambswool over rugs,' said Ted as the Silver Cloud moved out onto the road.

The car made its way through town with Dot looking down on the poor people, in their Vauxhalls, Fords, Nissans et al. She couldn't help, feel a twinge of guilt - here she was, left-wing firebrand (or so, she liked to think) being transported in the back of one of the symbols of capitalism, a Rolls-Royce. Her guilt was eased, however, by the look of starry-eyed wonderment on Bobby's face, and the innocent, inquisitive nature of his relentless interrogation of a relentlessly, patient Ted.

'Is tha' plastic?'

'No, it's called burr walnut.'

'Do de make it out of bears?'

Etc.,

Etc.

The car turned onto the M6 then surged silently to 100mph as it entered the outside lane with lesser mortals moving aside, allowing it to pass. Ninety minutes later it was crawling along Blackpool Promenade. Ted found the car park, and they left the car, then headed for the Pleasure Beach. The next three hours were an extravaganza of fun and thrills, candy floss and ice creams. Dot couldn't remember when she'd last enjoyed herself so much, Bobby had never enjoyed himself so much, and the experience brought back many pleasant memories of past times, to Ted.

Eventually, the pangs of hunger got the better of all three and brought the excitement to an end when they piled into a massive chippy, sat, and ordered cod, chips, and mushy peas, each, 'Sod all that olives and noodles malarkey, this is proper food, what sticks to yeh ribs,' said Ted, as he wolfed down a mouthful of chips and peas, thinking to himself how wonderful it felt to be eating a meal that didn't involve sprouts.

After a trip to the top of the tower, followed by a paddle in the Irish sea, the three headed back to Ted's bungalow. The Silver Cloud pulled onto the drive at 8.53pm. Bobby, wearing a plastic police Bobby's helmet and clutching a huge bar of rock, was stretched out asleep on the back seat. Ted switched off the engine. Dot turned to him, 'Thank you...' she said, with heartfelt sincerity. 'No... thank *you*,' he replied, then reached across and kissed her lips. As she looked into his eyes, she realized that this was the sort of life that normal people have – no, not galivanting around in a Rolls-Royce – the sort of life that ordinary people, who think the world or each other, have shared enjoyment, happiness. Not the sort of existence where you dread the sound of someone's footsteps entering the house.

'C'mon,' said Ted, 'we better wake the nipper up.'

The three of them walked up the path then entered the house. After a cup of tea, Ted and Dot's spirits began to wane. Their date was coming to an end. They arranged to meet again, and as Dot and Bobby were walking down the hall, toward the front door, 'hang on a minute,' said Ted, and he walked into a bedroom. Seconds later, he emerged carrying a motorbike model.

'There y'are, son, that's for you,' he said, to Bobby, as he handed him the model. 'That'll do to be going on with, 'til you get the real one...'

Bobby held the motorbike in his hands and looked at it, as if it was an apparition.

A moment.

'What d'you say...?' said Dot, as she smiled, appreciatively.

Bobby looked up at the smiling face of Ted. He raised his arms, and Ted bent down to meet him. He wrapped his arms around Ted's neck, 'Tankyou, Uncle Ted.' Emotion gushed through Dot.

Ted waved, as he watched the Astra disappearing down the road. He closed the door then entered his living room. He moved dispiritedly to the armchair, sat, stroked Toby's head, heaved a sigh, then resumed his life of loneliness, as Kenny chirped.

* * *

Monday morning, and Dot's head was full of Ted. She could hardly concentrate of the mundane task of filing off a minor burr, from a stock bin of four-inch copper tubes, a task that required the concentration of a gnat. Charlie was beavering away with the brush, tidying the place up. Dot looked across at her. As Charlie diligently brushed here, there, and everywhere, her head was full of Rick. She was going to make a determined effort today to rekindle their friendship, and she hoped this would be the start of a relationship between the two of them. As Charlie brushed some oily grit onto the shovel then threw it into the crisp box, Dot was overcome with a feeling of guilt. She still couldn't allow

Charlie to find out she knew about *Operation Dotted*, but she failed to see how she could keep the secret to herself, such was her feeling of gratitude. *Sod it*, she thought.

'Charlie...'

'Yes, Dot...?'

'Here, a minute...'

Charlie approached.

'Yes...?'

Dot paused, then breathed in.

'I know what you did...?'

'What are you talking about...?'

'Set me an Ted up, on a date...'

'Oh...'

'Yesterday, him, me, an Bobby, went to Blackpool for the day out... an I've never enjoyed meself so much, in all me life...?'

'Good,' said Charlie, firmly. 'That was the whole point of the operation.'

'What operation?'

'To bring Ted out of his loneliness and...'

'Wha...? Wha...?'

'To cheer you up - and stop you being such a miserable bugger. There. I've said it.'

There was a pause, then a smile crept across Dot's face.

'Jokin apart... I know we didn't gerroff on the right foot...'

'*Who* didn't get off on the right foot...?'

'Alright, *me*... but I want you t'know how much I appreciate what y'did. Thank you, very much...'

'Thank you, for saying thank you.'

Both women looked at each other, then shared a smile.

'So, from now on,' said Dot, 'if there's anythink I can

do for yeh, anythink I can help y'with, anythink y'want to know – just ask, an if I can help yeh, I will...'

'Anything...?'

'Yeah. I'm indebted to yeh, for what y'did. I've never seen little Bobby so happy in all his life...'

'Anything, you said?'

'You've only got to ask, just say the word.'

A moment.

'What do I need to know, about Rick...?'

Dot froze... She began to tremble inside...

'Well...? You said *anything* so, I've asked you... Or didn't you understand the question...? What do I need to know about Rick...?'

There was a pause.

'Anythink, but tha...'

Charlie gave a short, derogatory laugh, 'So, you're all talk. I might have known.'

She walked back to the corner and continued to brush it.

'You must promise me...'

Charlie turned, and Dot was there, next to her.

'Promise you, what...?'

'You must promise me... you'll never breathe a word to anyone... about what I'm goin to tell yeh... Promise me...'

'I promise...'

There was a pause.

'Bobby...'

'What about him...?'

Dot inhaled, then the words gradually escaped from her lips.

'He's Rick's...'

Charlie became dumbstruck, as Dot's words began to

sink in.

Dot slowly continued her confession, guiltily.

'We got bladdered one day, after a mass meeting... went back to his, one thing led to another... and it went too far... I was half-tidy in them days... not like I am now... You must never breathe a word, to anyone... especially Rick.'

There was a pause as Charlie gazed down at the work bench, then, without raising her eyes, she said in a whisper, 'Does he know... about Bobby?'

'Yes... But, I've laid the law down... I've told him, he must never come near that child, as long as he lives.'

Charlie turned her head and faced Dot.

'That's wrong. You're depriving them of each other.'

'Tough...'

And with that parting sentiment, Dot turned, walked back to her bench then carried on, with her work.

Charlie felt her world implode, as the enormity of Dot's revelation impacted viciously on her recuperating state of mental stability. As she stood gazing at the floor, she felt an inkling of stress begin to take root in her mind. Her life felt as if it was beginning crumble once again. Her breathing gradually became heavier, faster, as anxiety took a hold. She squeezed hard on the brush and closed her eyes. She let go of the brush, and it was all she could do to walk to the toilet, such was the feeling of creeping debilitation that began to spread through her limbs. The shock of Dot's unexpected words had triggered what she had hoped she was managing to defeat. She locked herself in the end cubicle, sat then closed her eyes tightly. She curled her hand into a fist and punched the tiled wall. 'No... No...' she wasn't going to give in... he wasn't going to win again...

Whore... Bitch... burn in Hell, you twat...
Concentrate... concentrate... seared into her mind.
You killed me... you killed me...
Concentrate... concentrate... her mind whispered, as she clawed at the past, in search of happier times, before the madness engulfed her life, and now here she was, trying her best to rebuild her existence, become normal again, find happiness, only for it to be dashed to pieces, once more... Slowly... through the whispering foul obscenities, her eyes closed, then a state of torpor descended and covered her like a blanket, as she searched for his face. *His eyes... his smile... he's there... I know he's there... Where are you...? Please help me...* a vision began to emerge, through the mist of fear that shrouded her mind... his face... his loving face... and there, he was, standing before her. He gave a cheeky wink and blew a kiss, then, *Sir Reginald... make him go away... please, make him go away... take me back... take me back to those days... I love* you... She reached out, and their fingertips touched. He smiled back at her, then, slowly, placed his hand upon her head and gently stroked her hair.

She woke. Her muscles had relaxed, her breathing regulated. She no longer felt the panic, the anxiety. She had tackled her demon head on, but this time *she* was the conqueror... with the help of her beloved, Sir Reginald.

'CHARLIE! ARE YOU IN THERE?' shouted Dot, from outside the cubicle door.

'Yes!'

'Get yourself back to work. It doesn't take twenty minutes to have a shite,' Dot said, huffily. Then she ambled out of the toilets. Charlie couldn't believe she'd been asleep for twenty minutes. She came out of the cubicle then walked

back to the area. Dot was nowhere to be seen. She sat at her
bench and thought of Rick.

22

Joan had returned to work.

The initial elation of her positive blood test had now settled, and the whirlwind of her emotions had calmed. Trying her utmost to give the outward appearance that all was just a normal pregnancy, she did allow herself the guilty pleasure of wondering whether the baby was a boy or a girl. Then, there was the spare room that would need redecorating, as a nursery… there was a cot to buy… then a pram… No, no matter how much she tried to play it down to herself and others, she was completely absorbed.

At ten to ten, that morning, Rick had arrived home with it. He'd parked it in his makeshift garage and couldn't stop looking at it. It was a dream come true. A mischievous grin spread across his face, as he thought of the ruse he was planning to play on Charlie. *Touche!* He'd already been next door and thanked Mrs Givin, with a tin of Manx fudge and a pot ornament of a Manx cat, for looking after his birds while he was away. She'd informed him that one of the goldfinch chicks had died. She'd removed it from the nest and buried it in the compost heap.

* * *

He drove into the car park and parked the Volvo. His appointment with Hardcastle, was ten minutes away. He freshened up, then made his way to the office. He wanted to get the formality over as soon as possible so that he could get out of there then make a beeline for Charlie.

'Morning, Rick,' said Zeta, as he walked in. 'Take a seat. I'll see if he's ready for you.'

Seconds later, Rick entered Hardcastle's office.

'Hello, Rick.'

'Hello, Mr Hardcastle...'

They sat opposite each other, and Hardcastle pained his way through the rigmarole, then showed Rick his redundancy package. At £12,870, it was slightly less than he was expecting, but he wasn't bothered, now. Just getting out of that place was the main priority.

'When d'you need to know by?'

'The end of the month at the latest. As soon as you've made your mind up. We've been over-subscribed with applications, so the sooner the better.'

* * *

'Alright, silk knickers. How's it goin?' he said, as he approached her.

Charlie finished off unscrewing a rogue bolt, and tossed it to one side, into the stock bin. She picked up another component and positioned it on the bench.

'Hello,' she said, coldly, without looking at him.

'What's the matter...?'

'I don't really have time to talk, Rick.'

'Don't you want t'know how the TT went?'

'I know how the TT went I've been following it, on the news... You didn't tell me you were going. Was it a secret?'

'No... I just forgot, that's all.'

'You didn't forget to tell Dot.'

'I didn't tell Dot she must have heard.'

There was an uncomfortable pause. Rick's heart began to sink. Charlie was giving the impression of indifference, but she was crying, inside.

'I got you this...' he said, quietly, as he took a small packet out of his pocket. He handed it to her, and she realized she could no longer keep up her show of apathy. She opened the packet, and it contained a silver, Celtic circle pendant with the three legs of Man in the centre.

A moment.

'Aren't yeh gonna put it on, then...?'

She began to put the pendant on, and he fastened it for her.

'I've got something to tell yeh...'

Please, Rick, please tell me about Bobby, stumbled through her mind.

'I've put in for redundancy... I'll be going in a few weeks...'

There was a pause.

'Thank you, for my pendant...'

'Are you doin anything at the weekend...?'

'Probably... Why?'

'A mate of mine's bought a new bike, and he wants me to take it for a run, into Wales. Try it out for him. Wondered if you fancied coming?'

'*Not BikerBreak?*'

'Why? What's wrong with BikerBreak...? Too down-

225

market f'you, is it?' he said, sharply.

'I'll think about it…'

He turned and walked away. Charlie's heart was breaking. She loved him, but felt she'd been betrayed. But then, how could he have betrayed her, when it happened years ago, before they'd ever met. If he would only tell her about little Bobby, it would go a long way to healing the hurt she felt. She carried on working.

* * *

Miserable Monday morphed into tedious Tuesday. The thrill of the unknown had begun to lose its gloss. In the few weeks since she started work there, Charlie had been the *Antichrist*, run the gauntlet, been accepted, become a hero, found love… and was now on the verge of losing it. Her zest for tackling the most mundane of jobs had lost its sparkle, and she was now experiencing the feeling of apathy, shared by most of her other Lowry People workmates.

Dot's spirit on the other hand, had soared. In the same length of time, she'd gone from existing as a miserable, cantankerous witch to being a friendly, happy-go-lucky woman, who was becoming the talk of the factory. Many of the cognoscenti were trying hard to understand what had brought about her transformation. Maybe she'd won a stash on the lottery and wasn't cracking on? Maybe she was on drugs? Ironically, now that love had found its way into her heart, it was the last thing she wanted to talk about. She had no need to talk about it when she could *feel* it. And all along in the back of her mind, she knew that the transformation had arrived on her doorstep the day Mrs Rose said, *'There's summat down here.'* But she did of course, acknowledge to herself that the whole story would never have reached its conclusion without the unstinting effort of Charlie.

Tuesday dinnertime arrived, and with it saw Charlie gazing down into Joan's heated cabinet at the mouth-watering array of grub: Cumberland sausage, Aberdeen Angus beefburgers, huge chunks of breaded haddock... A far cry from the cardboard crispbread she brought when she first started there. She took her tray and began to thread her way through the mass of chatting, burping, chewing humanity. There were a couple of empty tables down the far end, where the unadventurous fear to tread. She made her way toward the one next to the window and sat. No sooner had she cut into her sausage than Dot appeared, carrying her amply laden tray.

'Is anyone sittin here?' came her superficial query. As Charlie was about to say *no*, Dot sat. 'The sausages look nice...'

'Cumberland...' said Charlie, with a cold, token acknowledgement. 'I find it odd that they've not been renamed Cumbrian... bearing in mind that Cumberland doesn't exist anymore,' she said, sarcastically.

Dot shot her a look, *what the fuck is she on about...?*

'Boundary changes...' she continued.

A moment, as, *Y'don't say,* ambled through Dot's mind, then, 'Look...' she said, submissively, 'I know y'think I'm a twat...'

'Whatever gave you that impression?' said Charlie, dispassionately.

'But... it's for the good.'

'How exactly, did you reach that conclusion?'

There was a pause.

Charlie continued, 'Do you want that child to grow up thinking that his father's a drunkard, and a serial wife-beater...?'

Dot remained quiet and there was a pause, as Charlie's words began to sink in.

'Well...?'

Dot speared three chips with her fork, smeared them with baked beans, pushed them into her mouth and began to chew, ruminantly. Charlie continued eating her meal. There was a cold silence between the two, for a couple of minutes.

'It's not right, Dot,' said Charlie in a mildly submissive tone. 'A child needs to know who its true parents are...'

'I'll tell him at some point...'

'How many years will pass before then...? How many years will Rick be deprived of showing love for his son – and little Bobby? Showing love for his father...? Have you any idea what effect that could have on the child...? And you – how will he look upon you, knowing that you've deprived him of his father, his father's love, for all that time...? Dot... you're building up a can of worms for the future.'

Dot stopped chewing, Charlie's words having penetrated her heart, she sat in silence, gazing at the table, as Charlie continued,

'You've got to let go of this grudge... It's not your place to tamper with other peoples' lives. This isn't some petty management versus the workers squabble, *it's two people's lives*. Just let it go. You've found happiness with Ted, spread it around, starting with Bobby and Rick. The past is the past, you can't change that, but you *can* change the future - for your son, and for Rick.'

A long pause followed, as Charlie's words reverberated around Dot's conscience. She knew that Charlie was speaking the truth. She'd just repeated, almost word for word, what Joan had been saying to Dot since the day Bobby was born. The voice of her conscience began to echo through her mind, *time to let go... let it die... you can't change the past... just let it go...* She stared down at her food, then in a monotone, dropped a bombshell, 'Rick's a good bloke... I know that...' Charlie sighed, *the penny's dropped, at last.* Their eyes met. A pause. The vague hint of a gentle smile graced Charlie's lips, and through the smile, she whispered, 'Dot... please... just do it...' Three seconds passed, then Dot, impassively, began to cut into her hash brown. Charlie, defeatedly, heaved a sigh. Three minutes passed as the two women continued to eat their meals in silence, then,

'Is anyone sittin here?'

Rick had taken them by surprise. As he sat with his tray, the silence continued, as the two women carried on eating.

'Has someone died?' he said, sarcastically.

A moment.

'Yeah...' said Dot.

'Who...?' asked Rick, concerned.

Dot shot Charlie a glance. Charlie looked back at her.

A moment.

'Me...' said Dot.

'I thought you were serious, then,' said Rick, as he began cutting into his beefburger. Charlie finished off the last of her chips and looked at Dot. The two women made eye contact, then Dot, almost imperceptibly, gave a slight nod, as Rick, oblivious, lustily gazed down at his bulging plate.

'I'm going to catch a bit of sun before the bell goes,' said Charlie, diplomatically.

'See you later, crocodile' said Dot.

Rick grunted through a mouthful of food.

Charlie stepped out onto the field then wandered toward the embankment. The late June sun was a welcome friend. Inside, Rick carried on eating his food. The silence between them was broken when Dot said,

'He loves his new bike...'

'Good...'

'How did y'know which one he wanted?'

'Charlie told me... She was laughin, about the time she went 'round to yours, after - you know - and she told me about the one he'd painted...'

'*Jesus Christ,*' Dot said with a smile, 'I was hopin someone'd rob it.'

'She said he had his heart set on a Carrington Gurkha, so I got him one.'

'Thanks...'

'It's alright, he's my lad, isn't he...?'

'Yeah...' she said, 'he's your lad.'

'Charlie's been a bit off, lately. Have you told her about him...?'

A moment.

'No... It's not my job to... but I'll tell y'this much...'

'Wha...?'

'She loves you...'

'Don't talk daft.'

'I'm tellin yeh.'

'Has she said?'

'No.'

Chapter 22

'Well, how d'you work that one out?'

'I can tell by the look in her eyes when she talks about yeh.'

'I think you're wrong.'

'I'm not wrong... But you mark my words...' they made eye contact as Dot lowered her voice and spoke sternly, 'If you dare break that girl's heart... the way you broke mine... you'll be sorry...'

* * *

Eyes closed, she lay on the grass, absorbing the warm sunshine, half-listening to the distant hubbub from the canteen. She heaved a sigh; in a few weeks, he'd be gone. She felt as if she'd hurried past the ticket collector, rushed onto the platform only to watch, as her train was heading, into the distance. Maybe she'd fare better in the army. Push this factory episode into the past and find a new life somewhere else. Sod's Law – once shackled to a man she didn't love, and now the one she does, she's about to lose.

'Have you give anymore thought to the weekend...?'

She opened her eyes, and he was standing a few feet away.

'Not really...'

'Well, the offer still stands... if you're interested.'

There was a pause.

'I'm gettin back,' he said, and just before he turned,

'How are the goldfinches doing...?'

'One died, four fledged. She's started her second clutch.'

'How many eggs?'

'Two...'

'And what do you do with all these birds that you

breed, sell them?'

'I don't breed them t'sell, I set them free.'

He turned and began walking back toward the canteen. She waited until he entered, then stood, patted the muck off her jeans, and began to walk back. Feeling downhearted, she passed through the canteen, then out onto the shop floor.

* * *

Mid-afternoon Charlie, and Dot, were busy at their respective benches when Zeta came prancing into the area.

'Charlie...' she said with a chirp, on approach, as Dot meandered out of the area.

'Hi, Zeta.'

'Are you doing anything, Thursday night?'

'No.'

'Do you fancy a drink with the girls? Well, when I say *the girls*, I mean me and Petra. God love her, she's a bit down in the dumps at the moment, and I thought we could take her out and cheer her up. You know, have a good gab. Girl-talk.'

'That sounds great. Time? Place?'

'Same again, The Red House. Eight o'clock?'

'I'm looking forward to it already.'

'Right,' said Zeta, 'I'll see you when I see you, then.'

And with that, she walked off, as Dot reappeared, having been searching in her locker.

* * *

The afternoon dragged on, Rick making one appearance

when he brought a bin of fixings to be sorted – a tool having chipped, halfway through the machining process. Another suspense-filled task to accomplish. He'd now accepted the fact, that Charlie wasn't interested in him, and Dot's implication was a load of bollocks. She's probably got the weekend boxed off with one of her upper-class, twit boyfriends, but was keeping him in reserve in case it all went tits up. He considered cutting his losses and calling the whole thing off but couldn't quite bear to pull the plug. Hope springs eternal. Two hours later, as another Lowry painting came to life and a stream of humanity poured out of the factory, Charlie slumped into Cooper, started him up, and headed for home.

She entered the house, threw off her puffer jacket and trainers, then mixed a Campari and soda. She was alone. She went upstairs and into her bedroom, flopping onto the bed. She closed her eyes and listened drowsily to the silence of the empty house. How could she clear up this mess with Rick? What could she do? The more she thought about it, her mind began to crumple until, once again, she heard an evil voice in her mind, whispering...

'*Whore... Twat... Burn in Hell...*'

She tensed her eyelids and grabbed bunches of the duvet in her clenched fists, as she screamed...

'*GO AWAY... YOU'RE NOT GOING TO DESTROY MY LIFE, ANYMORE.*

GO ON - FUCK OFF! FUCK OFF! LEAVE ME ALONE.'

She began to run down a tunnel: faster... faster... he mustn't catch her. He'll never take control again. The walls streaked past as she ran faster and faster. She had to escape this. She *would* escape this. The room began to spin. Faster and faster. '*Away, go away, FUCK OFF, BACK TO YOUR GRAVE. FUCK OFF*.... Sir Reginald, stop him... please make him go away... I am lying on the bed. I am lying on the bed, the bed, the bed... It's metallic blue, the rain is bouncing off, I am lying on the bed. I am lying on the bed...' The spinning room began to falter... slower, slower, slowly, like a spinning top, about to lose its momentum, and flop to one side, rolling in a circle, clinging precariously the last remnant of its energy, then... the vison began to appear, in her mind: a little girl... a little girl lying on the bed... *listening intently for the sound of his footsteps, coming up the stairs. As they appeared, she drummed her heels excitedly, against the mattress. Seconds later, he entered the room, walked over to the bed, and glared down at her,*

'*Have you brushed your teeth, young lady?' he said, sternly.*

'*Yes, daddy.*'

'*Daddy? What have I told you about calling me daddy? Use my real name. What is it?*'

'*Sir Reginald... Fortescue... Bogpipe.*'

'*Correct. Now, I'll ask you again: Have you brushed your teeth, young lady?*'

'*Yes, da – Sir Reginald.*'

'*Oh, for Heaven's sake. How many times, have I warned you about brushing your teeth? Do you wish to grow into a beautiful, young princess, with sparkling teeth – or a toothless, old witch?*'

'*A toothless, old witch - Sir Reginald.*'

'*Exactly. So – if I catch you brushing your teeth again, I shall put you over my knee and spank your bum, until it's as red and as swollen, as a baboon's.' She giggled.*

'*Right – who is it tonight, then...?*'

'Jemima, please, da – Sir Reginald.'

His finger skimmed along the row of books, until he came to Jemima. He lifted the book out, sat on the edge of the bed, opened the cover, then, in his best ecclesiastical voice, pretended to read, 'And, the Lord said unto Moses: come forth – but he came fifth, and only won a balloon.' She shrieked with delight... As the story of Jemima came to an end, he closed the book: 'And so endeth tonight's sermon.' He stood.

'Sir Reginald – please. Once again – our song,' she implored.

'Oh... alright, then...'

He glanced through the partially-opened door, making sure the ogre wasn't lurking within earshot, sat back on the bed, and they began to sing in unison: 'A million housewives every day, pick up a tin of beans and say – beanz meanz FARTZ!' She shrieked with laughter as her daddy tickled her tummy, and the ogre walked into the room: 'For goodness sake will you stop this ridiculous carry-on and allow the child to go to sleep?'

'Jawohl, mein fuehrer.'

She stomped out of the room. He stood. 'Night, night, sweetheart. Sweet dreams.' He kissed her, gently, on the forehead.'

'Night, night - daddy... I love you.'

He pushed Jemima back into her slot, between Tom Kitten and The Flopsy Bunnies.

'I love you, too...'

She smiled as he gave her a cheeky wink and blew her a kiss, then - he was gone.

An hour later she woke. Her body was drained of

energy, but her mind had reached an oasis of peace. She heaved a sigh, and after a few minutes, sat up, picked up her Campari and soda and drank it. She glanced at her bookshelf, of Beatrix Potter books, and smiled. She felt normal.

She had no idea at the time, but she was approaching the end of her demons. Within a month, they would be gone, never to return.

23

The following day, Dot was elated. To say she was like a kid waiting for Christmas morning would be an understatement. Following on from her day out to Blackpool with Ted, they'd arranged for her to go around to his for a relaxed evening together, with a film, and a bottle of wine. At 7.02 a taxi pulled up outside her house, and she almost ran down the path to get into it. Young Bernie was looking after the rest of them, and Dot had promised to be back home for 11.00 on the dot. Ted, being the gentleman he was, had organized a taxi from Cresta Cabs to pick her up and take her home, so that she could enjoy a few glasses of her beloved Chardonnay, not having to drive.

The taxi arrived at Ted's bungalow at 7.36. He ushered her in as Toby came bounding up, tail wagging toward her. Ted took her coat, pecked her on the cheek and commented on how lovely she looked (in her RSPCA dress and Oxfam heels). They entered the living room, sat, and chatted over a glass of wine and a bowl of *Bombay Mix* as Toby settled down on the carpet, next to Ted's feet. As 8.00 approached,

'Well, I suppose we'd better start watching a film,' he said. 'I tell you what we could watch,' he said, enthusiastically, 'Three Amigos. Have you seen it? It's one of my favourites. Y'know, the first time I watched it, I nearly choked with laughter.'

'Go on, then.'

Ted loaded the DVD into the player then pressed *play*. He poured her a second glass of wine, she kicked off her shoes, and they snuggled up on the couch, bathed in the subdued lighting of the room. Dot took his hand in hers and squeezed it. He squeezed hers, in return. She rested her head on his shoulder and felt at peace with the world. Ted kissed her on the head, then rested his against hers, and his heart melted. The only minor hiccup to this scene of romantic bliss came when Toby farted. 'Sorry about that,' said Ted, embarrassedly. 'It's OK,' replied Dot, mischievously, 'I thought it was the dog.'

Two hours later, after much laughter and the rolling down cheeks of tears, the film had ended. A bonus being that Dot had added a new word to her non-extensive vocabulary: *plethora*. She'd also discovered a new talent within herself, that of being able to accurately mimic with devastating results, a Mexican bandit accent. She laid it on with a trowel, sending Ted into shrieks of laughter every time she said, *'you wanna die with a man's gorn, not a l'il seesy gorn, like thees.'* But when the laughter had faded, Ted looked into her eyes and said, 'I'm really glad you came into my life.' 'Me, too,' she replied, then took his face into her hands and gave him a lingering kiss. In return, he gently wrapped her face in his expansive palms. He pressed his lips against hers with a long, passionate kiss. When he released her, she stood, her breath trembling with desire. She took him by the fingertips and pulled gently. He stood, and again took her face into his hands. This time their kiss became more passionate, urgent, as a fire of lust began to rage within them. As they pressed against each other, she felt the length of his thick, hard shaft, against her thigh. She reached down and began to rub her hand up and down it, gently, slowly tantalizing and massaging him into a frenzy of heavy, desirous groans. His trembling palm engulfed her expansive breast, and he began to squeeze its plump softness between his fingertips.

'Hey, Mister Currie,' she said, desirously, into his ear, have y'gorra bedroom tha doesn't involve models?'

'Who needs a bedroom...?'

He began to feverishly tear at the buttons of his shirt, whipping it off and throwing it onto the carpet. Dot lay down, shoved her hands up her dress and pushed her thumbs into the waistband of her knickers. She slid them over her knees and down to her ankles. As she lifted one foot out, she glanced up at Ted. He stood before her, completely naked, except for his socks. Her eyes focused on his erect rod and hanging balls. She flicked her foot into the air, sending her knickers flying over the back of the couch. Leaning up, she cupped his balls in her palm and gently began to squeeze them together.

'Come on... do me,' she panted, through a trembling voice 'do me, now...'

She lay back down, and he knelt between her legs.

'I've waited so long f'this,' he breathed, lustfully.

'So, have I...'

They glared into each other's eyes with a mutual, desirous lust.

A moment.

PARP... PARP, PARP... PARP...

'Who's blowing that bleeding horn, he said, annoyed.

'Ted, sod the horn, just shag me, will yeh?'

'Right oh,' he replied, about to squeeze himself into her moistened slit.

PARP, PARP, PARP.

'*For God's sake!*' he said with a snarl, feeling his erection beginning to drain.

'*OH NO!*' shrieked Dot, the terror of realisation crashing into her with the force of a runaway bin lorry. '*It's me taxi. Wha time is it?*'

'Twenty to eleven.'

'*Jesus wept!*' she shouted, jumping up. 'I've got to be home for eleven, I promised me daughter - I'll have to go.'

She began to frantically search for her knickers, as Ted, disheartened, gazed into space as he heaved a sigh: *so near, yet so far…*

'Where's me knickers? Where's me friggin knickers, d'you know?'

'How do I know where your friggin knickers are? You had them last.'

Their romantic tryst showed signs of descending into a marital squabble, as Ted pulled his boxers back on. *PARP, PARP…*

'I'll have t'go home without them,' she said, frantically slipping her heels on.

They both began to calm down, as he helped her on with her coat, then at the front door,

'Better luck, next time, eh?' she whispered, with a naughty grin.

'You bet,' he said, before giving her a parting kiss, as she squeezed his balls, through his boxers.

'*C'mon, Dot, hurry up,*' shouted Alf, through the opened window, as the Mondeo ticked over. She ran down the path, turned and waved, got into the car, and, as she felt like Cinderella, her carriage clattered off in a cloud of dust. Ted closed the door. As the taxi turned out onto the main road, a couple of superfluous pleasantries were exchanged with Alf, then, apart from the crackling voice of the office, on the radio, silence shrouded her journey. She sat in the darkness of the back seat, her mind filled with Ted - the kissing, the rubbing, the squeezing, the sucking... Her breathing became heavier, as she felt her hand drifting down, under her dress, then, she began to massage her plump mound. Her middle finger found its way into her moist lips, then moved up to her eager nub. She continued to rub her middle finger. *Fast... faster...* as she fantasised about Ted - until... Her restrained groan caused her body to shudder in silence, as she reached her climax.

'Hey, Dot, did you hear the result?' said Alf.

'Wh-What result?' she said, through a trembling gasp.

'Liverpool hammered them, three - nil.'

'That's good,' her voice quivered, as if she gave a toss.

'Are you alright, Dot? You don't sound well.'

There was a pause.

'I'm fine, Alf,' she exhaled, relaxing into a gentle bliss. I've never felt this good for years...'

* * *

Thursday, 7.42pm, Charlie's Mini-Cooper turned into Summerhill Road, and began to accelerate. Fifty yards further on, Petra came into view, standing near their pre-arranged pick-up point, near the post box. Looking her usual stunning self, she climbed into the car and they headed for The Red House. The two women related to each other well, and Charlie wallowed in Petra's telling of many comical anecdotes regarding the mischievous escapades of reception-class rapscallions.

As they walked into the lounge, Zeta had bagged their usual table near the window, having made sure she was facing the door, and had started drinking her Bacardi and Coke. Old Tommy was sat diagonally opposite in his usual seat, with his usual half of Guinness in front of him. Petra sat and Charlie headed toward the bar. As she passed 'Van Gogh'.

'Would you like a drink, Tommy?'

'I've got one, ere.'

Charlie chuckled, quietly. Minutes later, all three were seated with a drink in front of them.

News of Dot's illicit sexual liaison with Ted had been relayed earlier in the day, from Joan, to *'her girls'* then passed on from Petra to Zeta, none of them, including Joan, believing in Dot's unshakeable insistence that they didn't have a shag. Or, to put it more accurately, in the delicate words of an unbelieving sister,

'Since when have you been a friggin nun? You like cock as much as the rest of us.'

At 8.14 the door swung open.

'Here's Rick,' said Zeta, a hint of excitement in her voice as Rick, and his mate, Ste, entered, walked to the bar and ordered a pint and a half of *Magner's*. Petra turned and looked at them. Charlie glanced, and felt mortified. Three minutes later, the two men were quietly sipping their cider as they discussed the previous night's football match. With their first round of drinks almost finished, Zeta stood and asked Petra to give her a hand, to get the next round in. As the four chatted at the bar, Charlie sat, vaguely feeling as if she was playing gooseberry. When Zeta and Petra eventually returned with the drinks,

'I've asked Rick and Ste to join us,' she said to Charlie. 'You don't mind, do you?'

Charlie shook her head, as if she had a choice. Two minutes later, Rick, and Ste, came walking across from the bar. After exchanging introductions, the two men sat. Rick and Charlie, both looking somewhat uncomfortable with the situation, Ste and Petra, showing an immediate interest in each other. Zeta had inherited the role that Dot had occupied last week, that of Mother Hen and her chicks. Ste was Rick's best mate. Thirty-one, he was six feet two, blond-haired with blue eyes, and immaculately dressed in a white granddad-style shirt, pale blue jeans, and a pair of black leather *Sneakers*. Petra was immediately attracted to his exceptionally handsome looks, mated to his softly spoken, but manly, voice, and likewise, he was captivated by her stunning beauty, and child-like, broken English accent. Zeta, noticing the reticence, or, was it defiance, between Charlie and Rick, to strike up a meaningful conversation, decided to help things along by stirring the pot with various snippets regarding, work, music, cars, anything she though they had in common. It was a different story regarding Ste and Petra. They were already joking and laughing with each other and, although they didn't yet realise it, they were falling in love. A smile tip-toed across Zeta's lips as she realised that the allotted time was almost approaching. Bang on the dot – 8.30 – her phone rang. She picked it out of her bag...

'Hello, mum... *Oh, no...* Are you alright...? I'll be there in twenty minutes...

Yeah... Everything's fine, here... Yeah... OK. See you

soon. Bye, mum.'

'I'll have to go,' said Zeta, with a groan. 'My mum tripped down a couple of stairs and hurt her wrist. I might have to take her to hospital.'

Words of consolation abounded, as Zeta finished her drink then gathered her belongings. 'I'll see yez tomorrow in work. Bye, Ste.' She headed for the door, exited into the street, walked around the corner, and taking out her phone, dialled…

'Hi, Dot… Yeah, perfect, it went like clockwork. They think I'm going to my mum's…

They're together now. A bit cold with each other, but they'll warm up…' She began walking down the street, as she continued 'There's been an unexpected development… Ste and Petra… they're all over each other…'

***

'Would you like a drink?' said Rick, knocking back the last mouthful of his pint.

'I've got one, thank you,' Charlie replied, coldly.

There was a pause, as Ste and Petra carried on enthusiastically chatting to each other.

'Have you give any more thought, to Sunday… Wales?'

'No.'

Another pause, that seemed like a year.

'Ste, are you ready for another…?'

'Another half, please, Rick.'

Petra asked for another wine, so Rick went to the bar to replenish the drinks. Ste was sitting between the two women. He turned to Charlie.

'He likes you y'know?'

'Really?' she said, indifferently.

'No, I mean... *really* likes you...? D'you know what I'm saying?'

When Rick returned with the drinks, conversation between him and Charlie gradually began to get off the ground. As stilted talking turned into relaxed conversation, then gradually progressed to smiles and titters, she started to think she'd been a little harsh in the way she'd been treating him. After all, there was no reason to think he wouldn't tell her about Bobby – maybe it was just a matter of time before he felt comfortable about it. But would he? As the creeping doubt began once again to trickle into her mind, she pushed it into a psychological box and closed the lid. Though at the same time, reminding herself that she could never have a relationship with someone who was prepared to sneakily hide secrets from her. She'd innocently endured that sort of carry-on in the past, and it had destroyed her trust.

An hour later Rick and Ste, having earlier veered from their original plan, steered a course back onto it, and invited Charlie and Petra to join them for a meal. They accepted, and the four left the pub, and crossed over the road, toward the cars. Ste waved, as his Citroen van pulled out from the kerb. As it drove past, *Ste Jones. Heating and plumbing engineer.* could be seen along the side. Charlie's car followed the van for a couple of miles as they made their way to the Taj Mahal, one of the better Indian restaurants in the district. Frequented by couples, groups of couples, and families, it was spotless, quiet, and beautifully laid out. Thankfully, because of its up-market appearance and gentile ambience, it was the sort of place that had no attraction for the usual crowds of pissed-up, foul-mouthed yobs. Ste opened the door for the women, and as they entered, he jumped in behind them, and mischievously let it shut in Rick's face. Each of the men lifted out a chair for their respective partner, a small gesture that wasn't lost on Charlie or Petra, and the four settled down over a drink, to peruse the menu.

The evening was going from strength to strength, and each enjoyed a delicious meal. Petra, being a vegetarian, ordered the mushroom course but wasn't so reticent when it came to drinks. Laughter abounded in plenty when she began slurring her words. Rick and Ste becoming an unexpected double act, with their, almost, never-ending comical anecdotes and self-deprecating humour, another feature of the evening which both women found endearing. Charlie and Petra did hold their own, however, mainly with tales of work, and, of course, Joan and Dot. Their coffee finished, the impromptu date began to come to an end with all of them having had a thoroughly, enjoyable time. Ste had fallen for Petra, and she made no bones about the fact that she had the same feeling for him. As they left the restaurant, and began to walk back to the cars, he suddenly stopped, took her face in his hands, and planted his lips onto hers. Rick and Charlie looked at each other. Then, as they looked into each other's eyes, Rick took *her* face in his hands and pressed his lips against hers. For ten seconds, each of the couples stood on the pavement, kissing, oblivious to passers-by. Before climbing into the Citroen, Ste and Petra had exchanged phone numbers and arranged a date for Saturday evening. As Rick got into the van he looked up at Charlie and winked,

'See yeh tomorrow.'

'Yeah.'

The cars pulled out and headed in different directions.

* * *

Charlie's car came to a halt, near the pillar box.

The two women sat for a few minutes, chatting, and laughing, about their unexpected encounter with the Terrible Twins, as they'd begun to call Rick and Ste. Charlie had joked about how Ste would come in handy if Petra ever needed her waterworks looking at, a comment that Petra rewarded with a polite smile, not quite sure where the humour came into such a practical suggestion. When the laughter calmed down to end of evening, polite goodbyes, Petra looked at Charlie, 'I am so happy that I find you, my dear friend,' she said, in a tender voice, though slurring her words.

'And me, you,' replied Charlie, with an appreciative smile and a friendly squeeze of Petra's hand.

'I must learn speak better Engleesh.'

'I can teach you - I mean, I'm not a teacher, but I can fill you in on the basics.'

'Fill me in? Like a hole?'

Charlie laughed.

'I'll explain in lesson one, when I'm teaching the teacher.'

They swapped phone numbers, then Petra gave Charlie directions to her flat, and they arranged a time on Saturday morning for her to go around and begin her teaching.

'You have truly kind heart...' said Petra, gazing into Charlie's eyes.

Before she had time to answer, Petra repeated, 'Truly kind heart...' She placed her hand onto the top of Charlie's inner thigh and began to gently massage it. Charlie's breath trembled out of her mouth as Petra continued the sensuous, hand movement. A moment – then, she made eye contact with Petra. 'And truly, beautiful face...' said Petra. She leaned across the car and cupped the side of Charlie's face in her palm. She placed her lips onto Charlie's, whose initial resistance evaporated in a second. The kiss was soft and gentle, and hardly felt, yet its true purpose did not go unnoticed. She then gave a second kiss, this time with more feeling, the tip of her tongue venturing between Charlie's lips. She drew back, 'I am sorry,' she said, averting her glance with embarrassment. 'I am so sorry, my dear friend... the wine... I must go, Goodnight... Please, forgive...' As Petra reached for the door handle, Charlie took her by the arm. She turned, with the look of a scolded child on her face. 'You don't have to rush off,' said Charlie, her stomach beginning to quiver. 'It was a lovely evening... I've enjoyed your company...' A couple more pleasantries were exchanged as the small talk got smaller and smaller, each woman developing a desire for the other. When the idle chitchat finally dried up there was a pause, then Charlie reached across and cupped Petra's cheek in her hand. She placed two, tentative kisses onto her lips, then, closing her eyes, rested the top of her forehead against Petra's. 'It's OK,' she said, with a gentle whisper, not wishing her to leave. 'It's OK...' Petra drew her face back, and the two women looked into each other's eyes. '*I said*... it's OK,' repeated Charlie, tremulously, followed with a slight nod. The silence in the car was broken only by the heavy breathing, stumbling from Petra's mouth. She reached forward, curved her hand around the nape of Charlie's neck and drew her face to hers. Their lips met, and they shared passionate kisses.

24

The following day was a sad one for Dot, it was the final day for the first tranche of twelve workers who had accepted redundancy. She'd made a point of seeing each one and wishing them well, while still harbouring the thought that they'd knifed the union, and their co-workers, in the back. Hypocritically, there was still the conundrum in her mind of how to accept her redundancy and leave, with her head held high. There would be a way out somehow, she just had to find it. Not an easy task when every time she began to assimilate a cohesive strategy, her mind became trampled with thoughts of Ted.

Charlie was going through a similar, psychological dilemma. Over the past few weeks, she'd grown closer to Rick. Their night out had broken down the final barrier, and they'd shown their true feelings to each other, they both knew, now, that they were in love. He was kind, caring, generous, treated her with respect, had a brilliant sense of humour, and his muscular body wasn't half-bad, either. So why, when she'd eventually found her Mr Right, had she begun to dither? As she'd lain in bed the previous night, it wasn't Rick's lips she'd imagined kissing hers, it was Petra's. In fact, it wasn't just her lips, that she'd imagined Petra kissing and sucking. Over and over in her mind she kept re-running her fantasy of having sex with Petra. Just twelve hours ago everything had seemed so simple: man chases woman until she catches him, man and woman fall in love, live happily ever after, The End. Now, a complication had arisen that she'd unsuccessfully tried to bat to one side. It was a stupid misunderstanding. Another 'schoolgirl' crush. How on earth could she possibly be sexually aroused by Petra? She was a work colleague... She was just... a beautiful, gentle, softly spoken woman that... smelt divine... had sensuous lips... breasts to die for... and she was *so* sexy. *Christ!* She *did* fancy Petra, and the more she thought of her, the less she thought of Rick. Once again, the dormant, bi-curious side to her nature had been awoken. She thought she had left all that sticky fumbling behind, in her teens.

As the day passed, she'd seen Rick a couple of times, and they'd shared laughter, but her mind had kept wandering back to Petra. As she'd stood in the canteen queue at dinner time, her eyes had been constantly scanning the entrance to Joan's kitchen area, to catch a glimpse of her, to no avail. She'd now worked herself up into such a tizzy that she could hardly face the possibility that Petra was straight, and that the kissing was a one-off. Her mind was in complete turmoil. How could this be happening in such a late stage of her relationship, with Rick? She was acting stupidly. She decided that she'd been carried away by the whole incident and had allowed her imagination to run riot. Right. That was it; she'd confirm with Rick she'd love to join him on Sunday, testing his mate's new bike out, in Wales. Then, she'd phone Petra, and cancel her going around on Saturday morning to give her some pointers as to how to improve her English. That was it. Infatuation over. Job done, end of.

* * *

She'd finished work early, driven around to the florists and picked it up. She arrived at the cemetery at 4.16, parked the car then made her way to the grave. It was over in the far corner, to the right, a section of the cemetery reserved for children and babies.

As she approached, her breathing began to tremble. She arrived, stood at the foot, and looked down at the headstone.

'Hello, my little boy,' she whispered, tenderly. 'Happy birthday...'

She reached forward and placed the teddy bear wreath on his grave. She picked off a couple of pieces of leaf debris and threw them to one side. 'Aunty Dot's got a new boyfriend,' she said, to stop herself from crying, 'and mummy's having another baby... but there'll never be anyone else to take your place... My little darling... I love you...'

As she felt the sobs beginning to rise in her throat,

'Hello, Joan...'

She turned, and John, holding a wreath, was standing behind her.

'Hello, John...'

'How are you keeping...?'

She smiled.

'Stupid question...' he said.

'Gettin by...'

John reached down and placed the wreath onto the grave of his son. Twenty seconds passed as they both stood, gazing down at the headstone.

They'd been married for three years, before taking the life-changing decision to make a better life for themselves and emigrate to Australia. John, being a joiner, had no difficulty finding a job and so, with hearts full of enthusiasm, they took the step into the great unknown and departed these shores. There was a honeymoon period of twelve months when their lives were a constant whirlwind of work, finding a house, making new friends, making mistakes, laughing, crying. When the maelstrom began to slow, and the daily attraction of azure blue ocean and hot sunshine started to lose its grip, Joan would sit alone in their large lounge, and think of miserable, old England, with her crap weather, postage-stamp houses, moaning inhabitants and, with a nostalgic smile, her dear sister, Dot and her rag-tag brood of unruly kids. As each month passed the pull of the Mother Country became stronger: family, friends, the sense of humour, the feeling of belonging. Many was the night when Joan would quietly sob herself to sleep, after John had dozed off. It came to a head when she told him she could no longer remain living in Australia. After a monumental row, he knew that he had to return with her, or the marriage was over. They arrived back, having sold everything they owned to raise their fares. After many job applications being rejected, he managed to find work as a school caretaker. Dot put in a word for Joan at Nelson's and she was taken on owing to her past experience as their canteen supervisor, to replace Sandra Brimble, who'd sought pastures new and gone to manage the café in a local M&S. They moved into a rented, two-up, two-down Victorian terrace, and after a couple of months of John licking his wounds, they once again began to see that there was more to loving each other than blue ocean and hot sunshine. So much, that, ten months later, Joan gave birth to their only child - Thomas.

* * *

'What would you like to drink?' he said, as she took a seat.

'Fresh orange, please.'

As John walked to the bar, he heaved a sigh and thought of their little son. How quickly the time had flown since his death.

He returned with the drinks, sat, and they began to talk. Smiles were gradually coaxed out of each other, as the fragility of their unexpected meeting began to evaporate. They were in the pub for close to an hour. Neither of them had anything other than an empty house to go home to. They were both comfortable with the situation, and as the minutes ticked away the past bitterness, recriminations and hostilities were pushed aside, if not completely forgotten. The passage of time had eased the heartache and grief of losing their child, and now they found themselves in a place where they could accept that the tragic consequences leading up to his death, were neither of their fault. He already knew that she was pregnant again, but it was news to him that she'd been abandoned. Similarly, Joan had reluctantly acquired a potted history, gained from the mutual friend grapevine, about John's couple of amours, since they'd separated. Over the last hour each of them had felt a warmth rekindle inside toward each other, and as they parted in the pub car park, he pecked her on the cheek:

'Look after yourself...'

'You, too...'

'Bye the way, congratulations - *mum*.'

She smiled.

Joan's Corsa turned left, out onto the road, John's Focus turned right. Seconds later, once again, they'd gone their separate ways.

* * *

Joan wasn't the only one who'd finished early, that Friday afternoon. Dot had bunged Zeta a load of bullshit about having to finish at four o'clock, and Zeta being Zeta, knew that Dot's heart-rending stream of verbal diarrhoea was, in fact, just *another* load of bullshit. But, sympathizing with the fact that Dot was still going through the agonizing throes of fledgeling, middle-aged love, she rode to her aid, turned a blind eye, and spun Hardcastle some cock and bull story. Hardcastle, on the other hand, while listening to Zeta's cock and bull story, had somehow managed to keep a straight face, while thinking to himself, '*what a load of bullshit.*'

At approximately 4.30 Dot trespassed breathlessly onto the hallowed ground that was C&A. Twenty-five quid in hand, borrowed from Joan, she made her way to the ladies'

department, and twenty-seven minutes later had kitted herself out with a denim Bardot dress, a pair of black, Jersey joggers and a pair of floral, embroidered Chelsea boots. And, she still had two quid left over, which was rapidly exchanged for a Holland's steak and kidney pie, out the chippy, on the way home. Oh! The sheer bliss she felt of being able to spend, spend, spend, whilst retaining a clear conscience. The reason for this last-minute, panic-stricken shopping spree was, of course, the fact that later that evening she had another date arranged with Ted, and this time there'd be no taxi to interrupt the natural flow, so to speak, of things. Joan had volunteered to stop the night and babysit. Ted was looking forward to a night of unbridled passion with his new amour, and Dot was straining at the lead to finish what they'd started the previous week.

At 8.08 Alf's Mondeo stopped outside Ted's bungalow. Immaculately made up and wearing her newly acquired finery, Dot got out, paid Alf, and hurried up the drive. After a warm welcome during which he cheekily bit her on the side of her neck, Ted hung up her duffle coat then complimented her on her new outfit, 'And it's all brand new, out of a proper shop,' she said, absent-mindedly. Ted looked at her, quizzically, then came back with, 'Glass of Chardonnay?'

'I suppose a bottle with a long straw would be out of the question?' she said with a cheeky smile, then, wine in hand, they settled down on the couch. They decided on The Pink Panther. Ted pressed play. Toby had already been out for his walk so he, too, was happy. As the evening came to an end, the film and the wine were both finished. Ted led Dot to the bedroom then left her to get into bed as he undressed in the bathroom. The room was lit by a side lamp as he, wearing just his boxers, entered. Dot was naked, lying under the duvet. Her heart pounded as he climbed in. Tentatively, they began to peck each other. He placed his mouth against her ear and whispered,

'What's the cut-off age for falling in love...?

'A hundred and fifty,' she replied.

'This is how it should be,' he said, quietly. 'Not scrabbling around on the carpet, like two animals.'

'I know...'

She turned her head and kissed him gently, on the cheek. He turned and placed his mouth onto hers. Slowly, he planted a succession of small, tender kisses onto her lips and around her mouth. She began to gasp quietly, as she felt his lips move down to her neck, sucking gently. As he moved onto her, she opened her legs, and he lay between her thighs. She felt his mouth move to her breast, and his tender, gentle kissing continued from one to the other. Her eyes closed, she began pant, *'Ted... Ted...'* He pushed his boxers down to around his thighs and lay upon her. She could feel his thick, stiff shaft pressing against her, his muscular chest pressing against her breasts.

'Oh, Dot... I've needed you so much...'

'I'm here, now... I'm yours...'

Her breathing began to tremble as she felt his erection slowly enter her. He placed his cheek against hers and gave a tender groan, as he slowly pushed forward. She whimpered as she felt him penetrating deeper. She wrapped her legs around the backs of his calves and they both began to pant tremulously, as he started to make love to her; slowly, at first, then he gradually began to increase in speed. Two minutes later they shared the exquisite delight of sexual ecstasy. Their climaxes reaching an end, he lay beside her as they rested, both with eyes closed, hardly daring to believe what they had just shared. Three minutes of silence passed, during which their breathing relaxed back into normality, then,

'I could murder a mugga cocoa,' she said, quietly.

'I've got no cocoa, but I could do you a mug of Horlicks.

I'll go and put the milk on.'

As he pulled up his boxers and was about to climb off the bed, she grabbed him by the wrist,

'Come here, you daft bugger. I was pullin your leg...'

He flopped back onto the bed, wrapped her in his arms and kissed her.

'Night, night, Dottie...'

'Night, night, Tiger...'

She pecked him on the lips. He reached across and turned the light out.

25

She knocked three times, half-hoping there'd be no response. She was about to turn and leave when the door opened.

'Charlie...' she said, mildly surprised. 'I was not expecting you to coll.'

'I said, I would,' she replied, guiltily.

After two seconds of uncomfortable silence, 'Well, are you going to ask me in?'

'Sorry, pliz come in,' said Petra.

She closed the door as Charlie glanced around the attic flat of a large, Victorian semi, casually furnished in a Bohemian style that was typically Petra.

'Pliz excuse my attire, but I was about to get into the shower,' she said, indicating her dressing gown and bare feet. 'Would you like a cap of tea?'

'No, thank you.'

'Pliz, sit down.'

Charlie sat in an armchair, Petra took a seat on the sofa, opposite.

'I am *very*, sorry.'

'For what?' replied Charlie.

'Thursday night... I am very, sorry, I dringing too

much wine. It make me...'

'It took two, to tango,' said Charlie.

'I do not dance,' replied Petra, to Charlie's imperceptible smile.

'It's OK.'

'It not OK... It was wrong of me, to act in such a way to my best friend.'

There was an uncomfortable pause.

'It was my fault I lead you astray. I feel ashamed of it.'

'You didn't lead me astray, and here's nothing to feel ashamed about...'

'I should keep my feelings under control... Sometimes is feeling for one, then sometimes is feelings for other... My dear, sweet friend, you are very, beautiful woman... but only as friend. I must control my feelings... I do not want lose you...'

'Of course, you won't lose me. What are you saying...?'

'You pliz... go now.'

'Why should I go...?'

'I do not want lose you. You are my dear, sweet friend. I am scared I will lose you.'

'Petra, you're not going to lose me. What's the matter...? Tell me...'

'I cannot... I will lose you...'

There was a long pause as Petra avoided her eyes meeting Charlie's, who, sat impatiently, curtailing her desire to speak any further. Petra hesitated, uneasily, then her mouth began to tremble with emotion, and she wiped an emerging tear from her eye.

'Petra... what's the matter...?'

There was a pause.

'I understand... if you call me freak and walk away.

You no longer be my friend.'

'Why would I do that...?'

Another pause.

'I did not get redundant made... They fire me... I am freak...'

'What are you talking about...?'

Petra was breathing heavily with trepidation.

'I am of the two sexes...'

She paused, then slowly, uneasily, continued 'I like the men, and I also like the women... My boyfriend was lazy slob. He spend all my wages each time, and not working himself, so I finish with him... He spread my secret around, and then... the parents in my village, find out, and they wait for me, outside the school... They do not want I teach their kids no more. They do not want that I touch their kids, in case I infect them... They wait for me... Three days, each day, they attack me, they punch me... they pull me by hair to the ground and kick me... They spit on me and shout *FREAK - Die, you fucking FREAK*. The headmaster coll me to office, and say I causing too much trouble. He say he give me good reference, then he fire me...'

Charlie was boiling with anger as she listened to the words emerging from Petra's lips.

'I wanted die, because is true, I am freak... I wanted move to nother village, nother town but, it will follow me wherever I go. They will always be there, waiting for me... Government say is OK, to be freak, but many, many people in my country, do not agree. They are backward people in small villages, the church rules them, not the government. Then, I read about Great Britain... Is good place to be free. To be, as was made by God... I am no freak. I read of *LGBT.* and the people of Great Britain, they treat them as friends, not freaks. So, I come England...'

There was a pause, then Charlie moved to the sofa and, sitting next to Petra, wrapped her arms around, and pressed her cheek against hers.

'You're safe, now... No-one will ever do that again, to you.'

They separated, then Petra put on a brave face as she said,

'What want you? Coffee or cap of tea? Is Yorkshire – Joan teach me, like Yorkshire tea.'

'Yes, please,' said Charlie, then, as a tender smile graced her lips, 'I'd love a cup of Yorkshire tea...'

'I put kettle on, and get dressed...'

Petra walked into the tiny kitchen, put the kettle on, then went into the bedroom. Within a minute, she'd returned, wearing a flowery summer dress and a pair of leather sandals. She moved to the kitchen, made the tea then brought it in, on a tray. They sat and continued talking.

Charlie was disgusted at the way Petra had been treated but, gradually, the story of her harrowing experiences came to an end. As they sipped their tea the conversation moved into a more light-hearted vein, and they relaxed. Eventually, when their tea was finished,

'Right,' said Charlie, 'let's get started on your lesson...'

'I can hardly wait. You make English lady of me,' she said, with a smile.

'The first thing I noticed was that you say, *What, want you?* You're saying it the wrong way around... The correct way of saying it is, What, do you want?

'What - do - you - want?'

'That's right... but a more polite, British way of saying it is, *What, would you like?*'

'What – would – you – like?'

'That's it. Now, cap is pronounced cop: *a cop of tea…* A cap is something you put on your head, and you'd be in trouble if you tried to fill a cap with Yorkshire tea.'

They both saw the funny side, then Petra, once again, became serious:

'*What… would you like… coffee, or a cop of tea?*'

'No, thanks. I've just had one,' said Charlie, with a giggle, that Petra returned.

The lesson lasted for an hour, with Charlie going over the primary elements of diction and pronunciation. She skimmed over nouns and adjectives but, didn't want to confuse Petra with an information overload. Petra was hungry to learn, and when her lesson came to an end, she almost begged Charlie to carry on, but she put her foot down. Then she relented and promised to call around one evening during the week, before which Petra would have armed herself with an exercise book, in which to make notes.

Petra walked Charlie to the door. As she placed her hand on the handle, she said,

'Tank you, for all, sorry, *thank you*, for eve-ry-thing.'

'It was a pleasure,' replied Charlie, as her breathing became heavier.

Petra leaned forward. Charlie's heart leapt, but all she received was a polite peck on the cheek.

She looked into Petra's eyes…

There was a pause as Charlie's breathing began to tremble out of her mouth, and her heart began to pound. She didn't want to leave. Gathering the courage to speak, she said, hesitantly,

'You know… there was nothing to feel ashamed

about... on Thursday night... It was lovely... I haven't stopped thinking about you, since...'

A moment.

'I think, you must now go... Is just infatuation. You are but a curious, young woman... I do not - *want* - destroy our friendship...'

'I don't want to go...'

There was a pause during which, Petra's eyes took on a look of concern, as Charlie continued, 'It won't destroy our friendship... I don't want to go... I want to be with you...'

Their eyes met, then Charlie reached across and placed her hand around the back of Petra's neck, bringing her face forward. She placed her lips onto Petra's and kissed her gently, for a few seconds. Their lips parted.

'Please... I think you must go... I am not predator... I am very sorry...'

'You wouldn't be a predator...' said Charlie, not realizing that it was *her* that was being the predator.

'It is not right... You are my dear friend...'

A moment, then Charlie sighed.

'Very well... goodbye, Petra.'

As Charlie made a move to turn,

'So, now you blackmail me...? I take you to bed, make love, or I never see you again...? You no longer be my dear friend...?'

'Of course not,' said Charlie. 'We still remain good friends. I promise. Bye, bye...' She took Petra's hand and gently kissed the back of her middle finger. Petra stood in silence. Charlie turned and walked across the landing as Petra watched her go, then she closed the door. As she descended the three flights of stairs, Charlie felt humiliated. How could she possibly have made such a fool of herself.

She wanted to crawl under the nearest stone and stay there for the rest of her life. She reached the hall then, as she crossed toward the front door,

'*Charlie...*'

She raised her head, to see Petra leaning over the banister.

'Come...'

As she walked back up the stairs and crossed the landing, her heart was pounding with anticipation, her breath trembling out of her mouth. She entered the flat, Petra closing the door, behind her.

'You are curious... You must promise me, it will not go further than just today... it will not destroy our friendship.'

'Of course, it won't.'

'Promise me.'

'I promise... Please... I want to know... how it feels... Please...'

'You have been with same sex before...?

Charlie hesitated, slightly.

'When I was sixteen... my friend, Jenny Taylor... kissing... we just... played with each other's lady bits... a few occasions, nothing more... but... it was gentle... nice...

They looked at each other and gave a knowing smile. Petra hesitated, then...

'Very well – come with me...'

Petra led her into the small bedroom. An old, oak, bedside cabinet stood beside the single bed. In the corner stood an antique, mahogany wardrobe. A large picture of The Sacred Heart of Jesus gazed down from a wall, and a small statue of the Virgin Mary stood on a shelf. Through the window, the tips of an overgrown sycamore branch intermittently tapped gently at the pane each time a breeze caught it. Charlie's stomach was turning over with a mixture of sexual excitement and dread. She wondered if this was such a good idea after all.

'Take off your clothes and get onto the bed, said Petra. 'Throw off the duvet.'

She did as she was told and looked at Petra, who kicked off her sandals and pulled the dress up over her head, revealing she was naked underneath. Charlie was mesmerized by her gentle presence. Her hair tumbled down to her shoulders, her porcelain-like body was slim and beautifully proportioned. Her exquisite breasts were of a perfect size and shape and her long, slender legs reached up to a crotch that bore a neatly trimmed triangle of pubic hair. She looked as if she'd stepped out of a Pre-Raphaelite painting. Charlie moved over as Petra approached the bed. She paused, opened the drawer of the cabinet, and took out a small bottle of baby oil.

'Lie flat,' she said, quietly, and Charlie did so. She flipped the top open and slowly drizzled some of the oil onto Charlie's freshly shaved crotch. She gave a small gasp as she felt the cold oil creeping its way into her. The two women lay beside each other. Charlie was physically trembling.

'You are sure of this...?'

'Yes...'

'You are not like me... You are not of the two sexes – you would have know by now... from being little girl. You are just a young woman, who is curious.'

'Yes...'

'I am not predator... I will not take advantage of you...'

'I know...'

'Very well...'

The words had a calming effect on her, and she began

to relax. Petra placed her hand on the side of Charlie's face, lowered her mouth gently onto hers, and began a chain of delicate kisses, moving around her lips. Charlie responded by opening her mouth. They began to massage their tongues against each other. She began to pant tremulously, as Petra, also, felt herself becoming aroused. As the kissing continued, Petra's hand moved to Charlie's crotch, and her fingers began to gently explore, then slowly massage. The kissing became more passionate as the two women became more engrossed in each other. Petra moved across, and Charlie opened her legs, as she climbed onto her. Their two bodies slowly began to writhe against each other. Petra's mouth moved from Charlie's down to her neck, where she continued to kiss, then gently bite. As she felt Petra's mouth moving down to her chest, Charlie closed her eyes and panted nervously. She felt the kindly, playful kissing moving to her breast, where it continued teasing in a circle. Petra's tongue began to slowly lick Charlie's nipple, coaxing it to an erection, then she took it into her mouth, gently rubbing it with the roughness of her tongue. She moved across and repeated the action with the other breast. Charlie's hands gripped firmly onto the sheet as she felt Petra moving down the bed, and her mouth settling on her stomach. She tenderly kissed Charlie's navel, then moved lower, lying between her legs, her head placed between her thighs. Petra looked up and the two women made eye contact. Charlie's breath was trembling out of her mouth, and the only response she could muster to Petra's reassuring smile, was a whispered anticipation of, 'Oh, my God...' She felt as if it was a dream; it wasn't happening in real life, it was a beautiful, erotic fantasy. Then, as the top of Petra's head came into view, Charlie felt the opened mouth, settling onto her pubic mound. Her head slumped back onto the pillow as she felt Petra's mouth move lower, and the tip of her tongue beginning to gently lick.

'Oh, my God... oh, my God...'

***

The face of Jesus was gazing down at her as she woke. She felt no guilt, just a great sense of psychological and physical relief. She was warm, under the duvet and didn't want to get up.

'Petra...'

The door opened and she entered, now showered, and fully dressed. She smiled, as she looked down at Charlie.

'How long have I been asleep?'

'Forty minutes... Would you like a cop of tea and a slice of strudel?'

'Yes, please.'

As Petra prepared their snack, Charlie grimaced as she pulled on her briefs and felt them sticking to her oily crotch. Then she grinned mischievously; a small price to pay for such ecstasy. Fully dressed, she came out of the bedroom then sat on the sofa. For another thirty minutes the two women enjoyed their tea and apple strudel, as they chatted. There was no guilt, no recriminations. It was as if nothing had happened between them. Petra spoke enthusiastically, about her forthcoming date that evening, with Ste. Charlie told her how she was looking forward to her trip to Wales with Rick, the following day.

When the time came for Charlie to depart, Petra walked her to the door. They stopped and looked into each other's eyes.

'I want you to be happy with Rick. He is a good man. He will take care of you.'

'I know... and I want you to be happy with Ste.'

'Yes, so do I... I like him very much.'

'Goodbye, Petra...'

'Goodbye, Charlie...'

A moment, as they shared a knowing smile.

'Don't forget to buy an exercise book - before your next lesson.'

She cupped Petra's face in her hand, placed her lips onto her cheek and gave her an innocent kiss. She crossed the landing and walked down the stairs.

She reached the car, entered, and sat. She rested her head back on the headrest and closed her eyes. She heaved a great sigh. Her curiosity had been satisfied. The desire quenched. She had enjoyed every second, of what they had done to each other. She felt no guilt towards her actions.

The adolescent seed that was planted years ago, with her friend, Jenny, had now reached fruition, with Petra. It was finished. What she had done was completely normal. She felt no guilt until... thoughts of Rick entered her mind. She felt a sense of betrayal. How, on earth, could she ever tell him what she had just done? No, she couldn't... she wouldn't. She didn't want to risk losing him. *Yes* – she loved him. It was then, she thought that that was maybe the same reason he hadn't mentioned little Bobby. One rule for one, and one rule for another. She felt like a hypocrite. No, she could never tell him. Her bisexual curiosity was now in the past – and there, it would stay...

I hope... she thought, as she gazed through the windscreen. She began to think of Petra. Her stomach began to quiver, and the breath trembled out of her mouth.

Chapter 25

She started the engine, pulled the car out, into the road, and accelerated.

26

Sunday morning, ten o'clock, and Charlie's car pulled up outside Rick's cottage. She climbed out, lifted a large, sports bag out of the boot then walked up his sun-drenched path. It was a perfect biking day, and she couldn't wait to get back in tune with the road: the sights, the rush of the wind, the sheer exhilaration of a powerful motorbike. Dressed in his full biking gear, he opened the front door and greeted her with a kiss. In his bedroom she stripped down to her briefs then took from her bag, a pair of skin-tight, black-leather jeans. She pulled them on, and then a black T-shirt with NORTON emblazoned in gold and silver, across the chest. She finished off the look with a black-leather biker jacket and pair of biker boots.

'Have y'brought a skid-lid?' he shouted up the stairs.

'A what?'

'Have y'got a crash hat, cause, I've got one ere.'

'I've got one ere, an all – Van Gogh,' she shouted back, with a cheeky smile.

'Y'wha?'

'Nothing,' she shouted, as she pulled a black and silver crash helmet from her bag.

'*Whoa*,' he said, as he saw her, crash helmet in hand, come walking down the stairs.

As she reached the hall, he became serious. He took her face into his hands and pressed his lips onto hers, in a kiss that lasted two seconds. 'You look stunnin,' he said. 'What have I done, to deserve you?'

***

He opened the doors and entered, into the darkness of the garage. She stood in the sunlight, squinting, to see the bike. A powerful, muffled roar was followed by a quiet tick-over, then seconds later the beast slowly emerged from the shadows, into the sunshine. Charlie's jaw dropped open, as the sun caught its lustrous paint and sparkling chrome: a new Triumph Thunderbird. Her stomach flipped over with excitement. She couldn't wait to get her legs astride it.

'*A T-BIRD?*'

'Your steed awaits, madam. Would you care to wrap your legs around it?'

'The bike…?' she said, concealing a naughty grin.

'Hey,' he said, fastening his helmet, 'get your crash hat on, and let's be off.'

She shrieked with delight, feverishly threw on her helmet, then leapt onto the pillion with the excitement of a child jumping on a bouncy castle. Twenty minutes later, they were riding across the Runcorn-Widnes bridge, heading for north Wales. The miles flew by, and their first stop was the obligatory pause; the BikerBreak café, at the top of the Horseshoe Pass. After a short pause, and cup of tea, they rode down the Horseshoe into LLangollen, then onto the A5. The bike was swift, powerful, and smooth. She was impressed with Rick's riding style: fast, calculating, and sensible, not taking any risks or chances. He was obviously a rider of much experience. She felt sorry for him, knowing how great his love of motorbikes was, and here he is now, road-testing one for his mate.

'So, what's happened to you friend?' she said, as they rested in a layby, admiring the brooding majesty of Snowdon.

'He's broke his ankle. That's why he can't ride it...'

'And he's buying it?'

'Yeah - depending on what I say. D'you fancy a sixty-niner?'

'I'd rather have a Ninety-Niner...'

'*Oh, my God...*' he said, wishing the ground would open up and swallow him. 'That's what I meant.'

'I know,' she said, with an impish grin, leaving Rick feeling a right softy, as he walked toward the Mr Softee ice cream van.

Taking in the beauty of the Pen-y-Pass, they headed north towards Caernarfon, then along the coast road to Conway, where they arrived at 1.37, and were ready to hungrily devour their fish, chips, and mushy peas, washed down with a large, cardboard mug of tea, as they sat on a bench overlooking the picturesque harbour. Charlie felt that this had been one of the best weekends of her life. She couldn't of course, forget what had happened the previous day, with Petra, and still, if she thought about their liaison too much, she again became sexually aroused. But this trip with Rick, was proving to be a mixture of the things she *needed* in life, to help ease the memory of the horror from her past: a gloriously sunny day, an iconic powerful bike, the man she loved – and of course, fish, chips, and mushy peas with salt and vinegar, what's not to like? There was one point in her life after the disaster, where she'd convinced herself she'd never ride on another bike again, such was the debilitating effect his overbearing, bullying character had had on her gentle, submissive nature. But with his demise, she became determined to eradicate all influences of him from her life. And now with the passage of time, bringing new experiences, new friends, she felt it was beginning to, if not yet heal, then, at least, *dull* the hurt and anger that she once felt in her heart. And of course, there was new love, new hope, a new beginning. She was determined not to squander this opportunity. '*The most ridiculous thing I've ever heard in my life*' had turned into a triumph – in more ways than one. Having finished their feast, throwing the last few chips to the persistent seagulls (Herring gulls, as Rick had pointed out), they ambled, holding hands, to the end of the harbour.

'Did y'never fancy takin lessons... you know, passin your bike test, like...?'

'The thought did cross my mind, but... I'm just a woman. What do women know about mechanical things...? Well, you know, we're just: children, fashion, book clubs, aren't we?'

'Yeah... pity, you'd have liked it. It's never too late, y'know. I could teach yeh.'

'That would be nice...'

The following hour they spent exploring Conway castle. When the time came for them to depart. They walked back into the car park.

'Can I have a sit on it?'

'Which?'

'*The bike.*'

'Yeah, go on...'

She threw her leg over, then straddled the front seat.

'It's so confusing... all these switches and levers and things,' she said, sheepishly.

'It's straightforward enough,' he said, reassuringly. 'This lever is the clutch – just like on a car, but you pull it in, with your hand. That one down there, is the gear lever, and you operate it with your foot. And that one there, is the throttle – you twist it to go faster... That one, and that one, are the front and back brakes.'

'Oh, Rick, please, it's so intimidating.'

'Press that button. Y'can have a little go round the car park.'

She pressed the starter button and the bike roared into life.

'Will we be OK? Don't I need L-Plates, and things. I'm really scared.'

'It's OK, there's no cops about. Just a coupla minutes, then we'll go home.

She put her helmet on, he did also, then he climbed onto the pillion.

'Just don't go onto the road. Whatever you do, *do not* go onto the road... Now, first, pull the clutch in... that one, there...'

Before he had time to say anything else, she pulled in the clutch, kicked the gear lever into first, then, letting the clutch out gently, fed in the power, gradually twisting the throttle. The bike moved forward, slowly, but confidently.

'That's right, you're learning already.'

She gently rode the bike around the car park, making a big impression on him. Having completed one circuit, she began a second. As it was coming to an end,

'That was great,' she said. 'Can I have one more, little go...? Please... Teacher...'

'Oh, OK. One more, then we go home...'

She drove the bike around the car park, and as the circuit was coming to an end, lined it up with the exit.

'Don't go on the road...'

She aimed the bike towards the exit and gently accelerated.

'Don't go onto the road.'

She drove the bike out, onto the road, terrifying Rick, in the process.

'CHARLIE! STOP! FOR FUCK'S SAKE – FUCKIN' STOP!'

'HOLD TIGHT!' she shouted, as she twisted the throttle, then, with her movements smoothly, and perfectly, coordinated, wound the bike up. Rick's penny dropped.

'HAVE YOU BEEN PULLIN MY PLONKER?'

'NOT YET,' she shouted back in reply, and the two of them roared with laughter.

Minutes later, they were heading back into the heart of north Wales. Miles further along the A5, she turned off at Cerrig, to try it out cross-country, not noticing in the process that a speed cop had appeared from nowhere and was tailing her. She rung its neck, and it took off like a rocket. Lightning quick on the straights, when she came to the hairpins and S-bends she confidently threw the bike from side to side, taking them with undoubted skill. The speed cop was doing all he could to keep up with her, then, after a couple of miles, decided to pull her in. The blue light in her wing mirror caught her attention:

'SHIT, I'VE BEEN PULLED...'

Their hearts sank as the bike began to slow down, and

the speed cop gained on them. As he flagged her down, she pulled into the upcoming layby then turned off the engine. The copper pulled his BMW in behind her, got off and ambled slowly toward them. He approached her.

'Who do you think you are, mate, Rossi?'

Charlie and Rick removed their helmets.

'I'm sorry officer, was I going a bit fast...?'

'Can I see your licence?'

She rooted in her pocket, took it from her wallet and handed it to him. He looked at it: '*Class A*'. He handed it back to her, then gazed longingly at the bike.

'What do you think of it?'

'Handles like a dream.'

'How long have you been riding?'

'Since I was sixteen – coming up to ten years.'

'Yeah... it shows...'

'I was just teaching my boyfriend how to take bends,' she said, tongue-in-cheek, as she and the copper made eye contact, sharing a secret smile. The copper then turned to Rick.

'Can I have a quick word with you, mate...?'

He walked a few yards back, as Rick climbed off the bike, and followed him. Standing with his back to Charlie, the copper said, quietly, in awe,

'Rick, where did you meet her?'

'In work, why?'

'Can you get me one...? I've been looking for a woman like that, *all* me life.'

'Does Carol know?' said Rick, and the two men shared a quiet, blokey chuckle.

'Go on, enjoy your day,' said the copper.

'See y'Dick.'

'That's what you think.'

Rick climbed back onto the pillion.

'What did he say?' she asked.

'Just take it easy,' said Rick, as he turned and slyly waved goodbye, to his friend.

***

Later that evening they feasted on the contents of Rick's larder: beans on toast, followed by a bowl of Weetabix, each.

'You really must do something about your eating habits,' she scolded, mildly.

'I just eat what's there.'

'But that's it - there's hardly anything, ever there.'

'I had two bananas, until yesterday.'

She shook her head lovingly, as she realised he had to be taken in hand. The evening drew on, and after watching a video of Gladiator,

'I suppose you'll be goin home now, will yeh.'

'I don't have to... I can stay if you want me to?'

'What do *you* think?' he said.

***

They lay in bed, both naked. He seemed distant, pre-occupied.

'Are you OK?'

'Yeah. I'm fine...'

'What's the matter...?'

'Nothin...'

'What's wrong...?'

'Nothin… I'm OK.'

He turned, and put his arm around her, then began to kiss her gently on the lips. She began to breathe heavily. She returned his kisses, and they both became passionate. Against the side of her leg, she could feel the length of his erection. She turned to face him, and could feel its end, nudging its way into the gap of her thighs. She pressed herself against it, and his hand moved down to her crotch. He began to kiss her again.

'Come on… come on…' she said, gently.

He stopped kissing her and closed his eyes. Seconds later, he turned back onto the bed.

'Rick… What's wrong?'

'I love you…'

'And I love you.'

He paused then, 'I really do…'

'Prove it, then…make love to me…'

He heaved a tremulous sigh that was a mixture of guilt and trepidation.

'What's wrong…'

'I can't make love to yeh… it's not right… it wouldn't be fair…'

'What are you talking about…?'

There was a pause.

'Tell me what it is… I'll understand.'

Beware, your sins will find you out, crept through his mind.

He got out of bed, and walked out of the room, closing the door.

***

Chapter 26

'*RICK... YOUR BREAKFAST IS READY...*'

He opened his eyes. Was that a dream, or did he just hear a voice shouting his name?

'*COME ON, IT WILL GO COLD...*'

It *was* a voice, and it was coming from downstairs. It was Charlie's voice.

He didn't expect her to still be there. After last night, he thought she'd have packed him in, and buggered off home.

'*HURRY UP...*'

He leapt out of bed, threw on his boxers, dressing gown, and slippers, and headed for the stairs. Halfway down, a gush of golly surged into his mouth, as the tantalizing aroma of cooked food entered his nostrils. He walked into the living room, and over on his small table in the corner was a plate filled with, Cumberland sausages, a large, grilled tomato, fried eggs, beans, slices of back bacon, mushrooms, fried bread – there were other things as well, which he couldn't make out, because they were half-buried under the mini, *Mont Blanc* of food that Charlie had cooked for him.

'What's this?'

'What part of the word *breakfast*, didn't you understand?'

'Where did it come from?"

'Patel's, six o'clock, this morning. *Sit!*'

He sat.

'*Eat!*'

He began to tuck into one of the thick, hefty sausages. He couldn't get the stuff into his mouth quick enough. Through a jumble of chomping and slurping, he garbled, 'You shouldn't have bothered.'

'Really,' she replied, with an amused grin, 'that's not

the impression you're giving me.'

Twenty minutes later, the plate was empty, and he was knocking back the last mouthful of his tea.

'Why did you do that?'

'Why do you think?'

Once again, he became distant. Then,

'Thank you...'

'Thank you, for saying thank you.'

There was a pause, then he looked at the clock.

'We better get ready for work,' he said, quietly.

Charlie moved to the table and reached down to pick up his plate. As she did, he took hold of her wrist.

'What are you doing...?'

'I'll understand...'

'You'll understand, what...?'

'I just want you to know - *I'll understand*...'

'You'll understand *what*...?'

'If you go...'

He took a deep breath, then, eventually, after a pause,

'Little Bobby – Dot's son... he's mine... I'm his dad...'

A pause.

He looked up at her. Her heart was bursting with pride and admiration for him, but she kept it concealed, picking up his plate and mug, and saying nonchalantly, 'Would you like some more tea...?' She walked into the kitchen, then placed the plate and mug onto the worktop.

'You've only got three teabags left,' she shouted through. 'We'll have to get some more.' As she was filling the kettle, he appeared, in the doorway.

'Did y'not hear, what I said...?'

'Of course, I heard what you said, I'm not deaf...'

'Me... I'm Bobby's dad... he's my son... he's mine...'

'There was an offer on PG Tips, in Patel's. I should have bought some, while I was there,' she said, feigning mild self-annoyance.

He walked toward her, gazing at her as if she were an apparition. She turned, and their eyes met. She slowly moved to him, put her arms around his waist, then rested the side of her head on his chest. He wrapped his arms around her, hugged her tightly and placed his cheek onto her hair. He began to gently shake, as she felt his restrained sobbing.

'Shhh... It's OK... It doesn't matter... Thank you, for telling me...'

After a minute, he regained his composure. He cupped her face in his palms, and looked into her eyes.

'Thank you...' he whispered.

'Let's go back to bed,' she said.

'What about work...?'

'*Well,* if you'd rather spend the rest of the day at Nelson's, instead of with me...?'

'Don't you want to know about, how...'

'Shhh...' she said, pressing her fingertip onto his lips. 'The past is the past. All I want to know about is the here and now...'

She took hold of him by the fingertips then led him up the stairs. They lay in silence on the bed. She cuddled into him, and he kissed her on the top of her head. Five minutes passed, then he said, quietly,

'It's all gone...'

'Which...?'

'Everythin... the fear... the guilt... I thought I'd lose you, if you found out... I was so scared to tell you... I'd be punished for my mistake...'

'Rick…' she said, gently, 'how could such an adorable child be the result of a mistake…? He was meant to be… If you could turn the clock back, now, and be without him, would you…?'

'No.'

'Well, then…'

He looked into her eyes.

'I don't deserve you.'

'I don't deserve you,' she replied through a gentle smile.

She lay her head on his arm. He placed his other hand on the side of her face, leant across and kissed her, tenderly. She responded encouragingly, and they gradually became passionate.

***

They lay side by side in exhausted repose, eyes closed, breathing now beginning to regulate. He reached down, took hold of her hand, raised it to his mouth and kissed the back of it. She responded by gently stroking his bicep, with the back of her fingers.

'I love you…' she whispered.

'I love me, too.'

She punched him in the arm.

'*Ouch.*'

They spent the rest of the morning making love, drinking tea, making love, talking, making love, eating sausage butties, making love. As 1.30 approached,

'Don't forget, you've got to take the bike back.'

He paused, then,

'I'm not takin it back, I'm keepin it…'

'You can't keep it you'll have to take it back.'

'I'm keepin it.'

'Don't talk silly. That's theft.'

'It isn't...'

'What are you talking about...?'

'It's mine... I bought it on Saturday.'

A look of elation spread across her face, then it was tempered by a look of concern.

'How much was it...?'

'A lot,' he said, sheepishly.

'I thought you were broke.'

'It's on the drip... but I'll pay it off in full, in a few weeks, when I get me redundancy money. I'll have a couple of thousand left over. We can go on a little holiday.'

Her face drained as she went into a state of mild shock.

'Holiday...? You'll be penniless, with no job?'

'Yeah...'

'*Right*, we're taking it back – *now*. Get dressed.'

He became serious. She looked at him.

'What's the matter?'

He remained silent, then eventually,

'You can do a lot better than me, y'know... You're beautiful, classy, well-off... What do you see in me...? I'm a common or garden, workin class bloke. I've got no prospects, I'll have no job, I don't even own this cottage. All I'll have, will be the clothes I stand up in. What kind of future can I offer you...? Just treat me as your bit of rough then throw me away, when you've had your fill...'

'Is this a joke...? Rick... this *is* a joke – *right*?'

There was no reply. She glared at him, her eyes gradually beginning to bulge with anger and hurt,

'How dare you say that, to me... I love you... I want you for what you are, not what you've got. I want to spend the rest of my life with you. Or are you too stupid to see that...? Well?'

As he grappled with the dilemma of the massive, stupid mistake he'd just made,

'So, that's all I was?' she said. 'Just another fuck? Another notch on your headboard, who you can now throw away?'

Before he had time to reply,

'*Fuck you,*' she said, then jumped off the bed, and walked brusquely out of the room.

Stupid bastard... he thought, to himself. *I've completely balls'd it up. I should have just come clean and told her the truth, straight away.*

The bathroom door opened, and he entered. She was sitting on the lavatory seat, with her head in her hands. She looked at him, '*Go away...* go away, then... if you don't want me. Just cut the bullshit and fuck off. I'm going...' She stood. As she was about to pass him, he reached out and took her by her arms. Their eyes met.

'I've been crucified once already, Rick. That's enough. No-one will ever do it again.'

He looked into her eyes, 'I'm *so* sorry... You *really* do love me, don't yeh?'

'*FUCK OFF!*' she screamed.

'C'mon, let's go back to bed.'

'Why? Do you fancy another free fuck?'

'C'mon on... I'm sorry... I've made a right mess of this... I've got somethin t'tell yeh... Please, let me explain.'

'How many more children have you got?'

'None... let's just go back to bed, and I'll tell yeh... what I should've told yeh to start with...'

They walked back into the bedroom. Ten minutes later,

after she'd composed herself, and they'd got dressed, she was sitting with her back to the headboard, as he entered with two mugs of tea. He handed her one, then climbed on the bed next to her.

'Well...?' she said, curtly. 'What's the next load of bullshit, you're going to spout?'

He took a deep breath, 'Me visits, to the doctor... I wasn't going to the doctor's... I was going t'see a solicitor.'

'*Oh! God.* What have you done now? Murdered someone?'

'No.'

He paused.

'In the sixties... me granddad bought a little, second-hand van, an set up on his own, deliverin parcels for people...'

* * *

Three days before Charlie started work at *Nelson's*, Rick had attended the funeral of his granny. He was her only surviving relative. Over the decades, Rick's granddad had built his small, delivery service, into a large, heavy-haulage company. He'd also developed a talent for buying rundown properties, refurbishing them and selling them on, at a handsome profit each time. Then, there was the stock market, which his granny had the knack of dabbling in, accruing cash at an admirable rate, burning her fingers only a couple of times. From the day Rick was born, his grandparents doted on him, setting up a trust fund, to mature on his 30th birthday. After his granddad died, his granny kept the business going for a few years, eventually tiring of it. Then, when a large, nationwide chain of hauliers made a *serious* offer, she decided enough was enough and sold out - for a seven-figure sum. The upshot being, that, after the funeral, he received a letter from her solicitor asking him to go in to have a word. The content of her will was made known to Rick, and he was paralyzed with shock to discover that he was the sole beneficiary, inheriting her estate: a six-bedroomed, detached house in two acres, all the contents, plus her *Austin Maestro*, a huge amount of *FTSE 100* blue chip shares, together with a substantial amount of cash and further investments. Grand total of the inherited estate: £3.26 million. Plus, he was made aware of the trust fund, that was due to mature in two years' time.

***

Rick stopped talking, and Charlie eyed him, suspiciously.

'This isn't another load of your bollocks, is it? To stop me making you take the bike back?'

'No, honest... it's true... I couldn't believe it... I thought she was skint. She used t'go to all the dodgy supermarkets, buying cheapo, short-life food. Her clothes came from charity shops. I used t'buy her cardies and dresses and things, from *C&A*, because I wanted her t'look nice. She told me the business went bust years ago, her house was rented, an anything she had to leave, was going t'the cat's home.'

Charlie was silent, as the enormity of Rick's revelation sank in, then, 'So, that was the acid test, you set me...? To see if I really loved you...?'

He was too racked with guilt to answer.

'Was it not obvious...?' she said.

'Of course, it was, I'm sorry. Please don't go, I love you so much. You're the best

thing that's ever happened to me... apart from the *Thunderbird*, obviously.'

Their eyes met, each trying their utmost not to laugh.

Over the following minutes, as they sipped their tea, she gradually forgave him. Somehow, she managed to see through his jumbled, and somewhat naïve, logic, but issued a final warning:

'Rick... don't ever dare pull another stunt like that one? Do you hear...?'

He nodded.

'Because if you do, that's it. We're finished.'

'I'm sorry. I know it was stupid...'

She empathised with his obvious feeling of guilt, then proffered her final gesture of forgiveness, when she said, 'Well, the first thing you'll need to do, now that you're a millionaire, is...'

'Invest it?'

'No - get that bloody, wonky leg fixed, on your table.'

***

At approximately 3.20 that afternoon, the Thunderbird, being piloted by Charlie with Rick riding pillion, was slowly cruising down Lord Street, Southport, with her looking for somewhere to pull in. As she manoeuvred the bike into a parking space, then switched off the engine...

***

'Are you feeling OK, Joan?' said Petra.

'Yeah...' she replied, hesitantly.

'You are not looking very too well. I thing you must sit down.'

Joan walked into the kitchen area then sat on a stool.

'What's the matter?' said Lesley, concerned.

* * *

Dot was ambling down the alleyway, towards Hardcastle's domain. She didn't want to appear keen to sign away her job, livelihood, and many years loyalty to the firm. After weeks of *umming* and *ahhring*, weighing up the pros and cons, and more recently, talking it over with Ted she'd decided to do the evil deed, and accept her thirty pieces of silver. As she passed Zeta, pleasantries were exchanged (Zeta having been sworn to secrecy) she then walked into Hardcastle's office.

'Dot, take a seat,' he said, with a smile.

'Thanks, Bill.'

She sat, as he began laying out the various paperwork that needed to be read and indicating to her the positions where her signature was required. An atmosphere of tranquility descended onto the office. After all those years, it was finally coming to an end: their mutual hostility towards each other, the endless 'cat and mouse' shenanigans, the point-scoring off each other. A truce had been declared. Peace had broken out. Each one bore an inexplicable feeling of fond nostalgia toward the other. After a coffee which Hardcastle had livened up with a Scottish dram, clinking mugs in the process, it was time for the iniquitous deed to be carried out. A firm smile of admiration marched across Hardcastle's lips as he watched Dot reading the papers. As she reached the end, she picked up the pen.

'Where do I sign, Bill?'

'Two signatures - where the two small crosses are.'

As she was about to sign the form, the exterior door into Zeta's office burst open, and Petra, panic-stricken, ran in. *'Oh, my God,'* screamed Zeta. Dot and Hardcastle looked at each other, shocked, then Zeta came running into his office.

'DOT, MR HARDCASTLE – JOAN'S COLLAPSED'

Hardcastle sprang to his feet and ran through the door before Dot had chance to put the pen down. By the time she ran out into the alleyway, Hardcastle, Zeta and Petra had raced twenty yards towards the canteen. By the time Dot, gasping, ran through the rubber doors all Hell had broken loose, in the kitchen area. Dot ran in, and saw Hardcastle on his knees, supporting Joan's head.

'No... no...' Joan sobbed, almost incoherently.

Dot stood, trembling with shock, looking down at her sister.

'Lesley' shouted Hardcastle, 'get to security now. Get the gate open. Petra, open the concertina doors, wave them in as they approach. Carol, stand outside, make sure they see you... It's OK, sweetheart,' he said, to Joan, with tender affection, 'You're gonna be OK. Don't worry.' She screamed out with pain, as Dot's face contorted with emotion. Four minutes later the ambulance siren could be heard, as it raced down the main road then swerved into the car park. Lesley pointed the way to the paramedic, and she accelerated the ambulance without hesitation, then, confused by the industrial layout before her, she picked out Petra, frantically waving her through the concertina doors. She accelerated toward her, through the doors, then spotted Carol, standing outside the canteen doors, waving

her arms. A minute later, the two paramedics were in the kitchen assessing the situation. Four minutes more, and Joan accompanied by Dot, were in the back of the ambulance, as it raced out onto the main road, blue lights flashing, siren screeching.

27

'Charlie, have you met Jules…?'

Five innocuous words that were to have a devastating effect on her life. She wasn't supposed to be at the party, but she'd turned up, loaning some extra wine glasses to her older cousin, Rachel. He'd locked onto her, the second she walked through the door, '*Who's the cutie, carrying the box?*' The cutie carrying the box had inadvertently landed the biggest fish. Julian Osborne was quite a catch. Minutes before she'd entered the room there were three other women at the party, angling for his attention. All in their mid-thirties', assertive, successful professionals, they were exactly the kind of woman he had no interest in. He wasn't looking for a '*you're well-off, I'm well-off, let's hook up, get married, have an idyllic honeymoon in the Seychelles, then spend the rest of our lives discussing current affairs.*' No thanks. He was into the younger, slimmer, beautiful, impressionable type. The type that can after a period of suitable grooming, be made to bend over backwards, jump through hoops. Malleable. To be sucked in, used, abused, then spat out when she'd served her purpose. She was twenty-two, he was twelve years her senior. He kept always his cards close to his chest. His life was one of shifting sands, moving goalposts, always managing to stay one step ahead of the law, with his finger in many, dubious pies. He was divorced, drove a classic Bentley, owned a rambling, Edwardian farmhouse in fifty acres, and had a villa, on the Costa Del Sol. She had the knack of attracting run-of-the-mill, arrogant tossers, but could handle them, bat them into the long grass, but this one was in a different league. Cunning, heartless, patient, like a spider sitting in its web, waiting for its next victim to become entangled in its sticky secretions, he had time to spare. Time to set his trap and slowly, gradually, entice her into it. Softly, softly, catch a monkey. With gentlemanly grace and impeccable manners, he forgivingly insisted that she had just one drink before she left. How could she refuse, as their eyes met? He was tall, muscular, a sexy smile, streaked blond hair and piercing, blue eyes. As she sipped her Rioja, she mentioned it would be the last, as she was driving. The conversation then naturally, turned to cars.

'What do you drive?' he asked her.

'A Mini Cooper.'

'BMC?'

'BMW.'

'I have one of the originals, a Cooper S, actually.'

'You have an original Cooper S?' she said, greatly impressed.

'Yes, a '67. I keep it in the barn, with the others. Let's go outside.'

It was a warm, summer evening. The rays of the setting sun were filtering through the delicate branches of a silver birch, casting a dappled effect onto the table and chairs, where they sat. She'd now been well and truly hooked.

Having nonchalantly reeled off the classic sports cars he owned, with a completely non-bragging, brag, her eyes lit up. When she discovered that his collection also extended to classic motorbikes: Bonneville, Square Four, Jota, Gold Star, CBX, he continued reeling them off, she was in seventh Heaven, bikes being her first love.

'I ride a bike,' she said, with enthusiasm.

'A Raleigh Chopper?' he said with an appealing, mischievous grin.

'A Dominator,' she said, feigning annoyance, which melted into a forgiving smile.

'Ooh, a Dominator,' he said, raising his eyebrows. 'Would you like to dominate me?' his mischievous grin resurfacing.

'Maybe, maybe not. That's for me to know, and you to find out. Toodle-pip.'

She placed her empty glass down onto the table then stood. He swigged back the last mouthful of his wine, and stood, also.

'Can I walk you to the car?'

'If you wish.'

'As they reached the car, she opened the door, and turned.

'Well, it was nice meeting you, Jules.'

Without a word, he pulled her toward him, placing his lips onto hers. Her resistance lasted less than a second, then evaporated, as she tasted the passion of his kiss. As their faces parted, she opened her eyes. He was serious now.

'I do hope we'll meet again.'

She didn't know what to say, how to respond, other than with an involuntary, schoolgirl giggle.

'Goodnight, Jules,' she said, as she got into the car.

He leant down, 'Goodnight… you, beautiful woman,' he whispered, in a tone that sent a shiver down her back. She watched as he walked up the path. On reaching the front door, he turned and gave a polite wave. She waved back, then he entered the house.

'*Phew, my God…*' escaped from her lips.

After two seconds passed, she started the engine.

***

Within two weeks, they were a couple. Gradually, surreptitiously, he began to reel her in. He showered her with gifts, took her to see La Boheme, Swan Lake. She became infatuated. A month passed and he'd been introduced to her parents. Her mother was greatly impressed. A rich, erm… well, let's call him a businessman, for a son-in-law? That would impress family and friends. Her father was not convinced. He felt there was something that didn't seem right, didn't fit. But how could he speak out when before his eyes, he'd never seen his daughter as happy, complete. A month passed, and then it started… slowly… gradually. Firstly, it was her clothing. He bought her a navy blue, pleated mini skirt, that he asked her to wear, when they had sex. She laughed it off initially, but his insistence gradually chipped away at her resistance. The miniskirt was then followed by a pair of white ankle socks, then, a blue, school blouse. She could see where this was going, but couldn't build up the appetite for a confrontation, so went ahead: it was just simple, dressing-up fun, and if it made him happy, kept him quiet… He had her in the palm of his hand, and continued gently squeezing, moulding, manipulating. He persuaded her to grow her pubic hair. He didn't like the

California look. Wanted her to look tarty. After more pressurising, she gave in. Then, came the anal sex, which hurt her, but, if she truly loved him, she'd be prepared to do it, she'd get used to it, wouldn't she? Besides, he'd do anything for her, why shouldn't she reciprocate, if she *really* loved him? And all these incidents were interspersed with his built-in defence mechanism, crocodile tears,

'I am so sorry, I've hurt you. Please forgive me. I love you so much. I'll never do it again.' Until the next time.

He began to dissuade her from seeing friends, going out. She could only see the friends he allowed her to see. When she went out, he'd want to know where? When? Who with? What time did you get back? Why did you ignore my calls? Why are you treating me so callously, when I love you so much? Her mind was gradually becoming trampled, without her realizing it. Simultaneously, she was the envy of her friends. They understood why she was neglecting them, to be with the man she loved. Any one of them would have jumped at the chance to be the girlfriend of such a handsome, charming, not to mention rich, hunk. As the months passed, her studies at law college suffered. She couldn't concentrate on revision and her marks began to drop. She went into a downward spiral. The stress began to take effect, turning to anxiety, leading to her being prescribed *Valium*, and it didn't help when he said to her, on a regular basis:

'You really do need to lose some weight. God, you're getting so fat.'

She'd tried to resist his habit but, eventually she caved, and started to share his joints. Then, a couple of lines. When he hinted that they should try something harder – more exciting – which she vehemently refused to do, his reaction frightened her. He began screaming and swearing, eyes bulging. Threatening. As quickly as he blew up, he calmed down, and the apologies began to flood out, again. But she knew that once the seed had been planted in his mind, it would only be a matter of time before he acted upon it. She could now feel herself being drawn deeper and deeper into his depraved lifestyle. Panic would overtake her mind, as she tried to find a way out. She realised, she was now scared of him, sometimes terrified. But what could she do? She was too scared to stay and too scared to leave. She couldn't confide in anyone. She deeply regretted the day she met him. Why did she have to take those wine glasses? Why did she stay for a drink? Why didn't she just come straight out? And all the time, he'd be showering her with expensive gifts: a Patek Phillipe watch, a pair of Berry's diamond drops, a Loewe shoulder bag, then his Jekyll and Hyde character would emerge once more as he denigrated her with nasty, hurtful comments. The only time she came close to building up the courage to leave him, he surprised with a £2,000 solitaire.

'Put it on.'

'But we're not engaged.'

'I know we're not engaged but put it on anyway.'

Before she had chance to reply, he took it from the box, and pushed it onto her finger.

'There, that didn't hurt, did it?' he said, then laughed, maniacally.

She forced a smile not realising that he didn't buy it as a ring, but as a manacle.

The following night he told her that her sex had become boring. *'Same old, same old.'*

He wanted to try something new, different, a threesome.

He even suggested one of his friends, Derren. She was aghast. He wasn't joking, he *meant* it. That was it. She knew she had to get out of this. She refused point blank, hoping it would spur him to break off their relationship.

'No. I absolutely refuse. You can't make me do it. It's out of the question.'

Cunningly, he turned the tables on her. He burst out laughing and said, '*You thought I was serious.*'

She said, she had to go home, she wasn't feeling well. She'd see him Saturday evening. Then, she left.

***

Saturday evening, and she arrived at seven. They had a king prawn stir-fry with noodles, and by eight, had decided to watch a film. As she settled on the couch, and started to scan down the options, he went into the kitchen and returned with two large glasses of *Merlot*. They settled and began to watch the film. Thirty minutes later she began to lose it. She looked at him.

'Are you alright?'

'I... I... can't...'

She collapsed back, onto the couch. Still conscious but confused, as the disorientation took control of her mind, she felt herself being lifted from the couch, and carried up the stairs. After she felt herself being flung roughly, onto the bed, she felt fingers beginning to undo the buttons of her blouse. She closed her eyes and sank into oblivion.

***

Her face was buried in the pillow, when she woke. She was

dressed in a schoolgirl uniform, spread-eagled, face down on the bed. Completely helpless, with no feeling in any of her limbs, she could hear him panting behind her, feel his rhythmic thrusting, as he penetrated her, anally. As she managed to turn her head to one side. Her confused mind could not comprehend what she was seeing. He was sitting on a chair next to the bed, holding a video camera, while filming her being raped. Another one of his sordid business ventures that added greatly to the coffers: internet porn.

'No...', she managed to mumble, almost incoherently, 'no...'

He leaned over and glared into her eyes, as he said, 'I wanted this, and you refused me. You said, I couldn't make you do it. You were wrong... You will do exactly what I tell you to do. Because, if you don't, I'll ruin your life to such an extent, that you'll wish you were dead.' Then, he looked at Derren and said, coldly, without feeling, 'punish the bitch.'

* * *

'Rise and shine. Come on, darling, wakey, wakey.'

He threw back the curtains and sunlight flooded into the bedroom.

'How are you, this morning. Feeling any better? I must admit, I was a bit concerned last night, when you passed out on me, but you seemed OK when you stood up and went to bed early. So, I left you to it, didn't want to disturb you. You cried out during the night. I think you had a bad dream.'

She lay in a daze, staring blankly toward the ceiling.

A pause.

'What happened...?' she said, slurring her words.

'I think it was probably the effect of the wine on your tablets. How do you feel now, OK?' Silence, then, 'Here, I've brought you a nice breakfast, scrambled eggs, with smoked salmon and asparagus, and a Buck's Fizz. Let's get you fed and watered.'

'I can't remember anything. What's happened to me...?' She sounded drunk.

'We can stroll down to the pub at lunchtime.'

'I need to shower,' she said, eventually.

'I'll go and put the kettle on. I've got some new coffee I'd like us to try.'

She heard him stomping down the stairs as she stared at the food. She tried to brush her hair from her forehead and as she did, her hand fell limply to her side. She leaned back onto the pillow and closed her eyes. She tried to make sense of what had happened, but her mind was a complete blank. All she knew was that something was seriously wrong. Then the realisation began to penetrate her mind, from the pain that lingered. She began to breathe deeply, getting as much oxygen into her lungs as she could. Minutes passed then she heard him coming back up the stairs. He entered.

'I think you're right, that wine was strong,' she managed to force out.

'Fourteen percent.'

'I'll survive... But I'll give the pub a miss, if you don't mind, darling... I need to go home and do... a few things.' Her wording was strained and still out of kilter, but she was managing to string sentences together more coherently, now.

'Don't be driving, the state you're in.'

'No... I won't go just yet... I'll hang on for an hour...

I'm sorry, I can't touch this food. Could you please, bring me a strong, black coffee.'

'Of course, I can, sweetheart.'

He moved over to the bed, bent down, and pecked her on the lips.

'Love you.'

'Love you, too,' she said, then forced a smile.

**

The Mini pulled onto the drive. She entered the house then made her way to her room, picked up her laptop, sat on the bed, and switched it on. She typed into the search engine:

R O H Y P N O L

**

The following Saturday evening, she arrived at 7.06, carrying two Waitrose bags, in one: chestnut mushrooms, mange touts, baby sweetcorn, piccolo tomatoes, a pack of mixed salad, and a long, thick cucumber. The other bag contained a bottle of Pinot Noir, a packet of long-grain rice, and two, large, frying steaks.

'What's all this?' he said, genuinely pleased.

'I want to give you a special thank you, for the way you looked after me, last Saturday.'

'I'll give you a hand.'

'*You will not.* You're going to sit down, with a large glass, and I'm going to wait on you hand and foot.'

'But...'

'*Sit.*'

As pleased as Punch, he sat in the living room, flicking

through a copy of Autocar. Two minutes later, she appeared with a large glass of red.

'Be about thirty minutes,' she said, with a smile, handing him the glass, then she returned to the kitchen. He took a mouthful of the wine then began to read about the latest version of the Range Rover. Twenty-two minutes later, she was laying the plates of food onto the dining table. She returned with the wine and filled his empty glass. '*Cheers.*' She sipped her orange juice. 'I'll have half a glass of wine, later.'

'I must say,' he said, 'this steak looks... partic... ly...'

'Yes, darling...? You were saying...?'

'Thi... stay... lo...'

He looked at her through glazed eyes, as she smiled back. The last word he heard her say, before he hit the floor, was '*Touche!*'

Nonchalantly, as he lay spread-eagled on the carpet, she continued to enjoy her meal, until every last delicious morsel had been consumed. A minute later his phone received a text. She checked it. It was from Derren.

is she ther yet

She replied **not come. sick**

sick of havin sore arsehole LOL

She replied **BIG LOLS**

***

The following morning, he woke, lying in front of the fireplace, where she'd left him.

His hands were tied behind his back, with his knees and ankles also tied. A large dildo had been secured into his mouth with Gaffer tape. He was naked except for a pair of white, schoolgirl knickers pulled onto his head, a school tie around his neck, and wearing a pair of grey, over the knee socks. Next to him on the rug, was the mangled remains of the solitaire, her having bashed it bent, with the hammer. There was an excruciating pain coming from his rectum. Eventually, after much effort, and repeated fallings over, he managed to struggle to his feet and gradually, with a series of intermittent, agonising, bunny hops, reached the full-length hall mirror. Looking at his reflection, he wiggled around, to see what was causing the rectal pain. Six inches of the thick, twelve-inch cucumber, were poking out of his blood-stained arsehole. Later in the day he received an image on his phone: him, face down, spread-eagled on the carpet, cucumber sticking out, message:

It's rude to point. BIG LOLS ☺!!!

***

Monday morning, eight o'clock, happily married, father of two toddlers, Derren Watt, crunched his way across the gravel drive of his large detached. As he proudly approached his brand new, proceed of crime: a silver BMW X5, it seemed different, somehow. When he drew closer, he could see what it was. Someone had been around it during the night and covered it in paint stripper. It was down to the bare metal. As his jaw dropped open, and he began to tremble with shock, he saw a note, under the driver's windscreen wiper. He picked it up and read it,

HAVE A HAPPY DAY – BUM FUCKER – BIG LOLS
☺!!!

28

Tuesday morning saw Charlie rushing from the car park. This was going to be the first day she'd been late since she started working there. She almost sprinted to the clock, grabbed her card and fluffed shoving it into the slot: 8.00. Just as she pushed it down: 8.01.

She entered the area then began to put on her overall. Dot appeared from nowhere, with a face like thunder.

'Where were you, yisterday?'

Puzzled by Dot's hostility, she answered, 'I wasn't feeling well.'

'What a coincidence,' said Dot, with sharp sarcasm, 'neither was Rick.'

'Dot... is something wrong?'

'You're fuckin right, there's something wrong,' she replied, emotionally. 'Joan's lost the baby. You'd have known, if you'd been here.'

Before Charlie had a chance to react, Dot stormed off, down the alleyway.

She stood, one arm in the sleeve of her overall. Her breathing heavy with disbelief, she slowly pushed her other arm into its sleeve. As she sat on her work stool, gazing down at her bench, Rick, full of the joys of Spring, approached.

'Have you heard the news?' he said, with delight.

'I've just found out,' she said, trance-like.

'I thought you'd be happy.'

'What are you talking about – happy?'

'Ste... y'know. He's asked Petra to marry him. She said, yes. They've only known each other five days. Talk about a whirlwind romance – love at first sight.' She looked at him, 'Joan's lost the baby.'

***

The terrible news sent shock waves around the factory. Even people who weren't that keen on Joan (not many) had nothing but unadulterated sympathy; how could fate deal such a cruel blow twice, to the same person?

She lay back on the hospital bed of her side ward, sedated, eyes closed, tears trickling down each side of her face. Her world had collapsed. The only way she could find any solace from the tragedy was to keep drumming it into her mind, over and over, that her baby had gone to join its brother, and they'd be happy together. A simplistic thought, but one which was desperately needed, to keep her from screaming out with deranged grief. Dot was the first to visit. There was nothing she could think of to say to her sister. '*How do you feel?*' would sound stupid in the circumstances. Likewise, she didn't take in any chocolate, flowers, bottle of Lucozade, they all sank into the abyss of cliched visitor banality. She just took herself, to be there for her, at the lowest point of her life. She sat at the side of the bed, clutching Joan's hand, periodically giving a gentle, reassuring squeeze of sympathy. Reaching across, she wiped away Joan's tears from her face, when they became too much. When visiting time was over the nurses and ward staff turned a blind eye, in asking Dot to leave. Only when her family commitments called her away did she reluctantly go.

Over the three days Joan was in hospital, she had a succession of visitors. Charlie went with Rick, there was Hardcastle and Zeta. The second day her girls from the canteen had arrived with a huge and beautiful flower arrangement, that raised a feint semblance of a smile from her. But, however kind their intentions, she wasn't up to being the centre of attention. She just wanted to pull the bedclothes over her head and say goodbye to the world. After her girls had left, she had the flowers removed, and sent to the geriatric ward, their presence being a constant, flamboyant reminder of her grief, past and present. On the afternoon of the third day, her husband came to visit. John was devastated for her. Already having shared the heartbreak of losing a child, it was almost unimaginable for him to comprehend how she must be feeling now. His words were soft, gentle, and reassuring. She appreciated them very much. She knew that he, above everyone else, was the one person who could speak from the heart, with empathy gained from experience. When he stood to leave, he looked down into her eyes.

'Oh, I forgot,' he said, taking a Bounty bar from his pocket and handing it to her.

'I was going to get you a big box of Thornton's Continental, but then, I thought *Nah*, she'd prefer her favourite.' She smiled back and said, 'Thanks, for comin.' He reached down and kissed her on the forehead.

* * *

When Joan was discharged, Dot collected her from the hospital and took her home. After an hour of stilted talk, over a mug of tea and a box of Jaffa Cakes, Dot went home, leaving her sister to the cold silence of the house.

She walked upstairs, then into the spare room that she'd decorated as a nursery. She stroked the teddy bear curtains then picked up the lemon romper suit, out of the cot. She buried her face into it. She had no tears left to cry. She then continued into her bedroom and lay on the bed. Her mind began to ramble. Thinking... thinking... trying to understand why she'd never been able to find a lasting happiness, in her life. There was always something to derail it. She cast her mind back. Even as a child her innocence robbed from her, between the ages of seven and ten, being gradually groomed, then regularly encouraged to perform oral sex, on babysitting *dear* Uncle Harry, as Dot slept in the next bed. Then, there was the unmerciful hell she'd endured in secondary school, at the hands of the bullies, as her cries for help were answered with *just fight back*. Easier said than done. And, as a young woman, the breast cancer that took away her completeness. Then she met John, and they fell in love, got married. Planning their lifetime together, which culminated in their aborted emigration to Australia. But then, her happiness scaled the heights again, when along came Thomas. Her life was fulfilled, but for just two years. Until it fell apart again, with the loss of her beloved child. And now, her last hope of becoming a mother again had gone. The more she thought about it, the more it became obvious; she was never *meant* to find happiness. That was her life's plan from

God - to suffer. No matter how long she lived, that was how it was always going to be. She couldn't think of the great sin she'd committed in life, that warranted her to be punished in this way but, obviously, she'd done something wrong that had garnered God's wrath. So, the best way to go would be to resign herself to the fact that this was how the rest of her life was to be. It would be better if she never thought in terms of finding happiness, never thought positive thoughts, positive thoughts are for dreamers. Think negative, then you'll never be disappointed. She looked at the ceiling... she looked at the ceiling... she looked at the ceiling... It moved... It slowly, began to descend... Closer and closer, slowly and gradually... closer and closer... as it approached, a darkness began to envelope her mind... she closed her eyes, and heard a child's voice, whispering in her mind, '*Mummy... mummy... why did you leave me, mummy...? Why did you let me die...?*'

* * *

Friday afternoon, and Dot was driving to Joan's house. Charlie was following in her car.

They turned into the street and managed to find a couple of spaces between the lined-up wheelie bins, the binmen moving to and froe like busy ants, to the back of the bin lorry. As they approached Joan's house, Dot took out her key and pushed it in the keyhole. She tried to turn it but it wouldn't budge.

'She's left the snip on by mistake.'

She bent down, shoved the letter flap open and shouted through.

'*Joan, it's me...*'

No reply.

'Joan...! She's probably in the kitchen.'

She looked through the letterbox, and saw Joan, standing on the stairs landing. She began to climb over the bannister. It was at that point that Dot noticed the rope, around her neck. Joan stepped forward and dropped toward the hall.

'OH, MY GOD! OH, MY GOD! – NO.'

Charlie's stomach turned over with shock.

'What's the matter?'

'GET THE DOOR OPEN. GET THE DOOR OPEN, QUICK. SHE'S HUNG HERSELF.

GET THE FUCKIN DOOR OPEN.'

Dot turned and screamed at the binmen. They came running across the street as Charlie looked though the letter box to see Joan, jerking and kicking, as she hung by a rope, from the landing banister. Dot was screaming hysterically as the two binmen pushed Charlie out of the way and began to hammer and kick at the door. One of them smashed the glass, reached in and turned the snip off. They turned the key and pushed again but it wouldn't open.

'The bolts are on.'

Charlie immediately shouted at Dot, 'Call an ambulance.'

'How are we gonna get the door open?'

'CALL AN AMBULANCE, NOW!'

As Dot started to punch 999 into her phone, Charlie rushed to one of the wheelie bins and flipped its lid open. It was empty. She pulled it to the window and swung it to shoulder-height, then drew it back and threw it with all her might, at Joan's parlour window. The bin shot forward like a huge javelin, crashing through the glass, leaving a large hole, surrounded by jagged slivers. Charlie ran to the middle of the street, lined herself up with the gaping hole, then raced forward. As she reached the window, she launched herself like a dart, went flying through the frame and into Joan's house. She landed in the broken glass, sprang to her feet, and raced into the hall. She ran to the door, released the bolts, and by the time Dot and the binmen rushed in, she'd grabbed Joan around the legs and was taking her weight.

'*Help me,*' she shouted to the binmen. They ran to her aid, lifting Joan around the legs.

'*Dot, get a knife from the kitchen. Cut the rope,*' shrieked Charlie.

With the rope cut, they eased Joan down, onto the carpet.

'She's not breathing,' said one of the binmen, tactlessly.

Dot was trembling with shock. Charlie slipped the noose of Joan's neck and started giving her mouth to mouth.

'Charlie, don't let her die, please don't let her die,' uttered Dot, through a trembling mouthful of sobs. Charlie continued with mouth to mouth and heart massage. Four minutes later the shriek of an ambulance siren could be heard approaching, from down the street.

* * *

A week passed.

Joan's mental health was then assessed, and the joint decision was taken that she needed extra specialist care. She was transferred out of the general hospital to an Acute ward, in the annexe. She then spent another ten weeks in the Psychiatric Intensive Care Unit. John came to see her every day. Slowly, gradually, as the weeks passed by, the healing process began.

For the first time in months, she felt a shred of happiness moving gently back into her life, when she was transferred to a rehabilitation ward. She made good progress, surrounded, and supported by the love and affection she received, from what seemed like a never-ending series of visits from her friends, family, and workmates. And there was less supervision there. She was no longer locked in and had access to the garden area where she found pleasure in the simple beauty of everyday things, like the gentle, unrushed melody of a blackbird's song, or watching a peacock butterfly sunning its wings. Like the time she sat on the garden bench, closed her eyes and leant her head back, taking the warmth of the sun on her face, the moment of inner contemplation only to be interrupted when she felt a light tickle on the back of her hand. She opened her eyes, to see a ladybird walking toward her wrist. 'Hello, little one,' she whispered to it, then she smiled, as it opened its wing cases and took flight. There were more activities in the rehabilitation ward to keep the patients occupied, and the staff were like friends rather than nurses. One nurse in particular, Adele, had developed an uncanny knack of making Joan laugh. Sometimes unintentionally, mostly with surreptitious intent. They shared the same sense of anarchic humour and were both past masters of the art of self-deprecation. Gradually, Joan began to come out of her shell, as the shared humour flowed between the two women, and a genuine friendship began to develop between them. The band of two grew to three, when *Filipino* nurse Jasmine joined in the great conspiracy, whereby the plan was hatched to smuggle Joan out of the place in a laundry basket. Much hilarity then ensued as the dastardly trio's great escape, vocal shenanigans escalated to the point where Joan, as usual, ended up with a damp gusset. And with the passing of each smile, each laugh, each blackbird's song, and guided imperceptibly back to health by the unstinting devotion, and skill, of the doctors and nurses, Joan's day of discharge finally arrived. A glaze of tears covered her eyes as she said goodbye to her dear friends, Adele, and Jasmine, whose suggestion that the three met up again at some point in the future, was met with a facetiously withering, *'frankly, my dear, I don't give a damn,'* from Adele. During this touching departure, Dot had been waiting a few yards away, diplomatically allowing her sister to say her goodbyes. Joan turned and approached Dot, and the two made their way out, into the car park. After a couple of miles of stilted conversation, there was a pause then, Joan said, quietly, 'Can y'take me to the cemetery before we go home...?'

'Of course, I can,' replied Dot, and she turned the car around, and began driving in the opposite direction.

'Thanks...'

* * *

The sky was covered in a threatening blanket of angry, grey cloud, as the *Astra* drove through the opened cemetery gates, and headed for a parking spot. The two women got out of the car, then wended their way through the various rows of drunken gravestones, as they headed toward the area where Thomas was buried. Dot stood a couple of feet behind Joan, who stood in silence, gazing down at her son's grave. Dot, realising that she was unintentionally intruding upon Joan's privacy, said quietly, 'I'll wait in the car,' then, she walked back. There was a distant growl of thunder, and Joan felt a spot of rain on her cheek. As she looked at her son's headstone, there were no tears from her. The words came into her mind and she silently spoke to him. She promised him that she would never again attempt to take her own life. The growling of the thunder became juxtaposed with the laughter of children – playing on the opposite side of the perimeter hedge. Another couple of raindrops landed on Joan's face, as the impending downpour began to show itself in earnest. She crossed herself and was about to turn away when she looked at the sad, decayed remains of the two wreaths that she and John had placed on the grave, on Thomas's birthday. She picked them up, then, with a final glance, she whispered, 'Bye, bye sweetheart...' She disposed of the wreaths on her way back to the car, where Dot was patiently waiting for her. The two sisters sat in silence for a few seconds, then Dot said, 'From now on, I'm not lettin you out of me sight. I'm gonna watch y'like a hawk.' As their eyes met, Joan replied, with the hint of a sympathetic smile, 'Don't y'think you've got enough people to look after.' 'No!' came Dot's feigned, curt reply, then she turned the ignition key, and the engine churned over lazily, without managing to start. 'Oh! God. Don't tell me. Not again!' said Dot, in exasperation. Then, she turned the key once more, and the engine repeated its lethargic overture – a million miles from sparking the engine into life. 'This bleedin battery's got me deranged,' Dot said, with a frustrated gasp, that was the cause of Joan's smile becoming more obvious. 'Why don't you buy a new one, then?' she said, feigning innocence. 'They're only about a hundred quid.' Their Laurel and Hardy double act was surreptitiously beginning to bubble under, and about to destroy the solemnity of the occasion. 'I'll try, once more,' said Dot, and as she turned the key, the engine churned over once again, this time getting slower and slower, as the battery entered its death throes, which was highly appropriate, seeing as they were parked in a cemetery. *'Come on, you bastard, start up!'* said Dot, through a growl, as Joan began biting her bottom lip, to curtail a guffaw. 'Do us a favour, will yeh,' said Dot, through clenched teeth, to her sister, have a scout round, an see if y'can find an open grave, I can throw me fuckin self into...' 'Cut out the middleman,' came Joan's lightning reply, which garnered a much-needed smile from Dot. The smile lasted approximately three seconds before the battery gave up the ghost, and finally died.

'Jesus wept!' said Dot, with a final, frustrated exhalation.

'He'd weep if he lived in your bleedin house,' replied Joan.

Dot turned and looked at her sister. Their faces simultaneously began to distort as they tried, in vain, to maintain a dignified silence more suited to the surroundings, then, with unadulterated delight, the two of them burst into shrieks of hysterical laughter. It was just what Joan needed, and, to a lesser extent, Dot.

***

Joan's circumstances put Dot's situation into vivid focus. For all her troubles, financial or otherwise, the fact was seared into her mind that, compared to her sister, she didn't have a lot to complain about. Her growing love for Ted, which was being reciprocated, had had a transformative effect on her life. Then it began to dawn on her that despite her ongoing borderline poverty, she always, somehow, by hook or by crook, managed to put food on the table, and pay her bills, if not on time, at least they'd eventually get paid. The more she thought about it, the more she wondered what would be the eventual outcome of accepting her thirty pieces of silver? She'd have no money worries, she could afford to buy any food she wanted, all the bills would be paid up, she could buy a decent car. But what about her new job prospects? Pushing forty-one, with no qualifications. Kaykay had no suitable vacancy for her. Employers wouldn't exactly be beating a path to her door, to shower her with job offers. The last thing she wanted to do was to be living on benefits. How could she turn her back on her years-long service to the union and her workmates? How could she betray the legacy and family heritage passed onto her by dear Uncle Harry? And in two years' time, when the money had run out, and all her accompanying accoutrements of *'wealth'* had evaporated? Back to square one – but with no job. benefits beckoning. She had to think this one out, carefully. Maybe it still wasn't too late, to apply to the RSC. *Yeah – right!*

29

The waiting room was L-shaped, the short arm of the L being semi-occupied by several late middle-age to elderly men, invariably accompanied by their wives. The couples sat in silence, staring zombie-like, at the wall-mounted television, where a BBC newsreader was dishing out the daily woes of the world. The volume was just about audible, but nobody had the nous, or courage, to ask if it could be increased. The long arm of the L, which contained the entrance door, consisted of two rows of chairs facing each other. The walls of both arms of the room were dotted haphazardly with information posters that nobody ever read. In a corner stood a wire carousel containing information leaflets that nobody ever took. In the long section there was one man sitting down at the far end, near the full-length window, engrossed in his book. Near the apex of the waiting room was the reception desk, next to the double doors that led into a corridor that contained small, administration and consulting, rooms leading off on either side.

It was his favourite book: Treasure Island, by Robert Louis Stevenson. He'd read it numerous times over the course of his life. He first became enthralled at the age of nine, as a newly joined member of the local library. Treasure maps, the Hispaniola, Long-John Silver and, of course, young Jim Hawkins, who he immediately identified with, all took root in the imagination of this young lad, to such an extent that he promised himself when he grew up, he'd become a pirate, sailing the seven seas, plundering Spanish galleons for gold doubloons. He

ended up being a bricklayer.

'*Mister Currie...*' said the urology nurse, to nobody, as she held the corridor door open. Ted raised his head, and they exchanged smiles of recognition. She led him a short distance down the corridor, then guided him into the consulting room, where sat Mister Luff.

After pleasantries were exchanged between the two men,

'Well, Mister Currie,' said Mister Luff, 'leading on from your biopsy, I have to tell you, that we *did* find the existence of cancer cells. The nine samples that we took however, from the left, right and centre of your prostate revealed the cells were only present in the left and centre sections. And these are presently at such a stage that you are classed as intermediate risk...'

Ted sat, intently listening, matter-of-factly. There was no panic, no tears, no *Why me, God?* As the meeting came to an end, he was assured by Mister Luff, that the cancer would be monitored at regular intervals, the purpose of which was to ascertain if, there was any proliferation of the cancer cells, which would elevate the situation the next, *high risk*, level.

* * *

Toby approached, on the cadge for a walk, as Ted sipped his coffee. He reached down and rubbed the dog's head. Kenny chirped, then carried on preening his feathers.

'Eee...' he said, quietly, 'Toby, lad - what next, now...? Eh...?'

The reason for his consternation, being his inability to decide which course of action would be the best to take. OK, it's cancer – shit happens. He wasn't the first, and he wouldn't be the last, to receive a diagnosis of the *Big C* but, more than anything, it was Dot he was thinking about. Should he tell her the news...? What should he tell her...? How much should he tell her...?

He'd been assured by Mister Luff, that prostate cancer is a slow growing one, and, as in this case, if an early diagnosis is made, before any serious progression has taken place, it could be managed, sometimes even stopped in its tracks. All well and good – but, what if it did progress? How could he hide that from Dot? She didn't deserve to be kept in the dark, on such a serious matter, but on the other hand, how could he risk destroying their current state of happiness? And, having told her, how would she react? He began to wonder about her loyalty. Would she be prepared to carry on in a relationship with someone who had cancer, or would she finish with him? He became racked with guilt. He didn't want to lose Dot, but what if this bastard of a disease didn't halt its progression? What if he did become high risk? How long could he keep her from discovering the situation? And having discovered the truth, how would she react to his deviousness, in keeping it from her? How could he hide the series of treatments that were forthcoming? His mind became a labyrinth of questions. The more he tried to come up with a solution to the situation, the more confused he found himself becoming. If only he could wipe the slate clean – turn the clock back, start again, from day one. The notion began to take root in his mind and provide a glimmer of hope. That was it. He decided to finish with Dot – out of the blue. Leave things for a week to cool off, then contact her back. Meet up with her and tell her what had happened. She would then be free to choose, whether to take him back, or not. The ball would be in her court. She'd be the one making the final decision, and his conscience would be clear.

'Right, Toby, lad, that's it...' he said, quietly. 'That's the answer... That's what we'll do.'

30

How are the mighty fallen!

Such a case in question was that of Julian James Osborne. His life of excess having spiralled out of control, driven by his inevitable addictions to hard drugs and alcohol, finally culminating in his depraved descent into self-inflicted oblivion. All in the name of perverted, spite-filled revenge.

***

'Woodlands' was an Edwardian, half-mock Tudor, seven-bedroom detached, set in extensive, landscaped gardens. Located on the outskirts of Ulverston, her granny and grandad had bought the house fifty-odd years ago. It had served its purpose well, and, after their brood had been born, raised, and eventually flown the nest, they resisted calls to downsize. How could they? The house had played a substantial role their lives. It was part of them, and they were part of it.

Charlie had driven up to Cumbria to visit her grandparents and spend a few days of peace and quiet with them, combining some fell-walking with revision for yet another exam, on her way to a post-graduate, law degree. Throughout the previous week she hadn't been feeling well, as if something was building up inside her. Intermittent bouts of mild anxiety, together with occasions of breathlessness, and feeling dizzy, she'd put down to the dread of the inescapable exam, that was looming. She was wrong. It was the indelible ghosts of her past returning once again to cast their shadows, over her fragile mind. After an invigorating walk to the top of Coniston Old Man and back, she was sitting at the desk, in *her* bedroom. '*God! Why do I want to be a solicitor?* She loved children. What she really wanted to do was be a primary school teacher, but – no. Best not to let the side down. Don't rock the boat. Best to spend the rest of her life in misery, wondering *What if?* Her head began to swim as she, yet again, began to revise the four elements of tort law. Robotically, her eyes scanned the wording on the page, but nothing was being absorbed. The breath began to tremble, nervously, from her mouth. She closed her eyes and rested her head in her palms. *I need a glass of water.* As her breathing grew heavier, she opened her eyes and looked down at the pages. The words were jumbled, the sentences running into each other. She placed her head onto her fingertips and began to tremble. Her mouth began to quiver, and her eyes overflowed with tears, which dripped onto the book. She felt a sob about to rise in her throat, as, through the windowpane, a car engine began to rev. Muffled at first, but the revving became louder, intrusive. She heard a voice shouting. A man's voice. The revving combined with the shouting, to make it impossible for her to ignore. Almost relieved at the intrusion, she rose to her feet and made her way to the window. As she looked down into the avenue, her stomach knotted with fear. She began to tremble, it was *him*. Sitting in the big Healey convertible. As his eyes caught sight of her at the window, he floored the accelerator and began shouting.

'WHORE... FUCKING WHORE... BURN IN HELL,
YOU CUNT.'

She began to tremble as she looked down at him, his eyes bulging, face maniacally distorted by a cocktail of drugs and alcohol.

'YOU KILLED ME... YOU KILLED ME... YOU,
FUCKING TWAT...
HAVE THAT ON YOUR CONSCIENCE FOR THE
REST OF YOUR LIFE.'

Frozen with fear, she found it impossible to turn away, as he threw open the door of the car and leapt out onto the pavement. As the stream of obscenities continued, he reached into his pocket and pulled out a *Stanley* knife. Trapped like a rabbit in the glare of headlights, she felt her stomach beginning to tremble, then her body beginning to quake. He roared once again with maniacal laughter, as his clenched fist sprang up towards his neck, then with one, swift slash of the knife, the razor-like blade severed his jugular vein, immediately sending a fountain of blood spurting three feet in front of him. She became hysterical, as she watched the life draining from him. He fell back onto the car then slumped down the side of it and into the rapidly expanding pool of blood, that was surrounding him. She continued trembling and screaming, as she watched his kicking and thrashing body gradually come to a halt, then he finally sank into death. She collapsed, onto her knees, not being able to comprehend the horror she'd just witnessed. She started to pant heavily, as panic gripped her stomach, like a vice. Her body began to shake violently, and her eyes bulged in terror, as his words stampeded over, and over, through her mind,

'WHORE... FUCKING WHORE... BURN IN HELL, YOU CUNT.'

The room began to spin, rapidly, *rapidly*. She couldn't focus, *she couldn't focus*. She closed her eyes and plunged her face into her hands, digging her nails into her forehead as she screamed,

'No... no... dear God, no...'

Tears drenched her face, then she sobbed, and began to screech and wail uncontrollably, like a tortured animal, as once again his words raped her mind,

'YOU KILLED ME... YOU KILLED ME... YOU, FUCKING TWAT...
HAVE THAT ON YOUR CONSCIENCE FOR THE REST OF YOUR LIFE.
YOU KILLED ME... YOU KILLED ME.'

She started banging her clenched fists against the wall, as she continued screaming. Shock took over, and her body began to shake, violently. She slumped to her knees, then forward onto the carpet. Rolling onto her side, she curled into a foetal position, and carried on wailing and screaming. A cloud of darkness enveloped her mind, as she sank into the abyss of unconsciousness.

31

It was a crisp, October Sunday morning, eleven o'clock, three months after Joan's discharge from hospital. John and Joan, with Ted and Dot, were sitting in Dot's front room, finishing off a pot of Yorkshire tea and a plate of chocolate fingers. The four were about to embark on a day trip to Blackpool. Upstairs, little Bobby could be heard thumping about, as he finalised preparations, for his day out to Chester zoo. John's insistent attention to Joan, in the darkest period of her life, had rekindled their feelings toward each other, and, after a few tentative romantic dates they'd gradually, once again, become a married couple, him moving back in with her.

Dot on the other hand, had decided to stay at Nelson's. She couldn't correlate leaving there, her friends, and the only working life she'd known, with the fleeting extravagances that would, surely, soon fritter away any redundancy money. As she was about to sign the leaving forms, she'd put the pen down onto Hardcastle's desk.

'I can't do it, Bill... this is all I've ever known... I'm scared.'

Hardcastle smiled sympathetically, folded up the

papers then filed them away. She stood.

'Just before you go, Dot,' he handed her an envelope. 'Archibald and Reginald want you to have this, irrespective of your redundancy decision.' She opened the envelope. It contained a cheque for £1,000. Dot's jaw hit the floor. Dot, being Dot, spent all of it, within a couple of weeks. None of it going on herself, though. After paying off a half a dozen overdue bills, she blasted the remainder away, on her kids... Well, when I say, *'nothing of it going on herself,'* that's only half true. With her last fifty quid, she finally got 'round to buying a new *bleedin battery*, for the clapped-out, heap of junk, she referred to as *the car*, having refused, resolutely, to take any handouts from Ted. Then, it was back to being broke. But, three weeks before the following Christmas, she would receive a letter from a firm of solicitors, asking her to go in, and see them. They would ask for her bank details and make her aware of a substantial amount of money to be transferred into her account, compliments of an anonymous donor. She'd make Ted swear on the Holy Bible, literally, that he wasn't the culprit. She never would find out who it was, that performed the dastardly deed.

Ted looked at Dot, and smiled, reflectively. 'Are you OK?' she said, tenderly, before biting two chocolate fingers in half. 'I'm fine,' he replied, while thinking, *apart from the cancer*. Try as he may, he couldn't find it in his heart to finish with Dot; confide in her about the disease. The following Wednesday he had an appointment at the hospital for another biopsy on his prostate, to determine if there'd been any proliferation of the cancer cells. He prayed to God that there hadn't. He knew he must tell her, sooner or later, and he knew he would, but not just yet. They both deserved the chance of second time around happiness, for the time being, anyway. Yes, he would tell her... at some point... but not just yet.

'I'll make us another cuppa,'said Dot, as she stood.

She entered the kitchen, picked up her latest, ostentatious display of wealth: a new, Russell Hobbs electric kettle, and began to fill it from the tap. Joan entered, and stood next to her. They looked at each other.

'Hello, luv... are y'alright...?' said Dot, quizzically.

The hint of an enigmatic smile graced Joan's lips.

'Wha...?'said Dot. 'What's up...?'

There was a pause.

'I'm ten days, overdue...' she mouthed, in a whisper.

'*Oh! my God,*' said Dot, delightedly, as the kettle overflowed.

'*Shhh!*' said Joan, with a smile.

'Can I have a coffee, instead, please, Dot...?' said John, as he suddenly entered.

'Er – yeah. Orright...' said Dot, making eye-contact with Joan, who, almost imperceptibly, shook her head.

'Ta, queen. Milk, no sugar,' said John, then he left the kitchen.

'*Jesus Christ!*' Dot exhaled, secretively.

There was a knock at the front door.

'That'll be them,' said Dot, switching the kettle on, then exiting into the hall, excitedly muttering, '*Oh! my God. Oh! my God,*' under her breath, as she rushed past the Laughing Cavalier. Charlie's car was parked, outside. '*Bobby, they're ere!*' Dot shouted up the stairs. As Rick walked down the path, Charlie sat waiting in the car. Her happiness now complete, she was totally, undeniably, in love with Rick (although she still intermittently fantasised about the beautiful time, she and Petra had shared). She'd also made amends with her mother (although, she was never to discover that she was an adopted daughter). The bell rang, Dot opened the door, and Rick walked in. *'Bobby, c'mon. Uncle Rick's waitin!'* He came thundering down the stairs. After many smiles and laughter from all, Bobby was led up the path by his *Uncle* Rick, to the waiting car. He bounced onto the back seat, and they buckled up. Charlie started the engine, then smiled as she witnessed Rick's love for his son. As the Mini drove up the road,

'You like kids don't you, Rick?'

'Of course - I used t'be one.'

'Do you like stinky, puking, squawking, little babies, as well?'

'Yeah, why...?'

'I've got something to tell you...'

Printed in Great Britain
by Amazon